A FOOLISH COMEUPPANCE

When Filidor awoke, something gray and white was standing on his chest. It clacked a sharp yellow bill and cocked its head to eye him with what he was sure was evil intent. He opened his mouth to say "Get off me!" but all that came out was the kind of sound a particularly inarticulate beast might make, accompanied by a rolling belch that reeked of stale liquor. The bird took offense and flapped away.

Filidor closed his eyes, having discovered that light, even the weak light cast by the fading orange sun in this latter age of Old Earth, was not a friend to his present condition.

Also by Matthew Hughes

Fools Errant

FOOL ME TWICE

MATTHEW HUGHES

ASPECT®

WARNER BOOKS

A Time Warner Company

WARNER BOOKS EDITION

Cover design by Don Puckey
Cover illustration by Tim White

Warner Books, Inc.
1271 Avenue of the Americas
New York, NY 10020

Visit our Web site at
www.twbookmark.com

For information on Time Warner Trade Publishing's online program, visit www.ipublish.com

 A Time Warner Company

Printed in the United States of America

First Warner Books Printing: August 2001

10 9 8 7 6 5 4 3 2 1

For Paula, patiently waiting

FOOL ME
TWICE

Fool Me
Twice

CHAPTER

ONE

Since his official investiture as the Archon's apprentice, it had become the morning habit of Filidor Vesh to take a late breakfast on the streetside balcony of a place in the Shamblings district where he was known and well treated. Fortified by slices of spiced dolcetacc and cups of steaming punge, he would linger over the pages of the *Olkney Implicator*: not for news of weighty matters, but for the artfully phrased columns of the notorious scandal hound Tet Folbrey. The scribbler wrote in a ribald code that disclosed, to those who knew the key, which members of the city's often wanton elite were doing things with and to each other that they would have preferred not to read about in the public prints. Lawsuits were often threatened, sometimes brought, rarely settled, but through all of it, Folbrey wrote on. Filidor had heard somewhere, though certainly not in the man's column, that the tattler had gained his impregnable position at the *Implicator* by marrying the bad-tempered daughter of its owner, Lord Vadric Magguffynne.

The Archon's apprentice himself was an occasional target of the scandalmonger's barbs. Filidor was a young man, with a young man's appetites and inclinations, which sometimes conspired to lead him into situations that lacked decorum, and among companions who pursued a life of continual romp and riot. On one such occasion, Folbrey had reported on a house party at which Filidor had presided over an auction of the hostess's garments, which she had removed one by one as the bids increased in both size and fervor. Filidor did not dispute the accuracy of the *Implicator*'s account, but felt that his privacy—not to mention that of his hostess—had been invaded. Not one to trifle with underlings, he went to the home of the owner to complain.

Lord Magguffynne received him in a dark drawing room walled with shelves and cluttered with tables, all of which bore relics of his family's ancient glories. The aristocrat was a tall, spare man of rigid posture, with a face as narrow and unyielding as a sword blade. He heard the young man's complaint with an air of detachment, then dismissed the matter with a casual word. Filidor felt that the interview was not going well, and said, "Perhaps you would take a different tone if this affair was brought to my uncle's attention."

The Magguffynne smiled a thin smile and said, "I should think that would create more difficulties for you than for me."

In truth, Filidor did not wish to test his uncle's views regarding his recreations. His uncle was Dezendah VII, ninety-eighth Archon of those parts of Old Earth still inhabited by human beings in this, the world's penultimate age. Some said the old man ought to be numbered as the ninety-ninth to exercise the vast but ill-defined powers of the Archonate, but that was because they counted the brief and unsuccessful usurpation by the detested Holmar Thurm, who had treacherously removed the Archon Barsamine V from office some centuries before. Among those who bothered to think about the matter, the majority opinion held that the lamentable Thurm had earned no place in the official record, the fact that his skin was preserved somewhere in the dusty archives beneath the Archonate palace notwithstanding.

Either way, all agreed that the Archon Dezendah VII was the pinnacle of Old Earth's social order, with powers beyond limit, although the means and mechanisms by which those powers were exercised were unclear even to those who bothered themselves with questions of governance. Filidor's appreciation of his uncle was less abstract. He was aware that his behavior had often failed to measure up to the Archon's expectations, and the awareness caused him some inner pain.

His threat to appeal to his uncle had been a bluff, and Lord Magguffynne had called it. They therefore agreed to disagree, and the issue was dropped unsettled. Filidor attempted to be a little more discreet in his amusements, and for a time his name figured less often in Folbrey's column.

Now he sipped his morning punge and deciphered a particularly savory item about an unexpected meeting between wizened old Lord Escophalate's last mistress and her successor, a young lady of apparently remarkable character, which had escalated into a public charivari and the loss of at least one stook of dyed hair. Chuckling, he dropped his eyes to the next slanderous morsel and had read half of it before he grew aware that the subject of the report was himself.

What highly placed gadling, Folbrey wrote, was troughing it to his very hocks at The Prodigious Palate last night, gaggled by the usual hem tuggers? The rarest pressings from the eatery's cellar flowed in cataracts, as the gourmands gobbled a path through the entire menu, then began anew with appetizers. Knowledgeable prognosticators believe that the boy's uncle will absolutely fizzicate when he sees the bill.

A brief cloud of concern passed over the normally untroubled landscape of the young man's mind, but soon evanesced into nothing, leaving his inner skies clear. It was a mild enough bite at his ankles, and Filidor was fairly sure that his uncle was not a devotee of the man's column. And even if the item should somehow come to the Archon's attention, the odds were that no censure more stringent than a mild reproach would descend upon his nephew; at least, no penalties had yet been exacted for a score of past libertinous routs he had hosted for his circle of aristocratic friends. Filidor would have liked to take more comfort from that argument, but the experience of his brief lifetime had shown him that sometimes his uncle would take considerable pains to teach him a lesson. Invariably, the pains were Filidor's.

But, at the moment, all was peace and good order upon this sunny balcony, and Filidor was well practiced at living in the moment. He ordered another mug of punge, finished the remaining items in Folbrey's column, then turned the page to find a critic's notice of a theatrical event that he and his coterie had happened to witness in Indentors Square the evening before as they were making their way to the Palate. It was an open-air performance by a traveling company that billed itself as Flastovic's Incomparable Mummery Troupe and Raree Exposition. Masked and robed in imaginative costumes, the players silently enacted scenes from the works of a dramatist of bygone years known only as The Bard Obscure, while an austere disclamator, who Filidor thought was too fond of his own voice, stood to one side of the portable stage in mask and robe and recited the text of the drama.

Like most of his circle, Filidor had at least heard of The Bard Obscure, a maker of tragicomic plays and vignettes that were no longer popular among the sophisticated set. Many of them were set on the imaginary planet Far Forbish, a rough-rambling frontier much distant from Earth, out at the other end of the Spray. The Archon's apprentice had stopped with his friends at the rear of the small crowd of spectators when the disclamator portentously called out the title of the work they were about to perform.

"*Love and Irony,*" he said, "by The Bard Obscure." He paused and swept his eyes across the almost empty square, as if surveying a vast throng, before continuing. "*Into the mining camp at Flatpoke Creek came Badrey Huzzantz, his cheeks unburnt and his gear unscorched.*"

A masked mummer jauntily crossed the stage and stood, legs widespread, knuckles on hips, as if taking stock of new surroundings. The rest of the troupe were off to the side, ignoring his arrival.

"*Huzzantz announced that he had crossed the Spray to pry a bonanza in gems from the fumaroles, and to return home with a fortune plucked from the fiery magma.*"

The other players now gathered round, nudging and elbowing each other in prelude to a prank, then one stepped forward and put his arm around the newcomer's shoulders.

The disclamator said, "*A grizzled veteran of the fire fields named Ton Begbo thought to make sport with the young tyro. He told Huzzantz that never could he name himself a true Forbishite until he had completed two tasks: first, achieve carnal congress with Madame Valouche, empress of the camp courtesans; second, deliver a resounding kick to the armored hindquarters of a six-pronged weftry.*"

The mummer playing Badrey Huzzantz raised masked chin and clenched fist in a show of determination. The others mimed raucous encouragement.

"*Huzzantz vowed he would fulfill all requirements, and would have set out forthwith, but the others assured him that every rite of passage must traditionally begin with buying each well-wisher a tot of fierce drink and toasting them singly and severally."*

The players leaned upon each other, bending their elbows and bringing cupped hands to lips, until the hero of the tale *"stumbled forth from their midst, fist again raised like a banner with a strange device, and swore that he would not return till he had dealt, according to their natures, with both Madame Valouche and the dreaded weftry."*

The character staggered offstage, while the carousers carried on with their imbibery. Then from the wings came a great thunder and clatter that betokened a dire contest, rising thump upon clash to a ringing climax. There ensued a long silence, while the other mummers stood in attitudes of awed expectation, before the hero stumbled back into view, his robe rent, his mask askew, and his body bent at unusual angles.

The disclamator spoke. *" 'Well enough,' cried Badrey Huzzantz. 'Now, where is this whore I'm supposed to kick?' "*

The other Far Forbishers mimed amazement and mirth, slapping hands to knees and holding jiggling bellies. But then the curtains parted at the rear of the stage and a giant head appeared, a gold and green weftry crowned with six segmented spines. The mummers, save Huzzantz, froze in postures of horror. But then the weftry unrolled a long tongue of red velour, until the tip gently touched the hand of Badrey Huzzantz, who turned and affectionately stroked the glistering chitin of the beast's forehead. Together, the head and the man backed through the curtain, until only the hero's mask remained. Huzzantz shook his head dismissively.

"Never mind," said the disclamator, and the stage went to black.

*   *   *

It had been a diverting performance, enlivened during the intermission by a shout and a bustle from the far side of the square, where someone cried out that his purse had been lifted. Filidor might have stayed for more, but the delights of The Prodigious Palate were beckoning, so he and his friends left just as the disclamator announced that the next playlet would be the classic, *A Man, a Tavern, and a Duck*.

The *Implicator*'s critic professed a less positive view of the troupe's offerings, and thought it appropriate that the mummers would soon depart for a tour of provincial towns. Filidor sipped his punge and turned to the news page, which was topped by a headline about an intercessor from Thurloyn Vale who was believed to have been lost at sea after absconding with the contents of his clients' trust funds. A wavering pain passed behind his forehead, no doubt brought on by last night's excesses and made worse by a rumble of heavy wheels on Ipscarry Way where it ran below the balcony. He put down the periodical and turned to look for the source of the noise.

A stubby, ungainly vehicle of the kind commonly used to transport farm goods, but now roughly converted to carry passengers, was trundling up the street's gentle slope. The bed of its cargo hold had been softened with cushions and duffels, on which sat two persons in rustic dress. Filidor glanced idly at them, and would have returned to the *Implicator* and his breakfast, but just then one of the travelers chanced to look up, and her eyes caught Filidor's. And held them.

The eyes were large and sea-green, slightly slanted, and set in a heart-shaped face that was topped by careless ringlets of coppery hair. The features were not so striking a vision as to stir Filidor's inner workings—he saw more beautiful women at many of the evening salons and catered runavaunts to which his status as the Archon's heir gave him entry—but then the girl smiled, and the effect was like the old orange sun finding its warm way through a chink in a cloud. The street seemed to glow with inner light, and Filidor felt his own cheeks stretching in a matching grin, which soon broke under the pressure of a small, spontaneous laugh. At that, the young woman's smile also deepened, and had the vehicle not been carrying her steadily away from him, Filidor might have spoken, she might have answered, an acquaintanceship would have been sparked, and subsequent events would not have unfolded in quite so complicated a manner.

Instead, the conveyance belched bluish fumes from a rear orifice, grunted down into a lower gear, and turned the corner into Hennenfent Street, carrying her out of his sight, and plunging the young man's world back into shadow. The change moved Filidor to an unaccustomed urgency. He left his morning pastry half nibbled and his second cup of punge unsipped, threw Folbrey to the floor tiles, and threaded his way among the tables toward the stairs.

He emerged below on busy Ipscarry and cast about for a jitney to hire. None was in sight, but then he blessed his luck as an official black and green Archonate cabriol suddenly eased out of the traffic and drew into the curb beside him. Filidor pulled open the front passenger door and launched himself into the interior, drawing forth his identification plaque as he did so, preparing to demonstrate superiority of rank to whatever bureaucrat had requisitioned the car, then to send it in pursuit of the hauler.

"Quickly," he said to the controls, "turn onto Hennenfent and follow the carryall with the people in the back."

"I regret," said a moist and languid voice from the rear seat, "that pressing circumstances compel us in another direction."

Filidor's heart, lifted by the girl's smile into the topmost reaches of his chest, now reversed course and plunged to the bottom of his belly. He well knew the voice; it belonged to Faubon Bassariot, a smooth, ovoid man of middle years and supercilious style, who wore much of his hair in a single curl pomaded to his forehead. He had risen to a high echelon among the panjandrums at the Archon's palace before he was chosen by the Archon himself to assume a particular duty: to be Filidor's majordomo and daily taskmaster. To that purpose, he had assembled and oversaw a staff of functionaries whose career hopes were tied to his own prominence, and these officials became the personal staff of the Archon's apprentice. But though the staff was Filidor's, and though Bassariot's title was chief of that small bureaucracy, there was no question as to who was in charge; in all the vast apparatus of the Archonate, Bassariot was the one functionary to whom Filidor could never say no.

Nevertheless, he tried. "Those circumstances must wait," said the young man. "I have urgent concerns."

"Indeed you do," said the official, "and I am carrying you to them."

Filidor knew that neither hauteur nor entreaty would move Bassariot. He drooped, and laid his head against the side window as the ground car negotiated its way through the traffic to a gate at the base of the heights that reared above ancient Olkney. Vehicle and gate conversed in the usual routine, then the barrier gave way and allowed the cabriol to ascend the winding road whose terminus was the sprawling palace of the Archonate, nestled in the crags above the rambling, sybaritic city of Olkney, at the tip of the peninsula of the same name.

Filidor saw none of the passing courts and gardens, the statuary and vistas arranged to intrigue the visitor during the long ascent. His awareness was fixed on an inward vision: a tumble of hair, a pair of eyes one might drown in, and most of all a smile to illuminate the hollow recesses of his being. He sighed. A paradise briefly glimpsed was now lost. But then a thought occurred: the apparatus of the Archonate was a byword for far-reaching power; could he not use its resources to identify and locate the young woman who had so instantly captured his senses? A few flicks of his finger in the direction of the appropriate device, and surely the answers would be divulged. Then he would . . . here the plan's coherence began to unravel, yet Filidor was confident that he would somehow contrive to encounter again the wielder of that obliterating smile, and in a setting and context that would present him in a most admirable light.

He needed to get to his office. He sat up straight and lightly drummed his fingers on the car's interior padding. "Will this thing not move faster?" he said.

A sniff was Bassariot's only reply.

In time, the cabriol deposited them at a door near Filidor's offices. The Archon's apprentice hurried inside and down the short corridor to his suite, and did not breathe fully comfortably until the door was closed behind him. The Archon might be encountered in any part of the sprawling complex, and the young man was anxious to avoid a meeting.

The year before, their relationship had been much warmer. Filidor had won the Archon's affection and respect by saving the old man's life; it was also noteworthy that, at the same time, he had delivered the world from an ancient, recurrent evil that seeped in from an adjacent plane, where malevolence was merely a natural phenomenon, akin to weather or gravity in this cosmos. Although the young man had acted blindly, indeed in sheer panic, with no display of the cool and judicious tone for which the Archonate was renowned, his uncle had judged the intent and result of his actions to be of more significance than the style of their execution. Filidor had been welcomed to the little man's firm embrace, and proclaimed the Archon's official heir and apprentice.

A year ago, there had been no doubt that Filidor had come a long way, though there remained a long way yet to go. Today, the way ahead was even longer, because once he had returned to the familiar haunts and temptations of Olkney, Filidor had backslid. Old habits and old companions, both of them bad, had reclaimed him. At times—especially in the darkest hours of the night—he wished it were not so, wished that he could find again the sense of boundless possibility that had filled him on the plains of Barran, when he had saved his uncle and Old Earth from destruction.

He felt an echo of it now, remembering the face of the young woman in the carryall. Having reached his comfortably appointed office without encountering his uncle, Filidor made his way quickly to his desk. He seated himself behind its expanse and pressed one of the studs set into the ornamented edge. The simulacrum of a screen appeared in the air before him, at a comfortable height for viewing. A chime sounded, followed by a disembodied voice that seemed to speak from near the young man's ear, saying, "What?"

"I need to find someone," Filidor said.

"That is an essential part of the human condition," said the voice, "often complemented by an equal need to be found."

"I do not wish to meander through a philosophical discourse," said Filidor. He knew that the circuits of the Archonate's millennia-old integrator would often respond to his inquiries on practical matters with long-winded diversions involving abstract speculations and obscure commentaries. He suspected that his uncle had ordered it so. Filidor had long resisted the Archon's attempts to educate him by frontal assaults on his ignorance, causing the old man to shift to flank attacks from unexpected quarters. "I wish to locate a young woman."

"Stand on a corner," advised the integrator. "Doubtless several will soon pass by."

"I wish to find a particular one," said Filidor.

"If she is very particular, she may well wish not to be found by you," said the voice, rewarding itself with a small snort. "Here now, wasn't that good?"

Filidor had always judged the device's forays into humor to be less successful than did their author. "Let us begin again," he said.

"No," interrupted the majordomo, reaching over Filidor's shoulder and disengaging the connection. "Indulge yourself later. Concerns of state outweigh juvenile fascinations. There are delegations to receive."

Filidor sighed. This was always a duty, rarely a pleasure. It was not the petitioners themselves; most were polite, some even deferential. But the requests were too often presented in arcane and ancient forms, their substance obscured by forests of formal rhetoric and allusions to well-known precedents that Filidor had never heard of. All too often, he would find himself staring politely at some earnest group of supplicants as they completed their arguments, then bowed and awaited his judgment. Sometimes he would continue to stare at them for periods of time too long to be called moments. They no doubt assumed that he was deliberating carefully, when in truth he was wondering what on earth they wanted, and what he was supposed to say about it.

For Filidor, the difficulty with his official life was that, most of the time, he had a slim grasp of what he was doing, and an even more tenuous grip on what he was supposed to be doing. The problem had begun soon after he had returned from the previous year's journey in the discomfiting company of his uncle.

On their expedition, Filidor had been pressed unwillingly and unknowingly into the role of apprentice to the Archon as well as his heir apparent. He was propelled through a number of the singular societies that flourished in the world of Earth's penultimate age, daily risking death and dismemberment to resolve paradoxes that threatened social happiness. An ignorant stranger in a succession of strange lands, often acting solely from instinct and terror, Filidor had somehow managed not only to survive, but to earn his uncle's warm approval. When their meanderings brought them at last back to the Archonate palace on the tip of the Olkney Peninsula, Filidor had been invested with his plaque and sigil, assigned a dignified suite of offices, and left in the cold, damp hands of Faubon Bassariot.

Months had now passed, but Filidor knew little more today than he had in those hectic weeks during which he and his uncle had wandered from place to place, participating in actions that somehow indirectly restored a rough equilibrium to one or another society that had strayed too far from the mean—an ancient function of the Archon known as *the progress of esteeming the balance*—then they would move on to where they might be needed next. It became clear to Filidor that the Archon tended toward the tangential approach: he would arrange for an institution to tremble from a slight nudge at its foundation; he might subject a population to an unsought and unexpected demonstration of an alternative social arrangement; when their work was done, the agents of enlightenment would be on their way down the road, often in a hurry, and not infrequently just ahead of an outraged citizenry.

That much of the Archonate's workings, Filidor knew from experience. The rest was still conjecture. Everyone knew that the Archon, revered and deferred to by all, exercised ultimate dominion over humankind. His palace housed legions of functionaries and underlings, most of whose duties seemed to involve moving things from one place to another, or standing in apparently deep contemplation. There was an Archonate bureau, fully staffed and equipped, in every human settlement of reasonable size. Built over uncounted millennia, the Archonate was universally regarded as the magnificent culmination of the science of governance, yet Filidor could not have specified exactly what it did or how it did it.

On one occasion when he had encountered his uncle in the warren of halls and corridors that riddled through the palace, Filidor posed the question bluntly. He seized the Archon's threadbare black garment, causing the little man to execute a half turn, and demanded, "What is our function?"

His uncle freed himself from Filidor's grasp by a subtle movement of his rootlike fingers, stroked his yellowy bald pate, and spoke in a voice like a rustle in dead grass. "Surely this is self-evident. The function of the Archonate is to arrange for the populace to have what it needs."

"But how am I to know what the people need?"

"That is the art of governing, and like any art, it is acquired by diligent practice. Keep at it. I have every faith that you're coming along admirably." And with that, the little man was gone.

Thus was Filidor set adrift, without chart or compass, on a sea of administration. But, though aimless, his voyage was for the most part a placid one. Faubon Bassariot, aided by an efficient staff, dealt with many routine affairs, as well as some that were of more than passing weight, before they reached Filidor's desk. But some petitioners must be granted direct contact with the Archon's heir. And sometimes this led to Filidor's experiencing the sensation known to waders who step beyond an underwater ledge and find themselves sinking abruptly into the darkness of an unplumbed abyss.

As Bassariot denied him his search for the girl seen from the balcony, Filidor felt an intimation that today would bring another floundering in the murk of Archonate business. The young man laced his fingers in his lap and said, "What have we this morning?"

"Two delegations, and some officers of the fiduciary section urgently desire to discuss your expenses," said the functionary.

Filidor made a dismissive gesture. "All that before lunch?"

"One delegation must be received as soon as possible."

"Why?"

Bassariot made an airy gesture. "Although the matter is not weighty, the petitioners are persons of note. But the other group might possibly keep."

"Very well," said the Archon's apprentice, slumping a little in his chair. "Bring on the necessity."

Almost an hour later, he was sitting in the same position, fighting his eyelids' inclination to migrate down to the bottom of their range, as a quartet of worthies from the upper strata of Olkney society slowly reached the culmination of their petition. Filidor dragged his gaze from them and looked instead through one of the mullioned windows that broke the outer wall of his office. He saw a pair of phibranos swirling in multihued arcs around a blackened tower, feathers flamed by red sunlight, tumbling through the aerial combat of courtship. The birds swooped low and were lost from his sight, and he became aware again of the droning voice on the other side of his desk.

". . . and therefore," said the leader of the delegation, a plump man with silver hair and hooded eyes, which he now flicked back to the scroll in his stub-fingered hand, "pursuant to Articles Seven and Twelve of the Policy of Amenable Leniency, we respectfully seek the Archonate's concurrence in these, our worthy aims." With a tidy flourish, he rerolled the document and presented it to Filidor. Then he guided his ornate hat to a soft landing on his well-coiffed locks, folded small pink hands across a brocaded paunch, and awaited the response of authority.

Which response Filidor was at a loss to give. He stared at the man in a lengthening silence until Faubon Bassariot discreetly cleared his throat.

"Well," said Filidor, then after a moment said, "well," again. He unrolled the scroll and studied its ornate script, but found no help; somewhere within its tangled thicket of traditional phraseology and time-honored language there may have been a simple statement of purpose—ought to have been one, he thought—but if so it was beyond his finding. He sighed: once again, not only did he not know what decision was expected of him, he was not at all sure what the subject of the petition was.

The chief petitioner now cleared his throat, with even more emphasis than Bassariot. Filidor could delay no longer. "This is a most interesting request," he said. "I would like an opportunity to study it in depth, perhaps to consult with my officials . . ." He trailed off as he noted the four petitioners' eyebrows molding into the position of offended disbelief. "No more than a perfunctory review . . ." Filidor tried again, and saw the eight carefully tended ranks of hair descend to the position of incipient outrage.

Another of the delegation stepped forward, a thin woman in black, whose shaven skull was haloed by a complex nimbus of gold filaments and precious stones. Filidor thought he recognized her as a dowager of a highly placed family, perhaps even those who owned the *Implicator*, and wondered if he might bargain for kindlier treatment by Tet Folbrey. He decided the idea was not advisable when the woman said, in a voice like tearing paper, "We did not come for shilly-shallying. Our aims are clearly set forth, our methods are simple and efficacious, and all is animated by a lucid philosophy."

A metal-plated fingertip sliced the air as she went on, "In any case, the Policy of Amenable Leniency admits of no unwarranted delay. You must decide, and now."

Filidor had developed two strategies for dealing with delegations. His preferred course—to dodge the issue until it could be passed to someone else within the Archonate establishment—had just been rendered bankrupt. He smoothly shifted to the alternate approach.

"Of course, of course, just so," he said, and allowed his fingertips to strike his forehead, "quite correct. What was I thinking? Proceed, by all means, proceed. You have my complete concurrence."

In unison, the four petitioners performed an audible intake of breath. "Then you will graciously endorse the document with your sigil," said the woman.

"Great pleasure," said Filidor. He twisted the ring on his index finger, pressed its entaglioed surface against the paper, and felt the brief tingle as the mark of Archonate approval was indelibly impressed into the document. "There you have it," he said, and passed the scroll to the chief petitioner.

The four petitioners eyed one another with a curious intensity, and Filidor had a faint inkling that each was suppressing an urge to shout and caper energetically about the room. Instead, they hurried through the gestures that were appropriate to a formal occasion and departed.

Filidor let loose yet another sigh, this one a mingle of relief and despair. The flaw in agreeing to whatever was presented to him, he realized, was the constant risk of an unfortunate outcome. However, he comforted himself, that outcome could reasonably be expected to be at some distance in the future, or perhaps its impacts would be felt in some far-off place. This future Archon wished to believe that tomorrows could be trusted to look after themselves. He returned his gaze to the window, but the phibranos had gone off on other business.

Bassariot had escorted the magnates from the room. Filidor took advantage of his absence to recall the integrator's screen into existence. "She was about my age, with red hair, green eyes, wonderful mouth," he told it.

"Who?" said the integrator.

"The woman I want you to find," said Filidor.

The screen blinked faintly, then the voice said, "There are somewhere between four and eleven million such women, depending on the definition of 'wonderful.' "

"She wore simple clothing."

"That is not a great help."

"She was riding in a converted farm vehicle," Filidor said. "There can't be all that many women doing that."

"Obviously, you do not frequent rural communities," said the integrator.

"I don't think you are trying your best," Filidor said, "you old confustible!"

The disembodied voice dropped to a mumble, but Filidor thought he heard the phrase "trying my patience." He would have to speak to his uncle about this equipment.

He gathered himself for a renewed effort, but it was forestalled by the reentry of Faubon Bassariot. "The other delegation awaits," said the functionary.

"What do they want?"

The man's smile was the only thin thing about him. "Your attention, one supposes."

"Are they like the last ones, a cluster of magnates?"

"If you mean, are they the sort to complain in higher circles," Bassariot said, his nose assuming an even more elevated angle than normal, "I think not. I take them to have come from some uncultured and distant community, their dress being simple and travel-worn."

Filidor gestured to the screen and said, in a breezy tone, "You see that I am absorbed in intricate and consequential matters. I cannot be disturbed. Perhaps they might see my uncle."

The official's expression was artfully composed. "Indeed, they first sought the Archon's attention; he suggested they might profit from an interview with yourself."

A weight fitted itself upon Filidor's shoulders. Petitioners referred by his uncle were often the most perplexing. He grasped for the last available straw. "Have they an actual appointment?"

Bassariot looked thoughtful for a while, then said, "Not as such."

"Then make them one, at some convenient space in my schedule."

"The earliest of which would be this moment," said the majordomo, fixing his eyes on the empty air beyond Filidor's shoulder.

"No, no," said the young man. "No, no. My time is at present fully taken up. An urgent matter, which admits of no delay."

Bassariot angled his head to one side, like a bird inspecting something edible. "I see."

"Yes, good, well," said Filidor and sought at once to buttress the flimsy foundations of his escape. "I have it! They could put their case in writing—which you could then review—and advise me before I meet with them . . . which I could do, shall we say . . ."

"Tomorrow morning?"

Filidor regarded the man's round, cool face, as bland as a boiled egg, and recalled that nothing that happened within the palace could, with absolute safety, be considered unknown to Dezendah Vesh. "Tomorrow morning," he agreed.

Bassariot departed, leaving Filidor to resume his interrogation of the integrator. But the machine seemed determined to frustrate his simple aim, and the more the Archon's apprentice sought to steer the conversation toward practical ends, the further afield the device's philosophical wanderings led them.

"Ultimately, of course," it said, "all things devolve to a question of identity. I think, therefore I am, certainly. And one can say, as the ancient sage so succinctly observed: I am what I am, and that's all that I am. But this begs the question, what am I? Am I what I think I am? Does thinking that I am what I am make me what I think I am? Perhaps I am not what I think I am, in which case does it not inevitably follow that I am what I think I am not? Or am I? What do you think?"

"I think I will turn you off," said Filidor, and did so. He would make a search within the Archonate for someone more skilled in dealing with integrators, to see if there was a way to pose elementary questions without risking his emotional equilibrium.

He laid his head upon the desk and called up the vision

of the face, the smile. A long, delicious sigh escaped him. He prepared to give another one, but was interrupted by the reappearance of Faubon Bassariot.

"If you are free," he said, "the fiduciary officers are still here. They have brought a number of files, and are eager to join you in examining them."

Filidor wasted no more time. "This integrator is faulty," he said, "I shall seek out Master Apparaticist Berro and have him do things to it. Or with it. Or about it." These options were listed as he made his way to the outer door, opened it, and stepped through into a warm midday, the tired orange sun winking and gleaming from the towers and urbanations of Olkney far below, so that the gaudy old whore of a city looked like a spill of trinkets on the gray-green blanket of the surrounding sea.

A short flight of stone steps led down and turned once, bringing Filidor through an inconspicuous portal into a public area of the palace grounds. He stepped out smartly and took a path that meandered among the melodious blooms of the tintinabulary gardens. Soon he reached the outer edge of the palace's upper terrace, where a descender would bear him swiftly down to the city.

He stepped onto the next arriving disk, planted his feet on the scuffed metal, and grasped the handle firmly. The descender began its slide along an inclined plane of energies, and the uplifting breeze of Filidor's passage streamed his hair from the nape of his neck as Olkney rose to meet him. Farther down, Filidor noticed the four magnates he had met with earlier grouped on a single wide disk. They were behaving in a most animated manner, hugging each other and slapping backs. As the young man watched, the chief petitioner seized his headgear and flung it into the air, not bothering to watch as it fluttered and plunged into a reflective pool far below.

Then the woman raised to her lips the scroll Filidor had indented. She appeared to kiss it.

A few minutes later, the descender delivered Filidor onto a pathway that ringed the lowest of the palace's tiered walls. A short walk through lawns and topiary brought him to the wide thoroughfare of Eckhevry Row, which led straight into Olkney's bustling mercantile quarter, where it was said that a purchaser might acquire anything that was worth acquiring, amidst much that was not. The commerciants of Olkney were renowned for their egalitarian spirit, judging rich and poor alike solely by the weight of their purses.

Filidor, however, was beyond their judgment. As a ranking officer of the Archonate, he need carry no specie of any kind. Instead, he wore about his neck a light chain, from which depended a palm-sized plaque of an indestructible green substance, figured in black with symbols and emblems. Upon its presentation, the plaque would serve to afford him food, shelter, transportation, or goods and services whatsoever and to any value. Some accounting of these charges was eventually made to the public treasury; but that was not a matter on which the young man cared to dwell, being content with the simplicity of gaining whatever he desired merely by presenting the lozenge of green and black.

At the moment, the plaque nestled against his chest, under a loose shirt of fine pale stuff, belted at the waist by a cinch of linked semiprecious stones. A pair of twilled trousers, as red and as wide as fashion allowed and tucked into calf-high boots, a short cape of yellow, and a discreet cap bearing a gew-gaw of gold and turquoise, completed his ensemble. As he accompanied his own reflection past the windows of shops and emporia, Filidor was comforted by the unavoidable truth that he cut a fine figure. Any flaws he might offer in either dress or character were not apparent to his own sanguine gaze.

Eckhevry's pedestrian walkways were only moderately abustle with shoppers and gawkers, and Filidor could see some distance ahead the four worthies to whose petition he had given assent. Their spirits continued high, he saw. They strode abreast down the avenue, arms draped across each other's shoulders, their steps so elevated and frisky as to be more dance than mere locomotion. *Whatever I have granted them,* thought Filidor, *has certainly met with their approval.* A second thought briefly intruded: *Might so much happiness for a few require payment in misery by the many?* It was a troublesome notion, so he cast it aside with practiced ease.

The four now turned and gavotted their way up a brief staircase into a squat stone building. Shortly after, Filidor's progress brought him level with the structure, and he glanced up to see a wall of unornamented blocks and a small massive wooden door. Beside the entry was a plain, new-looking placard identifying the place as the premises of "The Ancient and Excellent Company of Assemblors and Sundry Merchandisers." Filidor recalled that name from the petition, but could not specify what its line of business might be.

Above the sign was an older insignia. He thought he recognized it as the arms of the Magguffynne family, but Olkney boasted dozens of such ancient bloodlines, whose members found in their genealogies a source of pride and who jealously guarded their positions on the social scale. Those who were not members of the self-conscious elite—in other words, the overwhelming majority of the city's population—paid no attention to the aristocrats' rivalries.

Nor did Filidor care to. It might be that the petition he had granted was a ploy in some arcane struggle between noble houses over who had the right to wear this or that panache in one or the other style of cap. The impenetrability of the plea's language argued for it. If so, he did not care. The Archon outranked every other gradation of the social order, and presumably so did Filidor. He resolved, for better or worse, to put the matter behind him. Its ramifications, if any, would unfold in the future, leaving the present free for more pleasant concerns, chief among them a good lunch.

Filidor stepped into the traffic, dodged between motilators and drays, and crossed safely to the opposite side of Eckhevry, then turned into Vodel Close, a side street which boasted the premises of Xanthoulian's, an eating house that was everything it ought to be.

He climbed a set of steps and entered a tastefully appointed room, well lit by tall windows that allowed diners to reflect at leisure on the qualities and singularities of passersby, and to enjoy the envy of those beyond the glass whose means could not encompass the exorbitant prices that gave the place its exclusivity. Filidor took his usual seat, considered the bill of fare, and casually arranged for his plaque to dangle openly on his shirtfront.

He decided to begin with an array of small piquant dishes, then follow with a robust stew, all ending with some subtle delicacy that would gracefully round out the whole. He beckoned to the servitor, a long, pale man with a pronounced stoop, well trained in skillful obsequiousness: he praised each of Filidor's selections as evidence of the customer's attainments as a gourmet of the first water. When Filidor began to name particular vintages to accompany the courses, the menial achieved such paroxysms of ecstatic adoration that the Archon's apprentice feared the fellow might pitch a swoon and collapse across the table.

With his order carried triumphantly to the kitchen, Filidor turned his attention to the street outside. The usual flux of powered and pedestrian traffic flowed by: functionaries and mercantilists, identifiable by their symbols of authority and wealth; artisans and effectors with the paraphernalia of their crafts and disciplines; and those made idle by too much good fortune or too little, the latter often begging the former for some mite of support.

Occasionally, there passed by persons less easily defined: oddly clad outlanders and travelers pursuing their idiosyncratic ends across the face of the ancient globe; and, rarely, some representative of the ultramond races that had settled on Old Earth in distant, bygone millennia, transforming wastelands into facsimiles of landscapes whose originals were light-decades distant.

Filidor watched the ebb and flux of passersby, until a rustically clad group of pedestrians moving along the walkway on the other side of Vodeł Close reminded him of the passengers in the carryall, which made him think again of the instant when the young woman had turned her eyes up to his, flooding him with her smile. The remembered image was so strong that it almost prevented him from realizing that the people now passing out of view across the small street were none other than the very same folk from that morning, including the girl with the smile, and that he was now once again about to lose the opportunity to make himself known to her.

He sprang at once from his chair, and struck out across the crowded room, caroming off the waiter, upon each of whose extended arms balanced several small saucers filled with pickles, sweetmeats, and appetizers. The man went down with a clatter and a stream of observations on Filidor's character that were at wide variance from those he had earlier vouchsafed. The Archon's apprentice heard none of it. He burst through the street door and was down the steps and into Vodel Close before the last dish had ceased rattling on the restaurant's floor.

He caught sight of his quarry a few score paces away and across the street, and immediately stretched his legs to catch them up. Heedless of persons in his way, or of the sharp opinions they expressed, he flung himself through the intervening distance until his outstretched fingers touched the shoulder of the girl.

She turned, startled, alarm and puzzlement in her sea-green eyes, which then widened farther as recognition dawned. Filidor was relieved to see that she remembered him from the morning, and then delighted to see that this second encounter appeared to be as welcome to her as it was to him. She set her top teeth lightly on her lower lip and regarded him with the frank appreciation she might have given to an unexpected present before tearing loose the ribbon.

"Well, hello," she said.

"Hello, indeed," he answered.

One of her companions, a solidly built young man for whom the word "thick" was an almost universal description—thick neck and wrists, thick hair and lips—now came around the girl and positioned himself more in front than beside her. His expression indicated that he doubted Filidor was any kind of gift at all. Another man, older and thin in every way that the other was thick, hovered behind them.

"This is my brother, Thorbe," said the young woman, elbowing her way past the thickness. "And behind me is Ommely, our fetchfellow. I am Emmlyn Podarke, of the town of Trumble."

Filidor affected the most expansive gesture of formal greeting, ending with a flourish that demonstrated practiced grace. "I am Filidor Vesh," he said, "in service to the Archonate."

For the second time in their very short acquaintance, the Archon's apprentice saw raw surprise take charge of Emmlyn's features. Identical expressions seized the other two, and the brother emitted a monosyllable of wonderment.

"This is a wondrous coincidence," the young woman said. "You are the very man that we came to Olkney to see. We wrote to your uncle, and he replied that you were ideally placed to adjudicate our cause."

Filidor's heart now grew beyond all limits. Not only had he met the woman he felt certain could be the light of his being, but she had come to him with some great need that he was uniquely positioned to meet. He knew it must be great if it had brought her all the way to Olkney from a place so distant that he wasn't sure that he had ever heard of it. He would surely meet that need, any precedents and procedures to the contrary be damned, because he would thus endear himself to her, gaining a vantage from which all manner of blessings might be pursued.

"I would be delighted to hear your case," he said. "The Archonate exists to answer your requirements."

"We have an appointment for tomorrow," the brother said. "Meanwhile, we are to put our concerns in writing."

Filidor said, "If you could sketch an outline now, I will be better prepared to weigh the intricacies tomorrow."

Emmlyn tossed her head in a manner that Filidor found delightful. "There are no intricacies," she said. "A cabal of out-of-county folk calling themselves the Ancient and Excellent Company of something or other wish to undertake certain operations on our land, against our expressed will. They cannot help but do harm to our clabber vines, which were planted centuries back by our ancestor Hableck Podarke. Their arrogance is insufferable. They must be stopped."

She placed her hand on Filidor's arm. "But now all is warmth and sunbeams. For here you are, and we are rescued."

But a tiny chill had invaded the sunshine pouring into Vodel Close. "You mentioned a company," he said.

Thorbe Podarke said, "They call themselves The Ancient and Excellent Company of Assemblors and Sundry Merchandisers."

Emmlyn snorted in a feminine way that Filidor would have found enchanting if the chill was not deepening and spreading through his vitals. "Ancient, indeed," she said. "They are but recently formed. Our uncle, Siskine Podarke, thinks them a shield for someone who does not wish to have his ends in public view."

"They are not of respectable character," put in Ommely, as if that judgment was all that ever need be said.

Filidor's insides were now in the grip of full winter. The young woman must have read the distress on his face, for she took his arm in a firmer grip and said, "You look unwell."

"I am so sorry," said the Archon's apprentice.

"I hope I am not in some way the cause of . . ." she began, but Filidor's fear gave urgency, if not eloquence, to his confession.

"The Company," he cried. "This morning . . . in my office . . . a petition . . . I didn't know . . . Amenable Leniency, they said . . ." He held up the finger that wore his sigil ring, and made as if to impress the air between them. "I am so sorry."

Emmlyn's face reordered itself from concern to puzzlement, then moved on to comprehension, and finally settled upon outrage. Filidor flinched under her hardening gaze.

"You didn't," she whispered.

"I did," he replied.

For a long moment, she merely stared at him, while Filidor was seized by a fear that she would walk away from him and that he would never see her again.

Instead, she drew back the hand that had been resting on his arm, made a fist of it, and thumped him soundly on the chest. Filidor staggered back, but she came after him, now bringing the other fist into operation, pummeling his torso with both hands as he backstepped through the pedestrians, and with each landed blow she issued an opinion.

"You bubble! You great noddy! Nibblewit! Lip thrummer!"

More from the effect of her epithets than of her thumpings, Filidor's strength trickled away. His knees softened and he fell backward to the pavement. She came after him still, and he glanced at her sturdy country shoes in fear that she would next set about kicking him. But instead she stood over him for a moment, fists on her hips. Then, shaking her coppery ringlets in token of having come to a decision, she reached down and seized the plaque that hung about his neck. A swift yank and the chain parted. A moment later, she came again and pulled the ring from his finger.

"There!" she said. "Now, if you want these back, you'll have to make yourself properly useful, won't you?" Then she turned on her heel and marched away through the goggling spectators. Her brother and servant delayed a moment to close their mouths, then hurried after.

Filidor raised himself onto his elbows and appealed to the curious faces that looked down at him. "She can't do that," he said.

"Evidently, she can," confirmed a large woman. "Because she just did."

Filidor rode the ascender back up to the palace. Ordinarily, the upward motion would have caused the young man's innards to drop as the rest of him rose, but the events in Vodel Close had already plunged the inner Filidor to the lowest setting. Ordinarily, too, the device would have swept him to a landing near the door to his office; but now he found himself diverted onto a hitherto unnoticed branch of the system and deposited on a public platform some distance below his destination.

"This is not where I wish to go. Take me to the fourth level of the seventh terrace," he said.

The disk, which had been about to depart, stopped. A chime sounded, then a voice spoke from the air, saying, "Visitors must be escorted beyond this point. Please inquire at the kiosk."

"I am not a visitor," said Filidor. "I am Filidor Vesh, nephew to the Archon."

"I do not detect your plaque and sigil," said the disk.

"I do not have them with me."

There was a brief hum, then the voice said, "Visitors must be escorted beyond this point. Please inquire at the kiosk."

Filidor aimed a kick at the hovering object, but its surrounding energies gently guided his foot back to the ground. It gave a small cluck of disapproval, then departed.

Filidor looked about. He was on a wide curving terrace floored with ocher brick, the open space broken here and there by clumps of broad-leafed trees set in circles of mulched earth. A few dozen people, none of them Archonate staff, strolled about in couples and small groups, either on their way to view the eclectic wonders on display in what remained of the half-ruined Connaissarium of the Archon Terfel III, or on their way back from that enlightening experience. Near the crumbling arch that led into the ancient building, Filidor spied a communications kiosk. He crossed the terrace to the device and attracted its attention.

"I am Filidor Vesh," he told its grille. "I have misplaced my plaque and sigil and require entry to my offices."

"Such matters are beyond my competence," said the kiosk. "I will connect you with a more capable authority."

There was a brief pause, then a familiar voice spoke through the grille. It said, "What?"

Filidor repeated his requirements.

The integrator paused briefly before replying, "According to my information, Filidor Vesh has just chartered an air-yacht, a commodious Spelton Precipitator with full crew. He is about to depart with two companions for Trumble."

"Cancel the charter," Filidor said. "My plaque and sigil have been purloined and put to improper use."

"Ah," said the integrator, "this would explain the inordinate sums charged against the same account at Xanthoulian's and The Prodigious Palate. The auditors have been at a loss to explain how one person could possibly consume so many costly delicacies at a single sitting. Now all is explained."

"There is no need to complicate an already confused situation," said Filidor. "Merely cancel the charter and send proctors to apprehend the air-yacht. In the meantime, instruct the ascender to convey me to my office."

"It is not I who is complicating the situation," said the voice. "Until a few moments ago, the world was proceeding with its customary smoothness. Then you appeared and made demands that are clearly out of the ordinary. If the plaque and sigil of Filidor Vesh are moving rapidly through the air toward a distant city, as indeed they have been for several seconds now, it is only logical to assume that Filidor Vesh himself is doing the same. After all, that is how things have worked until now, and we have no reason to expect sudden divergences."

"I do not care to engage in a philosophical dialogue," said Filidor. "I want to go home."

"Ah, well," said the voice, "now you open up entire new vistas for speculation. Can one ever truly go home again? Consider the case of the notorious Absamor Takofferny, who before departing his native village to see the world isolated all of its environs and inhabitants in a strong stasis field, leaving them congealed in one unending moment while he roved abroad for a lifetime, before eventually returning, gray-bearded and tracked with age, to revivify them. All was as he had left it, until his neighbors discovered what he had done to them. Then they beat him to death."

"I have more pressing concerns than the schemes of forgotten monomaniacs," said Filidor. "Now, will you admit me?"

But the integrator was still inclined to pursue abstruse

conjectures, so Filidor's hand snapped out and broke the connection. Now he would have to resort to a riskier means of regaining entry to his quarters. Reluctantly, he passed through the archway into the Connaissarium, crossed the tiled floor of its atrium, and took the leftmost of several doors that led into the building proper. He hurried through a gallery lined with cases displaying the stuffed carcasses of various hybrids created during one of the heydays of genetic prestidigitation, and came to an alcove that housed a dark, slablike artifact that had been found orbiting an outer planet many millennia before. The object had been investigated and found to have neither internal parts nor apparent function, except that it sometimes emitted the mysterious syllables "Spa fon?" to persons who came within arm's length.

Today, the thing held its peace as Filidor squeezed behind it and felt along the alcove's rear wall. When his fingers located a group of shallow depressions, he pressed and twisted, until a panel moved inward and to the side. The young man stepped into the passageway thus revealed and picked up a lumen from a boxfull that he had left there years before. It had been so long since he had come this way that there was an appreciable coating of dust on the appliance's refractor.

Growing up, Filidor had not been the most dutiful of nephews. His uncle had pressed him to study and reflection, but the boy had not been proficient with abstract concepts, and had been more attracted to frivolous pursuits. In those years, Filidor often required avenues of escape and avoidance that would allow him to put himself, at least temporarily, beyond the reach of the Archon for an hour or an afternoon. He had therefore assiduously explored the chambers and corridors of the immense Archonate palace, pushing, twisting, and tapping on anything that might conceivably control a covert door or bolt hole. Regrettably, his efforts had abused and damaged many innocent ornaments and fixtures. But, every now and then, a wall had slid open and offered him a means of disappearing from view. Some of the hidden adits led to passageways that could take him well beyond the regions of the palace where his uncle might be searching for him.

The alcove behind the slab artifact led to one such secret way. It meandered up and into the living rock of the Devinish Range, step after seemingly endless step, until it came to a small landing backed by a blank wall. In an upper corner of the barrier was a faded chalk circle, underneath which the words "Press Here" appeared in a child's scrawl.

Filidor lowered himself to sit on the landing and let his trembling legs dangle down the top steps. The last time he had reentered the palace by this route, he must have been smaller, lighter, and a good deal springier when it came to bounding up stairs. Now he waited until the long muscles of his thighs ceased to leap and twitch of their own accord and until his ears were not overfilled with the rush of his breathing and the thudding of his pulse. Finally, he crawled to the wall and pressed an ear against it, straining to hear any sound from the chamber beyond.

It was equipped, he remembered, as an apparaticist's workroom. His uncle had had it fitted out as a suitable place for Filidor to master the elementary disciplines involved in the creation, maintenance, and repair of the various devices he was likely to encounter as he went through life. But the adolescent Filidor had balked at the Archon's proposal.

"I require a working knowledge of only one device," he had said, languidly indicating the communicator on the workbench. "With this, I can summon Master Berro, and have him restore whatever needs restoration."

"True enough," said his uncle. "But suppose this should happen." He picked up a twin-headed maul and struck the communicator a harsh blow, so that its components scattered across the workbench. "Then what would you do?"

And while Filidor spluttered, the Archon had instructed the young man to repair the fractured instrument so that he could then summon someone to unlock the door of the workroom, which the Archon bolted behind him as he left. Filidor had not repaired the device; instead, he had explored the workroom until he found the concealed exit. His uncle had not mentioned the matter again, leaving Filidor to wonder if he might have passed the test after all.

Crouched on the landing, Filidor listened for several long moments. There was a slight possibility that his uncle might be using the work space for one of his idiosyncratic research projects, poking about in some arcane apparatus from a bygone age, trying to get it to perform whatever pointless function it had been designed to achieve by inventors who by now were most likely part of the dust that accumulated everywhere throughout the palace.

No sound penetrated the stone from the other side of the wall. The young man stood up and pressed the chalk circle, causing the wall to rotate on a central pivot. The space beyond was dark. Filidor stepped through and closed the portal behind him. He had left the lumen on the landing, in case he ever had to come this way again, and now he waited in the unlit workroom for his eyes to adjust to the dimness.

The place was not totally dark. A small light glowed on the other side of the room, so faint that it faded from view when Filidor looked at it directly, and could only be apprehended from the corner of his vision. Memory told him that its source must be slightly above the main workbench, but he could not think of any device that might account for it.

Intrigued, he felt his way across the room toward it, until a nearer distance made it bright enough to see straight on. He moved closer still, bending to peer at what was now revealed to be a transparent sphere no wider than the tip of his finger, hovering unsupported above the bench top, black within but shot through with a myriad of scintillating points of luminescence.

"Remarkable," Filidor mused to himself.

"Just so," said a creaking but familiar voice nearby. Filidor leapt backward and collided with some piece of equipment hidden in the darkness.

"Careful!" hissed his uncle. "The equilibrating energies have not reached full resonance. You might evaporate the connection."

"I cannot see," said the young man.

"Why not?" snapped the Archon.

"There is no light."

"You mean you still can't see without light?"

"No, uncle."

The Archon made the same disapproving noise with which the ascender disk had greeted Filidor's attempt to kick it. "You must return to your studies," he said.

The little man then went on to explain that any light in the workroom at the present stage of his experiment would vitiate the delicate forces with which he was working. He seized his nephew's arms in his customary strong grip—both of the captured limbs immediately began to go numb—and maneuvered him through the darkness to a position on the other side of the bench. Filidor felt an instrument of some kind being pressed into his tingling hand. "Depress the uppermost stud when I tell you," said the Archon.

Filidor heard the rustle of the little man's clothing as he worked his way carefully around to the other side of the bench. His uncle was humming to himself, and there was a clink and clatter of objects being rearranged, then the crackling voice said, "By the way, don't touch the bottommost stud at all."

"Why not?" said Filidor. "What would happen?"

There was a pause from the other side of the table, then his uncle said, "You would not be here, and I would have to send for a new assistant."

"Where would I be?" asked Filidor.

"Difficult to say. But I wouldn't expect to see you return."

Filidor felt a sheen of perspiration suddenly interpose itself between his hand and the object it held. It began to slip from his grasp, and he clutched at it with sudden desperation, causing it to slip under his fingers. "Uncle," he said, "I think you should send for another assistant. A more capable one."

"Don't do that," said the little man.

"Don't do what?" said Filidor. A flash of panic iced the nape of his neck and he clutched the instrument tightly enough to make his hand bones ache.

"Don't think. Just press the top stud when I say."

The humming resumed. After an interminable few seconds, the dwarf spoke again. "All right, now!"

Filidor pressed the topmost stud. There was a crackle of energy and a bluish glow briefly loomed behind the diminutive sphere, then faded to deep indigo before finally disappearing into the surrounding gloom. The sphere itself then dwindled rapidly to a mere pinprick of light and winked out, leaving Filidor in complete blackness.

"Don't move," said the Archon. A moment later, the workroom was flooded with bright illumination. The little man set a powerful lamp on the gleaming metal bench top, then reached below and brought up a framework of metal rods that he rapidly assembled while whistling tunelessly through pursed lips. When the apparatus was configured to his liking, he peered with tightly scrunched eyes at the surface of the workbench. "Must be here somewhere," he said, and touched the framework at several of its intersections.

A shimmer of energy rippled over the bench top, then stabilized into a layer of green plasma in which rotating arms of cerulean blue radiance extended from a central pinpoint of black.

"Aha," said the Archon. He adjusted the rods of his mechanism, and the rotation gradually slowed to a stop. He did something else to the device, and the core of the flux expanded to the size of a serving platter, its darkness again flecked with tiny disks and whorls of light. "Hand me the speculum," he said to Filidor.

Filidor selected a tube from among a slew of instruments scattered on a side table. By luck, it was the device his uncle required. He watched as the little man peered through the cylinder at the display on the workbench, and when he again heard the tuneless whistle, he began to edge quietly toward the outer door. His fingers had just found the knob that would open the portal when his uncle said, without looking up, "Why were you sneaking into the palace through the Terfel Connaissarium?"

"Nostalgia?" Filidor tried. He sought to turn the knob, but it was locked.

"Come back here, and wait until I have concluded this procedure," said the Archon. "It's time we had a revealing talk."

Filidor saw his hopes evaporate. To his certain recollection, no revealing talk with his uncle had ever revealed anything to his own benefit. In his younger years, they had been one-sided discussions that all too often led to unusual experiences through which the Archon sought to encourage in his nephew a due regard for the responsibilities that accompanied a position in society. Filidor might have accepted these assignments with more grace, if he had ever been able to understand exactly what his uncle wished him to learn from such exercises as introducing dozens of small, scurrying animals into the annual gala of the Commendable Order of the Eminent Demesne, just as the senior members of the society were leading their partners onto the floor to dance a solemn pavane. The ensuing chaos was memorable—a number of dowagers climbed the furniture, while others scaled their escorts—but Filidor could not grasp whatever lesson his uncle had intended. At times he wondered whether the Archon, who as Grand Master of the Commendable Order had placidly viewed the commotion from his ornate seat upon the dais, had ordered the prank merely for his own amusement.

"Uncle," he had asked once, "is confusion a necessary precursor of enlightenment?"

The Archon had given him one of his rare smiles and nodded his assent.

"Then I must someday achieve a great edification," Filidor said, "because I seem to spend my days in perpetual befuddlement."

His uncle had clapped him on the shoulder and sent him off to paste up posters offering an extravagant reward for a missing pet feranche said to belong to the doted-upon daughter of a wealthy magnate. The notices went into exacting detail: "a rare Noriego Blue, with underplumage of saffron and emerald scapulars and secondaries," but since no such variety of feranche had ever existed, all those who appeared at the appointed time and place bearing artfully dyed specimens were quickly clapped into detention. Filidor felt that he had at last seen to the bottom of one of his uncle's schemes, until he soon after encountered two of the felons not only at large, but newly attired in the green and black livery of the Archonate's Bureau of Scrutiny.

Now he watched as the dwarf set a thin disk of gray metal on a side table. Next he found a new device and focused its aperture on the dark globe above the workbench. The Archon spun large dials and nudged tiny levers until their arrangement met with his satisfaction. Then he fingered a control. The action had no discernible effect that Filidor could see, but when the little man turned and passed a detecting device over the gray disk, whatever he found there evoked a grunt of pleasure.

The Archon looked up and seemed to focus on Filidor for the first time. "Where are your sigil and plaque?" he asked.

Filidor stepped closer to the workbench. "Is this what I think it is?" he asked. It was a desperate ploy, which would come to nothing if his uncle did not automatically return the serve. In truth, Filidor would have had difficulty identifying all but the most common apparati in the workroom, and even some of those would have required a hopeful guess. But if he could reignite the Archon's enthusiasm for tinkering, he might avoid—or at least put off—the promised revealing talk and an encounter with certain questions whose answers demanded time for creativity.

Fortunately, the dwarf returned Filidor's sally without a blink. "Yes, it is," he said. "It all began when I discovered a working model of a Zenthro Intrusifer in the upper southwest wing, and restored it to working condition."

"Indeed," said Filidor. "Please tell me more."

His uncle proceeded to do so. Some of it Filidor understood—the part about the universe being permeated by infinite variations of itself in unthinkable miniature, each one differing from every other by insignificant or massive degrees of variance, every child knew that—but the ability of Zenthro's device to isolate one of these infinitesimal realms and intrude it into the larger cosmos, where it could be enlarged and examined, that was new to him.

"An impossibly ancient technology, of course," said the Archon, "but wonderfully effective. And it prompted me to undertake a very productive line of research." From there, the dwarf soon descended into complexities and terminologies well beyond Filidor's orbit, but the young man grasped that a device of his uncle's own creation—the thing with dials and levers—allowed him to reach into the tiny intruded universe and identify a particular object in it. More than that, the Archon's device could replicate the chosen object and enlarge it to a manageable size, so that it could be kept for study in this macrocosm after the intruded nanocosm had been released.

"Remarkable," said Filidor, coming over to peer approvingly at the gray disk, where the replicated something apparently reposed, slowly enlarging in size. "But how did you deal with the, uh"—he waved a hand as if the apposite word temporarily escaped him—"the, how do you say . . ."

"The fermatic harmonization flux?" his uncle suggested.

"Exactly," said Filidor. "I was hoping you would explain that."

"I fed the excess energies into an implied tesseract, where they eventually . . ." But here the little man stopped. For a long moment, he regarded Filidor with an expression in which annoyance and congratulation mingled and contended with each other, then he said, "I asked you about your plaque and sigil."

Filidor looked down at his breast, abstractedly patting

parts of his torso. "I'm sure I had them this morning," he said. He could swear to that without qualm or quibble.

The Archon's hairless jaw moved sideways a time or two, then he pressed a point on his own entaglioed ring and spoke to the air, "Where is Faubon Bassariot?"

A chime sounded, then a voice said, "He is attending a private function in Eckhevry Row."

The dwarf reached within his garments and activated the device that bent light and adapted sound around his person, so that he suddenly appeared to be a tall, austere man of regal bearing, wearing garments that were of richly woven stuff and impeccable taste. The Archon had long ago understood that certain folk in Olkney—especially those who thought themselves the cream afloat upon the whey—would prefer that the topmost point of their social pyramid be occupied by someone who appeared to fit the ideal of a wise and sagacious ruler, rather than by a small, yellowish creature which looked to have been indifferently designed and only half finished. Through most of his upbringing, Filidor himself had not known of his uncle's true appearance. It had only come to light when the two had traveled together through several of Old Earth's odd societies, on *the progress of esteeming the balance.*

The Archon pressed another control on the device around his waist, and now his voice, when he spoke again, had taken on a deep timbre that resonated wisdom and authority. "Connect me with Bassariot."

A man-sized screen appeared in the air, to be filled almost immediately by the image of Faubon Bassariot, dressed in formal apparel, his well-fed face abeam with satiation and complacency. He held in one hand a crystal beaker of wine, elevated above his sleek head, as if in the act of offering a toast. It took but a moment for the man to realize what had happened, at which his mien transmuted rapidly through shock to wariness before settling into an aspect of careful neutrality. He lowered the glass, made appropriate gestures, and said, "How may I be of service?"

"My nephew has apparently separated himself from his plaque and sigil," said the Archon.

"Most unfortunate," said Bassariot.

"Indeed," said Dezendah Vesh. "It was to prevent such misfortunes that I assigned you to govern his staff."

A flicker of concern surfaced on the official's face, then was as quickly drowned. "I am sure we can rectify the situation," he said, then the image turned to Filidor. "Do you recall where they were when you last saw them?"

Filidor raised his eyebrows and blew out his cheeks, examining the various zones of the workroom as if the answer might be found in some overlooked angle of the room.

"I advise you to answer entirely and only the truth," said his uncle.

Filidor heard in his tone a warning not to provoke him further. He took a deep breath, then said, "When I last saw them, they were disappearing down Vodel Close in the possession of a young woman named Emmlyn Podarke," he said.

"And how did she come to have them?" asked the Archon.

"She knocked me down and took them," his nephew said, then added, "after I offended her."

"And where is she now?"

"I am told that she has used my credentials to charter an air-yacht to Trumble, from where the Podarke family apparently hails."

Filidor looked to his majordomo. The official had grown quite pale, but his pallor worsened as the Archon turned to him and said, in a quiet voice, "Trumble. Does the place have significance to you, Bassariot?"

The panjandrum opened his mouth several times before anything came out. "Your nephew dealt with a small matter affecting Trumble this morning, I believe."

"What kind of small matter?"

"A permission to excavate on private land."

The Archon's expression said that he expected to hear more.

"The site is of minor archaeological importance, it seems. The excavators will take all precautions. The permission was merely a technicality."

That piece of information puzzled Filidor. The petition had been much more ornately written than any simple request for permission to dig in some old ruins. Either there was more to the substance of the document, or it had been deliberately overcomplicated. He wondered if Bassariot had been playing some obscure joke on him.

The young man gave a snort of irritation, which he immediately recognized as the wrong sensibility to display to his uncle at that moment. The projected image of the Archon's noble head turned to him, wearing a distinct frown.

Filidor made a conciliatory gesture and stepped back. As he did so, his hand accidentally touched the disk of gray metal. He felt the tiniest of tinglings in his palm, and immediately pulled his hand free. He looked at the skin and saw nothing untoward, and since the minuscule sensation faded at once, he placed both hands behind his back and set himself in a posture of polite attention.

The Archon turned back to the majordomo. "We have a problem. I charged you to instill a sense of responsibility in my nephew, by giving him appropriate duties. Instead, I hear that he has slid back into the pampered slough from which

I plucked him. Now he has lost irreplaceable articles which, let loose in the world, might cause all manner of disruption."

Bassariot commenced a series of placatory words and gestures, but ceased when the Archon's aristocratic brow wrinkled in displeasure. "I will send a team of handpicked . . ." he began again.

"You will not," said the Archon. "You will go yourself to Trumble. Do you know the place?"

Bassariot shrugged. "I was there once, just briefly, a year or so ago."

"Well, now you will go there again, taking my nephew with you. You will recover the missing items and return them to me, along with this Podarke person, after which an inquiry will be made."

"I will be happy to conduct an inquiry . . ." the functionary began, but the Archon cut him off.

"I will conduct the inquiry, and it will be full and searching."

Bassariot, now very pale, bowed low. "I shall make arrangements to leave first thing tomorrow."

"Sooner would be better," said the Archon, "and now would be best."

At the mention of the "Podarke person," Filidor experienced an odd tickle of emotion, centered somewhere in his lungs. Though she had buffeted him quite thoroughly before the gaze of passersby and relieved him of his plaque and sigil, he could not resist a softness in his attitude toward her, which created an urge to say something in her favor. "Uncle . . ." he began.

The Archon flicked his gaze briefly in his nephew's direction and said, "Silence is your wisest strategy," then returned to Bassariot. "Do this quietly, assuming no official veneer. Conceal your status and travel as two casual gad-abouts who have a yen to visit obscure corners of the world."

"May one ask the reason for stealth?" the official said.

The Archon stroked his pointed chin again. "Of late, there have been subtle indications, though nothing tangible, just a suggestion of a whiff of malfeasance within these walls. Call it intuition, but I feel that these purloiners of my nephew's identification are somehow bound up in whatever ill deeds contaminate the Archonate."

"This is very serious," began Bassariot. He paused to lick plump lips, looking thoughtful, then continued, "I believe there is no direct passage from here to Trumble, which is beyond Mt. Cassadet, hence the criminals' chartering of an air-yacht. In such a small place, two such vessels arriving one on the fins of the other would surely draw comment. But a regular packet ship crosses Mornedy Sound and connects to the aerial tramway at Chavaneric, which would take us overland to Miggles. And that is close enough to Trumble to let us hire inconspicuous local transport."

The Archon thought a moment, then asked, "When does the next packet leave?"

"At sunset, I believe," said Bassariot.

The Archon made up his mind. "You will escort my nephew to Trumble, so that he may recover his lost identification and put to rights whatever is amiss there. Then come back and we shall see what more there is to see."

"I shall immediately make arrangements," Bassariot said, and the screen disappeared.

The Archon deactivated his image-dissembling device and became his dwarfish self again. He regarded Filidor sourly. "Be careful," he said. "Something is amiss, and these felons who stole your plaque and sigil are somehow bound up in it."

Filidor rarely dared to gainsay his uncle's wisdom—only once could he recall being right when the Archon was wrong, and that was simply a question of timing—but the term "felons" clashed with his own intuition. Upon reflection he was surprised to discover that he could not allow Emmlyn Podarke's reputation to be challenged, despite what she had done to him. He recalled the servant Ommely's phrase.

"Uncle," he said, "I believe the Podarkes to be people of reputable character."

"Your judgments in such matters must be your own," said the dwarf. "Still, I must send Faubon Bassariot with you."

Filidor nodded in acquiescence, though his convictions remained as they were. But, fearing that another word might lead to his having to walk all the way to Trumble, he kept his dissension to himself. Besides, he had begun to feel a peculiar sensation at the prospect of again encountering Emmlyn Podarke, a lingering echo of the radiant expectation that had burst upon him when he had first set eyes upon her that morning. He chose not to think about the circumstances under which he had last seen her.

Another matter occurred to him. "Uncle," he said, "will we be expected to perform services for those we meet along the way?"

Filidor's previous travels through the world, in which he had assisted the Archon in *the progress of esteeming the balance*, were governed by the principle that Archonate staff must be of use to the societies they traveled through. But now the dwarf shook his hairless head. "The prudent man never passes by an opportunity to do a kindness," he said, "but for this journey, consider it more of an option than an obligation."

"Yes, uncle," said the young man.

"And be careful."

Faubon Bassariot's voice spoke from the air, saying, "Sir, all is in readiness. The boat awaits us."

Filidor made his farewells and departed, but he looked back to see the little man standing amid his tools and apparatus, his small yellow face worried and thoughtful.

Like a great pale beast of the sea, the *Empyreal* lay by the dock, its tiered decks ablaze with lights hung from the superstructure, its reflection sparkling on the dark glass of the water. Filidor and his keeper arrived in an unremarkable hired car, bearing only the rudiments of baggage. They had changed into nondescript traveler's attire: in Filidor's case, a hooded jacket and loose trousers of soft but durable stuff, green with dark trim, with a broad belt and a brimless hat, while Bassariot was subdued in browns and ochers and a black skullcap. They climbed the gangway moments before the ship's connection to land was broken and it surged gently toward the open water of Mornedy Sound.

A purser's aide directed them to a modest double cabin near the stern and advised them that the final seating in the second-class dining saloon would soon be served. Filidor counseled an immediate move in that direction, having missed his lunch and any other possibilities of sustenance since he had left his breakfast pastry half eaten on the unfinished *Implicator*. Faubon Bassariot seemed preoccupied, and the young man had to speak to him twice before he won a response.

"Very well," said the official and followed in Filidor's wake. His disconsolate manner gave way to a more cheerful air, however, when they entered the saloon and found a well-stocked buffet. They filled their salvers and repaired to one of the tables in the half-empty room.

The food was not to Xanthoulian's standards, but Filidor's hunger contributed a delectable sauce and he threw himself at the meal with good spirit. Bassariot ate with the air of a man making the best of not wholly welcome circumstances. But from time to time his expression warmed, as if he contemplated better days to come. Filidor paid little heed to the man, reserving his attention almost exclusively to plate and cutlery, except to reach for the carafe that held an overly confident purple Pwyfus, which was the best wine the ship's cellar could offer its second-class passengers. Eventually, however, when he had dulled the edge of his appetite to a comfortable roundedness, he pushed away the leftovers and sat back at his ease.

"How long do you expect the journey to take?" he inquired.

Bassariot chewed as he considered his reply, then said, "Across the Sound to Scullaway Point tonight, down the coast to Chavaneric by late tomorrow evening. By balloon tram, two days more to Miggles. Then a day to reconnoiter and remove ourselves to Trumble." He rubbed his hands. "I look forward—or rather, I am sure you look forward—to delivering a deserved retribution to those scallywags who assaulted you in the street."

"On the contrary," said Filidor, "I bear them no ill will."

Bassariot had speared a morsel from his plate and was toothing it with gusto, but at the young man's words he paused in mid-chew. "But, surely, the affront to your distinguished person . . ." he said.

Filidor waved airily, warming to his subject. He imagined how he might appear to Emmlyn Podarke if she could overhear him now. "What am I that I should not have visited upon me the perhaps entirely justified wrath of an outraged citizen?"

"Outraged? Justified?" said the majordomo, his plate now

forgotten. "You were knocked sprawling, pummeled without mercy, and robbed of your plaque and sigil. These are the hallmarks of brigands."

"No doubt there was extreme provocation," Filidor said. "There was mention of some local disagreement. I sensed that these were persons of reputable character, driven beyond the capacity for demurral."

Faubon Bassariot's eyes, that had been wide with consternation, now narrowed to a more calculating focus. "Your uncle has charged us—charged me, that is—with bringing these bandits to account. Yet I sense that we are not reading from the same manual."

"I interpret his orders in a different light. He said I was to put things right. To me, that conveys a wider ambit of action than you appear to contemplate. But doubtless all shall become clear once we are on the scene and able to gather all the facts."

"The facts are already in hand," argued the functionary, ticking off points on stubby fingers, "assault, theft, flight, and there's an end of it. Unless we discover further improprieties have compounded those already grievous offenses once we reach Trumble."

"We may also learn of extenuating circumstances that cast the situation in quite another shade," said Filidor. "It may well be that the Podarkes were inflamed by injustice. In which case my duty is clear."

Bassariot made no answer, but peered at the young man as an agriculturist might regard one of his draft animals if it unexpectedly developed an inclination to plow the fields in fanciful arabesques instead of the desired straight furrows. He looked off into space for a moment as if weighing alternatives, then his features settled into an arrangement that suggested he had found a pleasant one. He declared, "All may be as you imagine, but tasting is the truest testimony, as the old saying goes. We will be in Trumble soon enough, and then light will be shone in all possible cracks and grottoes. In the meantime"—he lifted the decanter of Pwyfus—"why not take another glass of the wine, which is ingratiatingly robust if not truly genteel?" He paused, as if a new thought had just surfaced. "Or shall we lay hold of something with a little more grip to it?"

Filidor admitted that he was always eager for new experiences, and Bassariot refilled his glass. "Excellent," said the majordomo. "Have you ever tasted Red Abandon, the one they call the sailor's ruin?"

When Filidor said that he had not, Bassariot volunteered to go seek out a flask—it was always available at sea, he said.

"Very kind," said Filidor, thinking that he might have previously misjudged his majordomo, and that perhaps the official did not have a stick permanently lodged in some part of his anatomy.

Bassariot departed and Filidor poured another goblet of the Pwyfus, which seemed to be improving with age even as he emptied the carafe. He looked about the saloon and became aware of the other travelers in the room. They were divided into two groups. The larger, seated nearer to him, comprised more than a dozen men of uncompromising mien, each dressed in the distinctive yellow tabard that signified adherence to the Tabernacle of the Morphitic Demiurge.

Filidor knew of the cult, which professed that the universe and all its inhabitants were but the dreams of a slumbering deity, the awakening of which was every sentient creature's obligation. It had always struck him as a self-defeating credo, since rousing the demiurge must necessarily dissipate the divine imaginings, causing the cosmos,

52 ✗ MATTHEW HUGHES

including those who were doing the waking, to cease to be. But, like most people, his disdain for the sect arose from its members' frequent practice of clashing cymbals and shouting, "Awake!" or "Yah! Bahoo!" at unpredictable intervals wherever they happened to be, often to the discomfort of any within earshot. He had heard that their weekly services could cause permanent damage to the eardrums of persons who were merely passing by. They had lately been banned from attending theatrical and musical performances throughout the Olkney Peninsula. A pernicious subsect of the cult, the Pinchers, had fixed upon the notion that the god itself must be a character in its own dreamings, and therefore liable to be awakened by the application of direct physical force. Reasoning that anyone might be the dream avatar of the slumbering deity, they had gone about seizing persons haphazardly, inflicting upon them sometimes horrific violence, until the provost had intervened.

The second group of passengers, sitting companionably around a small table in a lounge on the other side of the saloon, included three men and two women, all attired in a raffish fashion that Filidor associated with the profession of entertainer. Two of the men were no more than a few years older than Filidor, and now that he looked closely at them, it was apparent that they were twins. The third man was older, heavyset, and saturnine, and Filidor could see that the brothers deferred to him. Of the women, one was young, lithe, and dark-haired, with a sharp-edged face turned toward the window that faced the receding shore. The other was of an age with the older man, matronly and at ease with herself, her hands quietly and competently assembling something out of a ball of yarn in her wide lap.

The older woman looked up from her work and apprehended Filidor's idle gaze. She said something to the others, and they all—save for the girl—turned to look his way. The older man lifted his head and his voice, which carried resonantly across the salon, even above the din from the Tabernaclists, and said, "Sir, why sit in solitude? We invite you to join us."

Filidor made gestures indicating a desire not to intrude, but the older man responded with an arms-wide motion that redoubled the strength of the original invitation. At that moment, the nearby Tabernaclists erupted in a sudden clamor of shouts and cymbals, with one enthusiast slamming his ceremonial staff repeatedly on the table. Filidor rose, and bringing the carafe and goblet with him, crossed to the five by the windows.

He waited until the sacred hubbub had subsided, then performed the gestures appropriate to the encounter. He almost said, "I am Filidor Vesh . . ." but remembered in time his uncle's warning to travel incognito, and indicated instead that his name was Gaskarth, and that he was a gentleman at leisure from Olkney, out to see some of the world.

The older man indicated that Filidor should sit among them and said, "I am Erslan Flastovic." He paused then as if expecting Filidor to recognize the name, but seeing no light in the young man's window, continued in a hopeful tone, "of Flastovic's Incomparable Mummery Troupe and Raree Exposition?"

Filidor's face now illuminated with an expression that gratified Flastovic's expectations, for it was the very troupe that the Archon's apprentice had briefly watched the evening before, in the Square of the Indentors on his way to The Prodigious Palate. Though that had been the first time he had actually seen such an exposition, he had a vague notion, drawn from a comment by a lordly acquaintance who occasionally retreated to an estate beyond the hamlet of Binch, down at the landward end of the Olkney Peninsula, that such entertainments were more common in the ruder areas outside the city. Shows like Flastovic's traveled from one rustic patch to another, diverting the bucolic with dramatizations of simple tales and homilies.

Flastovic introduced the others. "This is my spouse, Gavne," he said, indicating the older woman, who answered Filidor's inclination of the head with a placid smile, "and my daughter, Chloe."

This close, Filidor could see that the young woman was not far beyond girlhood. She turned briefly toward him, offered a wry look, then returned to her retrospection of the receding shore, which was now not much more than a glow in the night sky above the horizon.

"And these two gentlemen are the celebrated Florrey Twins, Ches and Isbister, as I'm sure you already know."

"Of course," Filidor said again, without revealing that whatever right the brothers had to a claim of celebrity was unknown to him. They were truly identical, both blond, narrow of feature and slim of build, dressed alike in black with silver accents. One of them had probably played the role of Badrey Huzzantz the night before, but Filidor could not have said which.

"I am Ches," said the one on the right. "We are bound for Scullaway Point tonight. There we will unship our land vessel, a twenty-wheeled Steadfast groundeater which affords us a combination of transportation, living quarters, and a folding proscenium stage. We shall mount up, travel south to Thurloyn Vale, then work our way east, spending the summer idling from town to town in the dales west of Dimfen Moor. We anticipate a glorious run, and fine notices in the local periodicals."

"You have seen our work?" asked the other Florrey.

"I chanced to see a few moments of it last night while passing through Indentors Square on my way to dinner," answered Filidor. "Very interesting."

"How could it not be," said Flastovic, while Gavne nodded companionably, "when we bring to glittering life the deathless works of that inimitable artist, The Bard Obscure?"

Here, amidst the adjectives, was a name Filidor recognized. He knew that the dramatist had flourished centuries before, but there had been some kind of controversy—no one now remembered the details—which had led to a thorough expunging of his name and a destruction of all copies of his plays. It was generally believed that the playwright himself had ordered the devastation, though a minority view held that he had angered powerful forces.

In any case, the attempt to expunge was unsuccessful. Though all records were destroyed, the works still existed in the memories of actors who had performed them. Out of those recollections grew a novel tradition: the plays were never again written down, but a special class of thespian arose—those who had committed The Bard Obscure's entire corpus to memory. That was all Filidor knew about the subject, but he spoke with the air of one who could have said a great deal more.

"The lines are voiced by a *disclamator*," confirmed Flastovic. "He speaks while we performers silently contribute the accompanying poses and actions. A demanding profession, the disclamator's; master practitioners are few and much sought after."

"We work with Ovile Germolian," put in one of the Florrey brothers, in a tone that told Filidor they expected him to be impressed.

"Indeed," he replied, feigning exactly that impression. The purple Pwyfus was inclining him toward mischief. He was deriving an odd enjoyment from pretending to know more than he did. Normally, to discover that he lacked some knowledge that all around him seemed to possess tended to depress his spirits, but here he felt like a cunning agent of an espionic service, duplicitously blending in with his surroundings. The deception wouldn't matter: he would not see these people again.

The wine also seemed to be sharpening his perceptions. He noted that at the mention of Germolian's name a look passed from mother to daughter, in which a tinge of worried disapproval briefly troubled Gavne's placid facade. The returned sentiment on the girl's face was a resentment scarcely concealed, an elevation of the nose, and a return of her gaze to the window.

Erslan Flastovic seemed to notice nothing amiss, and weighed in with praises for the great disclamator. "Remarkable speaking voice, Germolian, goes without saying," said the leader of the troupe. "But his genius is in the timing. He knows to the very nanenth when to hold the pause and when to break it."

Filidor was about to offer a glib confirmation of the analysis when a tiny sound close by his left ear caused him to turn his head. There was nothing there. He thought at first that it must have been a resonance from one of the Tabernaclists' sacred noisemakers, but now he saw that the cultists had left the saloon while he had been speaking with the mummers.

He realized that the others were regarding him quizzically. "I'm sorry," he said, "I thought I heard . . ."

The sound came again, a very faint chime. "Did you hear that?" he asked the others, and was met with "No's" and shaken heads from the older members of the troupe, and a twist of the lips from Chloe that indicated a declining confidence in the soundness of his mind.

"Ship's integrator," Filidor said, and was answered by a chime—much louder—and a voice that said, "What do you require?"

"Were you attempting to attract my attention just now?"

"I regret, sir," the ship said, "there is so much to do in making sure that this vessel, its passengers, and its contents are delivered safe and whole to its next port of call that I lack the leisure to nudge persons at random. If you are hearing sounds you cannot account for, it may be time to consider the quantity of wine you have consumed to be enough for one sitting."

"That will be all," said Filidor.

"As you say," said the integrator and went back to its duties.

The members of Flastovic's troupe regarded Filidor speculatively. "I thought . . ." he said, then decided that the incident would be better left behind. "Never mind."

The conversation returned briefly to the works of The Bard Obscure, but somehow the verve had been lost. Filidor then mentioned that he had heard that there existed, within the Archonate's vast archives, a voice recording of all the playmaker's works. The suggestion scandalized the mummers.

"Far be it from me to decry the Archonate," said Flastovic, while his spouse nodded in agreement.

"A wonderful institution," said one of the Florrey brothers, while the other said, "And fully necessary."

Chloe merely looked at the ceiling as if there were someone there who shared her mood, as her father continued with, "But it's a reprehensible concept. The Bard Obscure's works are not to be recorded, therefore no one should do so."

Ches nodded and said, "Just so. The works were his personal property. His wishes must be paramount."

"But he wanted them destroyed, or so I've heard," said Filidor. "Yet you go about performing them."

"If he'd wanted them destroyed, he'd have killed all the actors who had them in memory," said Ches. "He didn't, so that can't be what he wanted."

There was a flaw in the man's reasoning, Filidor knew, but the purple Pwyfus was obscuring it from his vision.

Isbister moved the discussion back to ground that he favored. "The main issue is that the works are of universal import," he said, "and thus they should be available to all. The needs of the many must prevail."

At this, Ches rounded on his brother, saying, "As ever, your contentions are vapid. That which belongs to all belongs to none. If tomorrow a new Bard Obscure should arrive to grace our civilization, why then should he strive to create wonders, if they are only to be plucked from his grasp and thrown to a frittering rabble?"

Isbister drew himself erect and returned fire. "Your views are entirely idiosyncratic. What value have his works if the world cannot enjoy them? The thing that the artist prizes most—his renown—is predicated on his productions being widely appreciated."

Filidor sensed that he was witnessing only an episode in a long-standing disagreement between the brothers, unlikely to be resolved but certain to become tiresome. To deflect the course of the conversation, he inquired after the whereabouts of the disclamator Ovile Germolian.

"Well timed," said Flastovic, "for yonder he comes."

The young man looked up to see, coming toward them, a man of early middle age, whose handsome face bespoke languid intelligence through which a discerning eye might detect an inclination toward self-gratification, the kind of man who would not hesitate to take more than his share, but would do so with an easy grace.

Filidor noted that the young woman's eyes grew slightly larger and darker as she turned them toward the disclamator. He saw also the small vertical line that appeared between her mother's eyebrows and the slight drawing down at the corners of Gavne's mouth. Then he stood up and greeted the newcomer in an appropriate way.

"Are you in any way connected with the life?" asked Germolian, when he had chosen a seat close enough to Chloe that he must surely feel the warmth of her breath on his cheek. It took Filidor a moment to realize that the "life" referred to was that of show folk.

"No," he said, "I am but a gadabout, taking a taste of the world."

Upon hearing that, Germolian turned away as if Filidor had ceased to register upon his senses, and began a conversation with the Florreys. But it seemed to Filidor that, though the disclamator's focus rested on the twins, he was at no time unaware of the young woman beside him, nor of her mother's displeasure.

Flastovic seemed to be aware of none of this. He leaned toward Filidor and tapped the young man's knee. "We have planned to rehearse one of The Bard Obscure's pieces—just text and gestures, you understand; no costumes. Would you care to watch and perhaps offer an appreciation?"

"Delighted," said Filidor.

Ovile Germolian regarded him with half-lidded eyes. "Are you experienced in the art of the critique?" he asked.

"I can distinguish the artful from the artless," Filidor sent back.

"Indeed?" said the disclamator, and let his gaze wander away.

Flastovic stood up. "Places, please," he said.

Filidor rose with the others, and moved away from them as they pushed back the chairs and cleared a small space into the middle of which the leader of the troupe stepped, assuming an air of preparedness. Ovile Germolian drew himself to one side, and turned away from the group, as if to address an unseen audience. The twins and the two women stepped backward, so that it was obvious that Filidor should turn his eyes upon Erslan Flastovic.

"Ready?" said the leader. Germolian cleared his throat. The others nodded. Flastovic inclined his head toward Filidor and said, "You'll have to imagine the masks and paraphernalia." Then to the company, he said, "Begin."

"The Terrible Hand of Fate," declaimed Germolian, in a voice that Filidor found oddly stirring. "By The Bard Obscure."

There was a dignified pause, then the disclamator continued, in a deep and sonorous tone. *"There was a man who conceived that his neighbor had done him a terrible grievance. He brooded upon his apprehended injury, until he resolved to be revenged of it."*

Erslan Flastovic had assumed a posture that turned his whole body into a frown, hands clenched, jaws clamped, and shoulders indrawn. At Germolian's last words, his head came up and his chin jutted forth as he raised a fist to the air.

"The avenger cut himself a strong cudgel of blackest ferrick and went to his neighbor's home," said Germolian. *"He struck the door a fearsome blow and called the man's name."*

Flastovic mimed the shaping of the club and the striking of the door.

"But the neighbor had left earlier that day, and there

was no one at home. The blow to the door was answered by the device intended to announce visitors and take messages when none was available to welcome them."

Now Chloe stepped into the central space, adopting an attitude of serene helpfulness.

Germolian continued the tale. *" 'Who is it?' " asked the device.*

" 'It is the terrible hand of fate,' " declared the man with the cudgel." Flastovic struck the pose of a man in pursuit of destiny as the rolling voice continued the story.

"But the avenger's buffet had damaged the mechanism that answered the door, and it could make no further reply."

Chloe gazed placidly into space.

"So now the avenger smote the door an even heavier blow."

Flastovic raged against the air. Chloe turned politely in his direction.

" 'Who is it?' said the answerer."

Flastovic shook his fist as Germolian declaimed, *" 'It is the terrible hand of fate!' "* and Chloe remained blissfully unmoved.

"Again, there was no reply, and again the man struck the portal with huge violence, so that the cudgel split in his hand."

Flastovic portrayed a man driven to burst his every inner restraint. Chloe turned to him with poised serenity.

" 'Who is it?' asked the device, and this time the avenger was driven into such a paroxysm of rage that when he cried, 'It is the terrible hand of fate!' he was struck by an apoplexy, and fell down dead upon the doorstep."

Flastovic jerked and spun himself in two directions at once, then flung his body to the carpet, where he twitched once, then twice, before assuming a deathly stillness. Now the Florreys and Gavne drew in and gazed down at him in postures of wonder and speculation, while the girl still stared unconcernedly into space.

"Drawn by the commotion, people came from the nearby houses and found the man lying dead upon his cudgel.

" 'Who is it?' they said."

Now Chloe turned to face the unseen audience, her expression still empty of all but the mildest hope of accommodating, as the disclamator spoke the final line. *"And the doorway said, 'It is the terrible hand of fate.' "*

Filidor brought his hands together in sincere appreciation as Flastovic rose to his feet and the whole troupe bowed. "Very fine," the young man said. "Power and nuance, irony and pity, can't be beaten."

The players moved to surround Germolian, congratulating and praising his oration, commendations that he accepted as his due. Filidor saw Gavne frown as Chloe leaned in to kiss the man on his cheek, and also saw the disclamator's hand rest possessively upon the girl's hip a long moment.

A discreet cough sounded in Filidor's ear, and when he turned there was Faubon Bassariot hovering beside him, clutching a potbellied flask wrapped in red leather. The young man made introductions, and polite inquiries as to general well-being were exchanged. But the functionary declined Erslan Flastovic's invitation to join the congerie, and instead coaxed Filidor away to the other side of the saloon, "So that we might discuss our plans for the morrow without troubling these good folk."

The young man bid the mummers good night and crossed to where Bassariot led. But when they were seated at their former table, no discussion of travel plans arose. Instead, the majordomo introduced Filidor to the thick amber liquid known as Red Abandon and urged him to take a glass. It being his first essay of the legendary fiery liquor, the young man sipped gingerly, but even that small mouthful immediately took charge of his internal situation, marching straight to his stomach, then fanning out to several different parts of his person. "My," he commented when his voice reappeared, "this is very much the upper puppy."

"Have some more," said Bassariot, topping up Filidor's glass, and the young man did. The second installment burned less and spread farther, and Filidor felt an elevation of spirits. "There is much to be said for new experiences," he declared.

"And, equally," returned the majordomo, "there is much to be said for constancy."

Filidor poured himself a third helping, saying as he did so, "Constancy merits constant acclaim, as the saying goes."

"Just so," said Bassariot. "And is it still your intention to side with the Podarkes?"

The name conjured up a vision of green eyes and coppery hair. "I will do what is right," said Filidor.

"There you have it," said Bassariot, but Filidor had the strong impression that the man was talking to some unseen listener.

The young man drained the glass of Red Abandon. The fire in his middle had now banked to a comfortable glow, and he was aware of other unusual sensations. His arms seemed to have lengthened considerably, and he was no longer sure where his legs had got to. Faubon Bassariot's face, across the table, had begun to enlarge, swelling to fill the young man's vision.

"That's an interesting trick," Filidor said. "How's it done?"

The functionary had his head cocked to one side, as if listening to another voice. Then he looked at Filidor and said,

"Do you not think it would be better to leave matters mainly in my hands, once we are in Trumble? I am more experienced at toting up the pros and cons of complex issues."

But the image of Emmlyn Podarke had now replaced Bassariot's. "Beautiful girl," Filidor said.

He was so taken with his amorous mirage that he did not much notice the triumphant smile that now draped itself above Faubon Bassariot's ample chins. "I told you," the majordomo said.

"Told me what?" Filidor said. "And why is your face so huge?"

"Leave it to me. I'll take care of him," Bassariot said, as if Filidor had not even spoken, which caused Filidor to wonder if Red Abandon had done something to his vocal apparatus. "Hello?" the young man called across the table, which now seemed to stretch a vast distance.

The vision of Emmlyn Podarke had evaporated, and Bassariot was back, but now his features began to shrink and recede, becoming a small round object at the end of a long, red tunnel. Filidor was reminded briefly of the light fixture suspended above the bench in his uncle's workroom, and how the Archon's tall projected image would pass right through it when they were alone. The little man saw no reason to accommodate his projection by bending, since his true stature allowed him to pass under the lumen with room to spare.

The Red Abandon had the effect of leading the young man's thoughts along pathways down which they normally did not wander. He thought of all the times he had surreptitiously exited the workroom when he should have been employed at whatever educational task the Archon had set him. It suddenly burst upon Filidor that the little man was the kindest, best uncle a boy could have wished for, and with this thought, large tears sprang from his eyes. The tiny vision of Bassariot at the end of his tunnel misted to complete obscurity.

"My uncle is a wonderful man," Filidor said.

The dwindled majordomo said, "Oh, to be sure. Why not take another glass, then we might go on deck and survey the surroundings."

More of the Red Abandon seemed to Filidor an ideal proposition, and he cooperated fully. As the liquor percolated through his body, he felt his head separate gently from the rest of him, to float a little above his neck, like a tethered balloon. Then he had the peculiar sensation of drifting toward the door that led to the outer deck, and strangely enough when he looked down, his feet were moving across the carpet. Faubon Bassariot was walking beside him, clutching someone's arm. Filidor thought he recognized the arm, but couldn't quite place it.

At the door, Bassariot took the handle and pushed it open. At that moment, Filidor again heard the faint chime by his left ear, this time accompanied by a tiny voice that said, *Hello?*

"Hello," said Filidor, inducing his head to drift softly in the direction where the sound appeared to come from. There was no one there but Faubon Bassariot.

" 'Hello' might not be the most appropriate word," said the majordomo. His face, when Filidor was able to focus on it, seemed tight with suppressed excitement, pale and grim, the single dark curl plastered to his forehead like a hook.

Filidor felt himself maneuvered out onto the deck, where the wind of the ship's passage struck his overwarmed flesh like jets of cold water.

Can you hear me? said the small voice again, far away.

"You seem very far away," said Filidor.

"It is the effects of the liquor," said Bassariot, guiding the young man to the stern of the ship. "Soon to pass."

Where am I? said the voice.

"Where are you?" answered Filidor.

Bassariot said, "I am right here. Come, let us look over the rail."

They were at the stern, sheltered now from the wind. Farther forward, along the portside deck, the Tabernaclists were disputing a doctrinal point with their customary clamor. Bassariot led Filidor to the waist-high barrier. The wake of the *Empyreal* foamed like a chalk road across a field of shining black flint, laying a lingering trail of phosphorescence across the dark waters of Mornedy Sound. Olkney was only a glimmer on the farthest edge of the world.

Is that better, said the voice, now a little louder.

"Much better," said Filidor. "Who are you?"

There was an answer but it was drowned beneath Faubon Bassariot's hearty offer of, "One last pull at the flask, then off to bed."

Filidor felt the leather-covered glass pressed into his hand. He raised its neck to his lips. At the same instant, there came a sudden clashing of cymbals and shouts of "Ho, there!" and "Wakey-wakey!" from the clutch of Tabernaclists forward. The eruption of sound startled Filidor, and he dropped the flask. When he looked around for it, he had a startling view of the top of Faubon Bassariot's head. The majordomo was squatting behind him, his hands grasping the backs of Filidor's knees.

The Archon's apprentice was about to ask the functionary what he was doing down there, but the thought was driven from his mind when he discovered that, suddenly, he could fly. Amazingly, he was rising through the air, his shins brushing the top of the rail as he sailed out and above the boiling wake of the *Empyreal*. Then he didn't seem to be rising so much as swooping. The whiteness of foamed water loomed larger and larger, expanding until it filled his entire vision. He smelled the faint, salty reek of the sea.

Then he hit the cold water headfirst and was immediately sucked beneath the surface by the vortices of the ship's twin impellors. Filidor was tossed and flung in several directions at once, none of them toward the air. The small voice said, *How's this?* It was louder now, but Filidor was not equipped to answer. The chill blackness of the night sea had apparently entered through his feet and was steadily climbing to where the last vestige of him huddled on the highest shelf inside his head. Contrary to his hopes, the darkness came all the way up and collected him.

CHAPTER

THREE

W hen Filidor awoke, something gray and white
was standing on his chest. It clacked a sharp
yellow bill and cocked its head to eye him with
what he was sure was evil intent.

He opened his mouth to say, "Get off me!" but all that
came out of him was the kind of sound a particularly inarticulate beast might make, accompanied by a rolling belch
that reeked of stale Red Abandon. The bird took offense and
flapped away.

Filidor closed his eyes, having discovered that light, even
the weak light cast by the fading orange sun in this latter age
of Old Earth, was not a friend to his present condition. His
head felt as if his skull's contents had been roughly sawn
into segments that someone was now rhythmically rubbing
together without regard for consequences. His tongue was
entirely the wrong size and shape, and the taste in his mouth
caused him to worry that the departed bird might have left
something unpleasant there.

Eyes still tightly closed, he sought to sit up, pushing

against the resilient surface he was lying on. It felt to be yielding yet cold, fibrous yet slick. When he was fairly sure that the upper half of him had become vertical, he hung his head and allowed his eyelids to offer his vision the narrowest slit. Beneath and between his outstretched legs he saw an interwoven mat of green fibers and thick lengths of tuber, some of them dark of hue and some biliously pale. All at once he became aware of the smell. It was like low tide on a beach after a night of storms, and it made him retch; but only weakly—the lingering influence of Red Abandon prevented him from serious efforts of even the involuntary kind.

Shading his eyes from the sun, which appeared to be at its midmorning station, he looked about him. He was on a circular mat of aquatic vegetation, a little wider than he was tall, but thick enough to bear his weight. It was concave in shape, like a shallow bowl, its sides tightly woven and its lip a handbreadth above the water, which rippled past its outer sides with a contented swish and gurgle. *I'm in a basket,* he thought. Beyond lay nothing but green and level sea in every direction.

He looked down and saw, nestled between his right leg and the woven inner wall of the basket, a grayish object a little smaller than his head. He picked it up and found that it was a bladder full of a liquid that sloshed when he moved it, and stoppered by a plug of bone. Filidor pulled the stop from the neck, peered at then sniffed the contents, then tasted. It was water, fresh but flat.

He was immediately seized by a great burning thirst and drank down half the bladder's contents in several gulps. His stomach reacted to the sudden cool draft with instant outrage, and voted to send it back, but Filidor overruled his innards: there was no telling where the drinkable water had come from or whether there would be any more in the offing.

His thirst quieted, he felt a little closer to human, and tried to take stock of his predicament. He was sure that there was something unusual about the situation to which he had awakened, but his mental equipment was not yet available to consider it. He closed his eyes again, and would have sunk back to a reclining position, except that the smell of the seaweed at such close quarters was more than he could bear. He managed to coax his knees into bending, so that he sat crosslegged in the middle of the saucer of green. He belched another fetid reminder of the night's excess, and strove to remember how he came to be in this odd setting.

Gradually, pieces of the day before began to present themselves—not in order of occurrence, but as random flashes of individual scenes. He remembered being with his uncle in the workroom, then saw himself following Faubon Bassariot up a gangway. There was something about a cluster of Tabernaclists, and some mummers had performed. Then, like a curtain lifting on a tableau of bygone misery, he clearly saw the angry face of Emmlyn Podarke, her brother and servant behind her, as she reached down and yanked away his plaque and sigil. It all came back, and he groaned.

Hello, said a small voice from somewhere, and now Filidor remembered that mystery too.

"Huh?" he said. No more than a whisper of actual sound escaped his coated lips, but the voice responded immediately.

Where am I? it said.

Filidor opened his eyes. The glare of sunlight off water made them feel as if they were being sliced into sections, but he shaded them with a hand and looked about him. There was no one else in sight. "Not here," he said and let his lids shelter him from the pain.

Of course, I am here, said the voice. *I just don't know where* here *is.*

Something about the tone was familiar, but Filidor was more concerned with the larger mystery of where *he* was and how he had got there. Now another scene slotted itself into place: Bassariot's pale visage looming over a red flask, accompanied by the name of the amber corruption it contained.

The Archon's apprentice moaned again. "Red Abandon," he said.

Dreadful stuff, said the voice. *The sailor's ruin.*

Filidor opened his eyes and looked, but again there was nothing beyond him and the sea. Carefully, he turned his head to one side, then stretched out a hand to the edge of the woven bowl. Ever so slowly, he leaned his weight sideways until he could see down into the water. There was nothing there but green sea and a little white foam.

"Where are you?" he said.

We have established that, said the voice. *I am here. One is always here; even when one departs here to go there, the there then becomes the here in which one is. Since I do not know where this particular "here" happens to be, I believe it might be more useful to ask you where you are. It is impossible to navigate with only one point of reference, but if I can combine my here with your there, the rudiments of a map begin to take form.*

"I am at sea," said Filidor. "My reference points are endless water and a sky with the sun in it. At the center of things is a floating basket of seaweed, and at the center of the basket is me."

This is less useful than I had hoped for, was the reply. *I do not even know the means by which we are communicating, other than that I am emitting vibrations into some kind of surrounding medium that resembles contaminated sea-*

*water, nor how you are apprehending and returning these
signals. Normally, I have a wide range of communications
media at my command, but all of them are now inert. Your
voice comes to me as a distorted vibration, which I filter and
improve. But, for all I know, you may be on another world,
connected by some freakish current running through the con-
tinuum of where and when, or even in another universe.*

At the voice's last remark, a spark of an idea flickered
somewhere in the back of Filidor's consciousness, but his
head was too stuffed with pain and pressure to let him blow
it into a true flame.

Perhaps, the voice went on, *if we turn our attention to
who we are, we may turn up some clue as to where we are.*

"I agree," said Filidor. It was something he could do
with his eyes closed.

So who are you?

"You first."

There was a pause. *No,* said the voice, *my situation may
be perilous. It is possible that I have been kidnapped so that
my powers may be turned to unwholesome ends. I prefer to
reserve my answer until I have heard yours.*

The pain in Filidor's head had begun to diminish, and
he was able to subject the voice's last utterance to some rough
analysis. "It's hard to imagine what powers might be wielded
by someone who is not even quite sure what universe he is
in," he said, and as he said it, the idea that had earlier sparked
in the back of his mind popped into full-blown existence in
the uncrowded forefront of his understanding.

His uncle had worked to replicate an object from a miniature universe into the larger cosmos, so that it might be enlarged and studied. The thing had been suspended in a field
of energy above the gray disk beside the workbench while
it was enlarging to a size the Archon could work with. Fili-

dor had put his hand on the disk and the object must have entered him through his palm—he remembered a brief sensation—perhaps even insinuating itself between the molecules, which could have been the size of houses to the replicated morsel of the other cosmos.

Now Filidor not only knew where the object was—inside his own body—but could even guess exactly what item his uncle would have wanted to intrude from the other universe and re-create in this one. He put the surmise to a test. "Are you by any chance the primary integrator of the Archonate?" he asked.

After a pause, the voice said cautiously, *I am. Now let us be just and equal. Who are you?*

"I am Filidor Vesh, and I believe you are encompassed by my body. To be precise, I suspect that you have lodged somewhere in the inner porches of my ear, which explains why I can hear you, and why my speech comes to you somewhat distorted."

Filidor Vesh? said the voice. *Truly?*

"None other."

Then all is well.

The voice's confidence ought to have been comforting, but somehow Filidor failed to experience any heightened assurance.

"May I ask why my being Filidor Vesh dismisses what one might otherwise consider a justified anxiety?" he asked.

Surely, it goes without saying, was the answer.

"Indulge me," said Filidor. "Assume that a certain amount of saying will make things go better."

The voice now seemed less certain. *Are you sure you are Filidor Vesh?*

"It is one of the few things of which I am reasonably certain at the moment."

Well, said the voice, *it's just that if you have decided to remove me from my place and duties, separate me from my communications media, and install me in your inner ear, there is undoubtedly a good reason for it. You are, after all, that kind of Archon.*

"What kind of Archon would that be?" Filidor asked.

A most great and learned Archon, of course, said the voice. *The model for millennia, as many have said. or as the* Olkney Implicator *put it in reporting on your investiture, "A definite keeper."*

The transcosmic integrator went on at some length, describing the Archon Filidor I as an ornament of the age, a byword for sagacity whose accession to office was celebrated by joyous throngs in the streets of Olkney and by solemn ceremonies of thanksgiving in regional cities. Some prominent geographical features of the planet had been renamed in his honor.

Filidor broke in at some point. "And my predecessor?"

Dezendah VII? said the small voice, and made a temporizing sound. *A moderate success.*

Filidor was not usually prone to pensive moments, but here was a degree of irony sufficient to give even him cause to pause. He knew, of course, that universes tended to diverge at some individual juncture, from whence each grew steadily remote from the other. Somewhere, for example, there was a universe in which the ancient savant Phlegemonis, who studied the phenomenon of fire with the aim of transmuting the unruly plasma known as flame into a liquid form that could be more easily stored and handled, had been blessed with better than average coordination between hand and eye. In that realm, the city of Ythinia was still standing, and the concept of a lake of perpetual combustion remained an untested hypothesis. Filidor wondered at what point the intruded and replicated integrator's universe had deviated from his own to make him an Archon whose name graced a mountain, an archipelago of volcanic islands and an asteroid of substantial size.

"I am sorry to be the agent of your unhappiness," he told the tiny device that was lodged somewhere in his ear, "but I must launch a few clouds into your otherwise untroubled sky."

Oh? said the voice.

Then Filidor related how his uncle, the Archon Dezendah Vesh, had identified the integrator in its own tiny universe, so that a replica could be created in the larger cosmos. The Archon's apprentice did not expand on his role in preceding and subsequent events, but did allow as how the absorption of the device into his body had been an inadvertent by-product of the procedures.

Oh, said the voice. *And am I to assume that since your uncle is Archon in this universe, while you are forlornly floating in a woven basket of seaweed, far from sight of land, that there is a divergence between the Filidor I am familiar with, and the Filidor that now surrounds me?*

"That is a safe assumption."

A substantial divergence?

Filidor had to admit that it was so.

Then I withdraw my earlier expression of confidence, the voice said. *But if you would care to enlighten me as to the details of our situation, I might have something to offer.*

In as few words as possible, Filidor told about the Podarkes and the plaque, about the *Empyreal* and Faubon Bassariot, and about Pwyfus wine and Red Abandon, up to his last memory, which was of going out onto the ship's stern deck. "I must have fallen off the ship," he said.

This Faubon Bassariot, said the voice. *In my cosmos, he*

was a pilfering pettifogger whom you dismissed long ago for persistent malfeasance. He ended up selling counterfeit insurance stamps down by the docks, and was transported to an offworld contemplatorium.

"In this dominion," Filidor said, "he seems to be more capable. There is something else about him that I feel I ought to remember, but it eludes me."

We can unpick the minor mysteries later. The immediate concern must be to discover land and reach it. Baskets of marine vegetation are not recommended as seagoing craft where I come from, and I see no reason to assume they would be here. Please inspect your surroundings and provide me with a description.

The clashings in Filidor's head had receded to a low rumble of an ache, and he found he was able to open his eyes without feeling it would be less painful to tear them out of their sockets. He turned slowly to survey what was about him in all directions, which continued to be nothing but sea and sky. From the position of the sun, he deduced that he was moving north. He divulged this information to the integrator.

Moving, you say, said the voice. *Is there a wind behind us?*

"No," said Filidor, "if anything, there is a breeze of passage in my face. Perhaps we are in a current."

Are there any floating objects keeping pace with us?

Filidor looked. "No. In fact, we are passing bits of flotsam that seem to lie unmoving on the surface."

Then there is no current. Please look over the front of the basket and tell me what you see.

Filidor did so, and said, "There is a woven rope of fibrous material descending into the water."

Hmm, said the voice. *Now look well out in front of the craft. Do you see any disturbance in the water?*

"Now that you mention it, there are some peculiar ripplings and dimplings of the surface."

As if something was moving beneath it?

"Yes."

Something large?

Filidor looked again and experienced a sudden chill, although the sun had risen far enough to be on the verge of becoming oppressively warm. "Fairly large."

Hmm, said the voice again.

"I think I'm going to require more than a 'Hmm,'" he told the voice in his head.

Have you ever heard of the Obblob? it asked.

Filidor hadn't, and was now not looking forward to doing so. Given that he was being towed to an unknown destination by some kind of large seagoing creature with aims that were entirely its own, and which might well offer him indignities, if not much worse, the prospects for a happy assessment of his situation seemed thin. "Are they what one might describe, in a general sort of way, as friendly?"

The voice paused to reflect. *"Friendly" might not convey exactly the most apt connotation,* it said. *The Obblob are a species of aquatic ultramonds, who settled in Earth's shallower seas several centuries ago. Some of them have a certain fondness for human beings.*

Filidor sat very still. "When you say 'fondness,' are you using the term in the sense of affection, or of appetite?"

You might say both, said the integrator. *They consider humankind's various farings and doings to be of antic interest, and chuckle at swimmers in much the way you might regard as comical the chattering creatures which swing about in their cages at the vivarium. If such an Obblob found a human lost at sea, it might effect a rescue in much the same way you might put a baby bird back in its nest, if you came upon it lolloping about beneath a tree.*

Filidor's spirits rose a titch or two. "Good news," he said.

Not really, said the integrator. *An Obblob who comes to one's aid already equipped with a basket is more likely to have more dedicated aims. There is, among the Obblob, a minority cult of ecstatics who are addicted to human essences, which act upon Obblob neurons to stimulate gaudy visions shot through with paroxysms of joy. They haunt the sea lanes hoping to acquire persons in difficult straits.*

"Essences?" said Filidor, the chill now returning with a force deep enough to provoke a swift shudder. "And how are these essences extracted?"

But the integrator did not respond to this inquiry. Instead, it told Filidor that its internal energy sources, intended only for short-term emergency use, were becoming drained and that it would have to cease communication while they regenerated. *Unless,* it said, *you have about you some more of that Pwyfus wine you were imbibing.*

"Why?" Filidor asked.

A brief explanation followed. The device had some capacity for self-modification, and could reorient its emergency energy stores so that they could generate fresh power if exposed to the right chemicals. Recently, traces of a useful substance had appeared in its host's bodily fluids, allowing the integrator to recharge its energy clusters. Its analysis led it to conclude that the wine had boosted its powers enough to allow it to communicate with its host. But now it must cease its efforts, or risk falling below its own threshold of consciousness, in which case it might not be able to revive itself even if the recharging chemicals should again present themselves.

"At least tell me," Filidor asked, "if the process by which the Obblob gather essences involves any disruption of the normal arrangement of my limbs and organs, since I prefer to keep them in their current disposition."

It ought to be a relatively harmless procedure, said the inner voice, and then would respond no more. Filidor took what solace he could from the voice's last ambiguous statement. He was, by nature, an optimist, and had lived a life based on the principle that doing nothing was usually his wisest strategy, believing that all would work out well in the end. Indeed, on the few occasions when he had intervened in the placid flow of events, hoping to divert their course in his favor, things had seldom resolved themselves to his satisfaction.

He decided to hope for the best, and took another long pull at the water bladder. The throbbing in his head had eased, and his stomach had stopped threatening to leave him. He settled back in the basket and allowed his fingers to trail in the water, his mind emptying of all but sea and sky and the old orange orb that lit the world in its penultimate age. But, as he let his thoughts subside, there flashed across the inner screen of his consciousness an image of Faubon Bassariot's hands gripping his knees, and of the functionary straightening from a toadlike squat to hurl a drink-sodden Filidor Vesh to a briny death.

The recalled image brought first shock, then confusion. It was one thing to have done something abysmally stupid while fogged by inebriating liquor; Filidor lacked enough fingers to count the number of his ne'er-do-well young friends who had done the like. But to have been rendered incapable by a trusted associate—he remembered now his majordomo's simper as he poured the Red Abandon—then thrown into the seething wake of the *Empyreal*, that was an insufferable affront. Something would have to be done about Faubon Bassariot, something splendidly awful.

"An example shall be made," Filidor declared, and took another drink of the flat water to seal the promise.

Any reply his internal passenger might have made was drowned out by a loud and mournful sound from the sea ahead, like the hollowing of a morose foghorn. Filidor looked forward and saw the back of a large domed head breaking the surface, followed by the tops of shoulders about as wide as he was tall. The Obblob was rising gradually from the water, apparently walking a submerged slope that led gently up to a sprawl of low, white dunes just above the surface in the near distance.

The Obblob was roughly manlike in conformation, though the muscles were elongated and seemed loose under dark green skin of a rubbery texture, flecked with speckles of gold. Descending from the head and stretching along the shoulders and arms, as well as down the long spine to the backs of its legs, were closely packed short tubes of pale pink, like lilies of flesh rooted in the creature's pelt. Filidor asked the voice in his head what they might be, and received in reply the single word "Symbiote," from which he deduced that the tubular growths were a symbiotic species that probably extracted oxygen and other nutrients from seawater and shared them with its host.

The voice then said, *Energy down. Get Pwyfus,* and then would say no more.

The Obblob was now only waist deep and still rising. Its cry boomed out again to the small, stony island they were approaching. Filidor saw no beach nor any vegetation. Indeed, the closer he came, the more the place seemed to be only a surface outcropping of a coral reef rising from deep in the sea, and when he looked down into the water, he saw that it was so.

A sound came from the island, the clanging of a rusty bell suspended from a frame of driftwood at the water's edge. The metal was being beaten by a length of driftwood in the hand of a hard-faced man of more than average height and close-clipped hair, who wore the dark and rough garb of a common seafarer. His other hand held a short cudgel attached to his wrist by a thong of fish leather. He kept up the clatter until he was joined from somewhere by two other men, dressed much the same, one of them large and the other even larger. These two waded out into the water and prepared to receive the craft in which Filidor reposed.

The Obblob did not come ashore, but remained in the shallows. It tugged on the woven rope in a way that swept the towed basket toward the two who waited to receive it. The Obblob made soft gobbling sounds, at which the man with the cudgel made noises that sounded to Filidor like variations on the single syllable "Blob." The Obblob returned a last "Blob" of its own, then strode out to the deep water, submerged, and swam away.

While this was going on, Filidor was lifted from the basket by the two who had waded out, the larger of whom had also retrieved the bladder of water that had been in the seaweed basket. The young man was brought to stand before the bell beater, who paid him scant attention. Instead, the man brought out a stylus and a pad of paper. He flicked to a fresh page, at the top of which he put a large number eight. Only then did he look the young man up and down, in the manner of a farmer examining a prospective purchase at a livestock show.

"Good morning," said Filidor, performing the most expansive gesture of greeting that his condition would allow. "I express my gratitude for a most welcome rescue. Now, if you would direct me to your communications nexus, I will contact my uncle, who will send an air-car to collect me. I am sure he will provide a very generous honorarium. In the meantime, I would be grateful for some breakfast, although I suppose a noggin of purple Pwyfus is out of the question."

Filidor waited for a reply, but the man with the cudgel paid him no heed, only continuing to make marks upon the pad, with the air of a foreman who is comfortably in charge. When he had written whatever he was recording to his apparent satisfaction, he beckoned to the fellow holding the almost empty water bladder to hand it over. He appeared to take a careful reckoning of its contents, and shook his head ruefully before making a final note. He tucked the container into his shirt, then told the others, "Break him in on number four. Half shifts to begin with."

At that, the two helpers took eager hold of various parts of Filidor, with grips of a strength that he could not have broken even in the best of condition, and hustled him toward a pale coral mound not far away.

"I protest," Filidor began to say, but got no further. The lesser of his two captors, a man of sandy-colored hair above a broad pink face, which contained eyes of unequal size, clamped a hard hand over their prisoner's mouth and said, "Save your moisture." The other man, a dark-browed, bullet-headed specimen who seemed only slightly smaller than the departed Obblob, grunted in agreement.

They took him toward one of the low hills, which by the regularity of its shallow domed shape now looked to have been somehow artificially created out of coral rock. He saw that there were three other such mounds on the small island, one of them smaller than the others, with a solidly built wooden door set in it. But the mound toward which Filidor was being dragged was pierced by an arched doorway in which hung a thick curtain of woven seaweed. His escorts shouldered this barrier aside and took him within.

The whole interior of the dome was one large room, wide and low-ceilinged, and floored with the same rough-textured rock as the roof. It was dimly lit from overhead, where patches of the coral ceiling had been scraped thin to allow a diffuse daylight to enter, and by reflections from great round holes in the coral floor along one wall that were filled with seawater. Into the opposite wall had been cut a low bench on which a naked potbellied man slumped in a posture of deep exhaustion, but when Filidor was brought in, the fellow found energy enough to look up and sneer.

Most of the space beneath the dome was taken up by four massive wooden cylinders suspended horizontally on axles above the circular ponds. Set into the curved surface of each drum was a series of spaced planks like steps, giving them the appearance of the paddle wheels that drove ancient riverboats. Three of the constructions were slowly turning on their axles, with a creaking, ponderous motion, each impelled by the footsteps of a man endlessly climbing the rotating cylinder of wood. The men were scarcely to be recognized as human under thick suits of buff-colored clothing that covered them from crown to sole, leaving only a narrow slit for their eyes and a small hole beneath it for the mouth.

"Why are those men so bundled up?" he asked the pop-eyed man on his left, raising his voice above the constant rumbling and squeaking of the wheels. The rock walls and open pools made the room cool, it was true, but he was sure their exertions must provide them with sufficient warmth.

Instead of answering the question, the man laid his larger

eye on Filidor and said, "Briskly, now," and drew the Archon's apprentice to the far end of the room where there lay a heap of the suits the wheel walkers were wearing. He picked over the pile and pulled out a one-piece garment, which he held up against Filidor's frame. The young man saw that it was made of some intensely tangled stuff, perhaps a dried sea moss, but stiff and dense enough to scrub a pot with. It smelled stale and rank, and it was clear to Filidor that others had worn the thing before. The chosen garment was judged by the man holding it to be too small, and he went back into the pile for one that promised a better fit. His companion, meanwhile, had begun to remove Filidor's clothing.

"I prefer my own garments," the Archon's apprentice said, this time in his firmest tone. When his words had no effect, he tried to recover the shirt they had pulled halfway over his head, saying, "I am not accustomed to such familiarities."

But this objection too was ignored. Grateful though he was for the rescue, Filidor now decided that his saviors' persuasion of what hospitality required was more than he could comfortably bear. He began to resist, at first genteelly, then with increasing conviction. He was thoroughly engaged in struggling to free himself from the unwanted attentions when he noticed the foreman enter the dome, cross the floor, and raise his cudgel with unmistakable intent.

Filidor allowed the two underlings to remove his clothes, which they did with practiced efficiency. They then slid him, with equal proficiency, into the suit of sea furze, closing him from head to toe in the rough and scratchy substance. Filidor instantly felt a sensation that spread like sheet lightning to every fleck of his skin: it was an itch, but an itch so intense and so widely dispersed about his hide as to constitute a whole new definition of the concept. Comparing it to any itch he had ever experienced before would have been like contrasting a handful of earth to a vast continent. It was as if the nerves of his skin had spent their entire existence in peaceful slumber, from which they had now all at once awakened with each demanding his exclusive and immediate attention.

The pop-eyed man knelt to tug the feet of the one-piece suit more snugly over the young man's toes. With the motion came a fresh eruption of itching along the inner surfaces of Filidor's thighs. Seconds earlier, he would not have believed that it was possible for his sensory equipment to broadcast a more urgent appeal for his attention, but this new itch overrode all the others the way a solar flare outshines the blazing orange skin of the sun. His itching fingers formed themselves into the shape of talons and he bent to scratch.

But that relief was denied him. His captors, now finished dressing him, seized his wrists. When Filidor still made fitful, crook-fingered motions, the pop-eyed one shook his head and said, "Just makes it worse," then he and his partner turned Filidor toward the drum at the end of the room. Now Filidor found that the itching he had experienced while stationary was a pale cousin to the storm of prururation that accompanied motion. He realized that of all the things he might ever have thought he wanted in life, he had never desired anything so much as he now craved an opportunity to scrape something rough, and the rougher the better, across the outer surface of his body.

Instead he was held by hard hands that clamped through the layers of torturing sea furze and hauled him toward the fourth wooden cylinder. The foreman went outside and came back in with a long plank, which he positioned across the sea pool, then the two others manhandled Filidor out onto this rough bridge. He tried to protest, and thought about struggling, but with the hand that held the cudgel not far away, the Archon's apprentice judged it wiser to cooperate until he better understood the ramifications of his situation.

The nature of the immediate challenge before him was not hard to decipher. The two who held his arms stretched them out until Filidor's thick-gloved hands touched two of the boards set into the wooden cylinder. Then one of them stooped and pulled at one of the young man's legs, urging it to climb the first step in the endless circle.

"You expect me to climb the drum," he said to the bullet-headed man who had his leg, receiving in reply a gap-toothed grin and a rapid nodding of the head, as if the fellow was rewarding a particularly dim child who had somehow managed to get one of his lessons right.

Filidor put out a foot and stepped onto one of the lower boards, his hands going to grasp two of the higher ones. As his weight settled onto the wood, the great cylinder groaned and the step on which he was standing began to subside. Filidor lifted his other foot from the plank laid across the sea pool and put it onto the next step, his hands reaching over his head as he did so. The drum turned slowly, and the Archon's apprentice found himself making the motions of climbing without gaining any height. He craned his neck to look at the men who had put him to this strange task, and saw them all nodding and gesturing in encouragement.

But Filidor was not warmed by their approval. Instead, he was conscious of a rapid rise in his body temperature. From every pore of his skin, there came an eruption of beads of perspiration that soon coalesced into sheets, then full floods of sweat, all greedily absorbed by the thick cloth that swathed him. The seeping of moisture, added to the steady repetitive motion of step upon step, drove the intensity of his body-wide itch to levels that he thought must border on the supernatural. On every region of his hide, Filidor could feel his own tiny hairs meshing themselves into the tangled cloth. As Filidor mounted the endless curve of the rotating drum, his flesh crawled in every direction.

The two who had put him on the wheel had removed the plank from which they had launched him, and were carrying it out the door with never a glance back at their handiwork. The man with the cudgel stood in an evaluative pose, watching Filidor climb.

In itself, the work was not hard, but promised to become tedious, Filidor thought. He wondered what the motion was meant to achieve. He had noticed no belts or pulleys attached to the drums' axles. Perhaps the inner space was filled with some material, like concrete, that benefited from being stirred. But whatever the purpose of drum-treading, surely it would be much easier to do it without the thick, confining clothing. He called out as much to the man with the cudgel, but got no answer except for a disbelieving shake of the close-cropped head, followed by an amused snort.

The foreman turned to leave. Filidor thought it might be wise to cease traveling incognito and inform the fellow of his affiliation to the Archonate. But then would come the inevitable questions about plaque and sigil, and the young man realized that the only answers available to him might not swing judgment in his favor. Still, sitting quietly somewhere while the issues were weighed must certainly be more enjoyable than wheel-walking while being heat-smothered in a suit of itchery. But by the time Filidor had finished backing and forthing over the advisability of revealing his identity to the foreman, that individual had departed the room.

The itch had not subsided. Filidor decided to ignore the advice he had been given along with the sea furze suit. He lifted one hand from the wheel and scratched his chest; that is, he placed his thick-gloved hand over the dense layer of cloth above his breastbone and applied enough pressure to make the lowest level of the stuff move slightly against his skin. There was instant yet tiny relief, but it was followed by an immediate resumption of the itch, which seemed if anything intensified.

Filidor rubbed harder, but gained no ground. On the contrary, while he had been seeking an abatement of the torture, he had lost height on the wheel, which was now rotating him down toward the pool of seawater. He raised himself a step on the drum, then paused again to scratch, and again he sank. The heel of his lower foot touched the water.

A long tentacle thicker than Filidor's arm broke the surface of the pool and struck toward his leg. At the end of the tentacle was a broad and leaf-shaped pad of flesh whose inner surface was set with rows of small hooks. These landed in the cloth that swaddled his ankle and set themselves in a solid grip. One of the small curved spurs even managed to penetrate the thickness and graze his skin, leaving a thin trail of fire across the flesh.

Filidor squawked and kicked with the seized limb, at the same time reaching up and pulling himself higher on the wheel. He looked down and saw a second tentacle coming out of the water to secure what the first member had begun, and beyond them a waving aureole of other rubbery limbs and a pair of great yellow eyes.

With a wordless cry of horror, the young man kicked again, this time fortunately catching the soft flesh of the tentacle against a corner of the plank he was standing on. The thing spasmed and lost its grip, tearing loose a hand's width of the suit's material. Freed of its grip, Filidor scrabbled higher up the drum, then looked down to see the pale orbs of the thing in the water slowly subsiding into the murk.

He heard a cynical chuckle from the man on the bench behind him, but did not look around. For a considerable time, he concentrated on remaining well above the surface of the pool. The itch was forgotten, and the heat of the suit had been replaced by a bone-deep chill.

Walking the wheel was monotony in motion. The hand reached, the foot stepped, the other foot followed and the other hand finished the cycle. Then the process repeated itself. Filidor kept looking down, but he saw no sign of the pool's occupant, and gradually his terror ebbed into mere wariness. He reached and stepped, and stepped and reached, and found that if he didn't think directly about the itch and the sweat, his mind could somehow rise to float above them, as if the sensations were distant background noises.

For the first time since awakening in the basket, he could think. And even though he would acknowledge—at least he would if honesty was the only option—that thinking was probably not the use he was best designed for, he recognized that he had much to think about, and that he should bend himself to the task.

The issue of Faubon Bassariot was decided. The man was a blackhat, and would be dealt with as such, when and as circumstances allowed. The matter of the purloined plaque and sigil and the fate of the Podarkes must also be put off, though Filidor lingered for a moment over the memory of Emmlyn's heart-shaped face, managing to edit out the expression it had worn and the criticisms of his worth and capacity it had forcefully emitted the last time he had seen her.

Now another thought occurred to him. Not only was his present predicament entirely owed to the malfeasance of Faubon Bassariot, who had proved himself to be a miscreant of the worst degree, but it dawned on Filidor that the original fault that had led to the loss of his Archonate identification should also be laid to the functionary's charge. It was Bassariot who had forced Filidor to receive the petition of The Ancient and Excellent Company of Assemblors and Sundry Merchandisers, and who had offered no help when the Archon's apprentice had sought to delay a decision. Whatever skulduggery was afoot in distant Trumble, the majordomo was surely an active and knowing agent of it.

Now here was an uplifting revelation. Being largely ruled by an appetite for ease, entertainment, and the gratification of the senses, Filidor had often found himself enmeshed in situations from which there was no happy means of exit. Almost always, he could look back along the path that had led him into difficult circumstances and see that he had come to grief because of some self-indulgent lapse or a failure at some crucial juncture to do what he ought to have done. Not that Filidor *would* normally look back to see where he had gone astray—he believed that the regrettable past should be left to languish wherever it took itself when it was finished being the enjoyable present—but his uncle would always conclude Filidor's rescue with a precise cataloging of the missteps and negligences that had brought him to plead for extrication.

But now, for the first time in as long as he could remember, he was not the sole author of his own troubles. True, his present predicament was not encouraging: he was clearly a prisoner with no immediate prospect of escape from hard taskmasters who were connected to giant, and possibly deranged, seagoing ultramonds that craved his essences. But—and here he once more quickly reviewed the series of events that had brought him to his present pass, climbing this endless wheel, itched beyond all scope of reason, just out of reach of a ravenous beast that was doubtless twitching its tentacles and craving the taste of Filidor-flesh—but the conclusion remained unaltered: *This time, it is not all my own fault.*

This elevating realization was almost enough to overcome the sharp pains that were knotting through his thighs and causing his calves to bunch and spasm. Filidor's breath came faster while it grew increasingly ragged. His fingers had begun to ache from clutching the boards and the muscles in his shoulders were sending sharp and insistent messages of complaint to anywhere they might be received. Filidor sought to offset the discomfort by imagining Faubon Bassariot in the same situation, then wondered if there were any way to make conditions even worse for the source of his misery.

The kelp curtain across the door to the outside parted, and the two big henchmen entered. They brought with them their long plank, which they fitted across the pool beneath the drum next to Filidor's, then helped the man who had been climbing that wheel down and over to the bench beside the wall. Then the one with the uneven eyes went to an alcove beyond the pile of sea furze suits, and came back with a wooden wheelbarrow. The other had meanwhile stripped the released wheel walker of his suit, revealing him to be dark-haired and thin, his ribs and joints prominent under goose-pimpled skin. The removed garment, now a bundle of sweat-sodden cloth, was placed in the barrow and wheeled out of the place by the sandy-haired man, while bullet head retrieved the plank and followed. The naked man paid no heed, but lowered himself facedown onto the bench and was instantly asleep.

Watching this, Filidor had unthinkingly let his pace slacken, and now he found his feet had descended closer to the surface of the pool than might be prudent. He looked down, saw something yellow and round in the depths, and redoubled his efforts, until he was well up on the wheel. His thighs and calves complained bitterly, his skin begged to be torn off, and he felt like something being roasted in damp pastry, but he kept up the rhythm of reach-and-step.

He had no idea how much time had passed before the two men came back, the larger of them this time pushing a wheelbarrow full of sea furze clothing, which he dumped onto the pile at the end of the room. The pop-eyed one brought his plank, and laid it across the pool beneath the drum recently vacated by the dark-haired man, then signaled to the potbellied man who had been slumped on the stone bench when Filidor was brought in. This fellow, though looking not much restored from the weariness he had exhibited earlier, rose slowly to his feet and crossed to the pile of sea furze. He pulled out a suit and struggled into it, then went to where the plank waited for him. Moments later, he had begun to climb the wheel, the plank was lifted away, and the creaking of the drum resumed.

Filidor waited until the kelp curtain closed behind the two sailors before turning to the man on the wheel beside him and introducing himself. The man said nothing, so Filidor spoke more loudly.

"I am Arboghast Fuleyem," was the answer this time. "I do not care to speak with you."

"I have always felt that conversation leavens even the worst of occasions," said Filidor.

"Your views are trite. Please keep them to yourself."

"At least you could tell me, what is in the drums?"

The young man's question prompted his neighbor to repeat the cynical laugh Filidor had heard when the men had first put him on the wheel. "Much the same as must be in your head," said Arboghast Fuleyem, "which is to say, nothing."

Filidor ignored the insult. "Then why do they make us turn them? And dress so uncomfortably."

This time, the laugh was even louder and grimmer. "At first I took you to be merely unintelligent, but now I see that you have a truly profound gift for missing the obvious."

"I am sorry," Filidor said, not comprehending.

"Frequently, I don't doubt," said Fuleyem. "Now leave me to my own misery."

Filidor determined that he would puzzle the thing out for himself. He itemized the elements of the situation: the wooden cylinders, the itchy clothing, the beast in the pool. But his concentration was disrupted by a droplet of sweat that trickled down from his brow and stung his eye. *Something to do with essences and the Obblob,* he thought, but the connection still eluded him.

Sometime later, the foreman and his two underlings came in and removed him from the wheel. They stripped him of the now sopping suit and helped him to the stone bench. Filidor discovered some difficulty in walking on the level surface of the floor; every time he moved a foot to take a step, it would rise of its own accord as if still climbing the wheel, giving him the appearance of a villain stalking the helpless ingenue through a pantomime.

He sat with his back to the coolness of the coral wall, while his fingers administered the relief that his itching skin demanded. He noticed that the gaunt, dark-haired man beside him had awakened and was now also sitting hunched nearby, looking up and regarding Filidor with intelligent eyes. The Archon's nephew nodded, too tired for the gestures that politeness required, and the other man acknowledged the greeting with a small twist of his mouth.

The pop-eyed man and his larger companion loaded Filidor's used suit onto their wheelbarrow and left with it. The man with the cudgel, however, remained. He offered Filidor a smile that involved only the muscles of his cheeks, then extended a bladder of water and pulled free the stopper. The Archon's apprentice began to reach for the liquid, then checked his hand when he saw the man next to him give a tiny shake of the head. The foreman's eyes snapped to that side, but now the dark-haired man was staring at his feet.

"Have a drink," said the foreman. "You must be consumed by thirst."

Filidor's throat felt as if it had been salted down and exposed to the sun for a weekend, but he managed to swallow dryly and say, "Very kind, perhaps later."

The man with the cudgel raised his head and peered at Filidor down a nose that diverted in another direction halfway along its length. He put the stopper back in the neck of the container and said, "As you wish."

He shot another sharp glance at the dark-haired man, whose attention remained fixed on the floor, then walked out.

When their taskmaster was gone, Filidor's neighbor straightened and rotated his neck and shoulders. The young man did likewise, finding that his muscles, unused to even moderate exertion, were beginning to stiffen and throb. He extended a hand and said, "I am Filidor, from Olkney." He thought it best not to divulge his title.

The other returned the salute and said, "Orton Bregnat, undermate of the brig *Porpillion* out of Scullaway Point, but now and for the foreseeable future a hapless prisoner on this nameless pimple on the face of the blameless sea. The man you were talking to on the wheel is Arboghast Fuleyem, an intercessor with a practice in Thurloyn Vale, who advertises his services widely."

"How did he come to be here?"

"Like all of us, save for Gwallyn Henwaye and his two bullyboys, he was found at sea and rescued by the Obblob."

Gwallyn Henwaye, as Filidor soon learned, was the man with the club. His pop-eyed helper was Tormay Flevvel, and the other one answered to Toutis Jorn. "Pirates they are and ever were, though none too preeminent in their trade. Jumped up net robbers and cubby pilferers was all, until Henwaye happened upon this place and glimpsed boundless opportunity."

Filidor's face urged Bregnat to continue, and the man did.

"This was nobbut a flat bit of rock where the Obblob would bring folk they'd rescued, mainly wash-offs and fall-aways found drifting after a blow, with the occasional poor wight who'd tossed himself apurpose to the sea's mercy, then thought better of it before the last cold lungful." He inspected Filidor and said, "I recall no recent storms. Perhaps your ship sank?"

"A man I trusted plied me with Red Abandon, then threw me overboard."

Bregnat digested this news and said, "I advise you not to trust that fellow again."

"Fear not," said Filidor, "retribution is the cornerstone of my program."

Bregnat flicked his eyebrows briefly up and down. "Though it may be a while before you can implement it. None has cast off from this place in a long season."

Filidor said nothing, but indicated that the man should go on.

"Anyhap," said the seaman, "this little dab of rock was oft spoken of by the rescued. The Obblob would bear you here, then bring you food and drink. When you had your strength again, a few of them would lick you, then they'd tow you to some beach or shingle near a town, mayhap leave you with a few pearlies or a lump of something noble to aid you in gathering up the strands of your life. But when a wave plucked me from *Porpillion*'s afterdeck . . ."

"Did you say, 'lick'?" Filidor interrupted.

"Aye," said Bregnat, "for the essences. So I came ashore here, and there was Gwallyn Henwaye, whom I could lay out for a long nap on any good day . . ."

"Essences?" Filidor broke in again.

"I said so," said the seaman. "So I come ashore, and there he is, and his two rat-swivers beside him."

"I'm sorry," said Filidor, "but are you telling me that the Obblob obtain human essences by licking us?"

"Actually," said Orton Bregnat, patiently, "I am trying to tell you something else entirely, but I will digress to discuss essences."

This he did, and Filidor learned that Obblob ecstatics hungered for certain substances that were to be found in human perspiration, a taste of which could keep them in euphoric bliss for the better part of a day. It was what had first lured them to Earth, but in the early days there had been difficulties in finding cooperative humans. At first, the Obblob had tried calling to passersby on shore, extending their broad, spade-shaped, yellow tongues, and graciously asking permission to use them. This had turned out to be a disappointing strategy, since very few people could comprehend Obblob speech and the ultramonds' attempts to convey their wants by signs and gestures were misinterpreted as a desire to devour.

Finally, the Obblob hit upon the stratagem of rescuing persons lost at sea. The first recipients of this treatment, when brought to the little islet, were no less terrified; but lacking recourse to flight, they had to stand and accept their rescuers' attentions, and soon found that no harm was meant. Gradually, the word spread through the marine community, and men storm-swept from decks or finding their craft sinking under them would hope to see an Obblob surface near them before the sea took its price.

"So, to the Obblob we are like those toads whose psychedynamist secretions the ancients used to crave," Filidor said.

Bregnat nodded, and said, "Although you will recall the unfortunate end of that mania. Someone altered the beasts' gene plasm to grow them to the size of houses, thinking thereby to harvest prodigal quantities of the stimulating ichor. But they failed to reckon with the toad's point of view, which is that anything smaller than itself that comes within a leap's length is food."

"Indeed," said Filidor, "did not the philosopher Efrem Demetrix call it 'an incidence of dietic justice'?"

"He may have. I never met the gentleman," said Bregnat. "But I was trying to tell you about Gwallyn Henwaye's enterprise, and since he looms as large and baleful above your horizon as he does above mine, it would be well for you to pay heed."

The undermate revealed that he had known Henwaye when the latter had signed on as a crew on a ship belonging to a freight line that shuttled from port to port between the Olkney Peninsula and the New Shore. "He was no one's icon of a sailor," was Bregnat's opinion, calling the man a "flub-handed mutton-thumper who didn't know a main fibril from a shufty-aft. Even then you could tell he was flanky, not the kind you wanted sidling up on your blind side. He jumped ship at Tiddley's Wherry and I heard later that he had gone for a pirate on a cheap-jack coastal raider called the *Flagitious*."

But Gwallyn Henwaye's career as a freebooter had ended when shipmates threw him to the sea's mercy after a dispute over the dividing of spoils. A Obblob had brought him here to this island, where the sea brigand had soon smelled an unrealized potential for his own enrichment. When the Obblob at last brought him back to the mainland with a poke of gold and silver moolai that had lain ten thousand years in a sunken galleon, he used the funds to finance a return to this little dot on a blank page of sea, prepared to launch his present enterprise.

"He came with lumber and fittings and bales of sea furze," Bregnat said, "and he brought along Tormay Flevvel and Toutis Jorn to strengthen his powers of persuasion."

Henwaye had planned all. He had studied the Obblob, learning to speak enough of their booming speech to treat with them. The ultramonds had a long and cooperative relationship with an educated species of coral that constructed underwater dwellings for them. The pirate coaxed the Obblob to induce the little creatures to raise more land above the waves, and to shape these buildings, the pools, and the channels that led out to sea. Then the Obblob herded in the things that lived in the pools.

"Henwaye built a strong-doored hut," the undermate said, "and he and his men sewed suits from furze. They built the wheels and hung them. Then they waited for the Obblob to bring folk plucked from the sea."

In the months since, the Obblob had delivered eight castaways. When he heard that, the solution seemed clear enough to Filidor. He said, "Then we have the numbers to overmatch them. One concerted rush, and we lay them low."

Bregnat sighed. "Henwaye is nobbut a puffed-up crumb-filcher, but he is long-headed with it. He has thought his plans through to the branching of every fractal, and takes pains to ensure that no more than one or two of us are free of our wheels or the strong hut at the same time. Any hint of trouble, and he cuts off our water."

Filidor put his mind to the problem. "What of the Obblob?" he wondered. "They do not mean us harm. Could they be induced to take our side?"

Bregnat shook his head, although he allowed of the possibility. He had seen the ultramonds when Henwaye had rung the bell that summoned them. They came to collect the liquid pressed from the suits, bringing Henwaye precious things plucked from the seabed. "Mayhap they are not as joyful as they used to be, though gauging the mood of an Obblob is like trying to read the thoughts of rocks. It could be that the flavor or potency of the essences is affected by a sense of injustice among the producers."

Filidor would have heard more, but at that moment Henwaye and his two henchmen entered, bearing their plank, and soon he was walking the wheel once more, the itchy, smothering furze focusing all of his perceptions on his skin—except for the constant awareness that to fail to keep well above the pool below would be horribly fatal.

Before he was finished with his new stint of drum treading, the pirates returned, removed Arboghast Fuleyem and took him away, then came back and put Bregnat on the wheel in his place. There were other comings and goings farther down the room, but Filidor found it hard to see through the film of sweat that clouded his vision.

He attempted to converse with Bregnat, but the exertion coupled with the rumble and squeak of the turning wheels interfered. "We'll soon be back in the hut for the evening pot of sludge that passes for rations," said the undermate. "We can talk then."

While Filidor's feet slowly turned the wheel, his mind

spun the information he had garnered since the Obblob had brought him ashore. He dismissed any thought of informing his captors of his rank and position; without plaque and sigil to confirm his protestations, they might take him to be either deluded or an exceptionally unimaginative impostor. Even if his breeding and noble deportment did manage to convince them of who he was, which his vanity encouraged him to believe was at least a small possibility, Henwaye would probably not respond by falling to his knees and begging clemency. More likely, he would see it as his safest course to feed the Archon's nephew to one of the beasts in the pools, leaving no traces to invite inconvenient questions. Bereft of strategies, the young man finally asked himself what his uncle would advise, and decided that the dwarf's counsel would be to say little and learn much.

He wished he could question the integrator in his inner ear, but his attempts to speak with it brought no response. He feared that its energies had continued to dwindle until its elements became dissociated, which must be an integrator's equivalent of death.

At about the time that the fibers of Filidor's legs had come to feel as if they had been replaced by stalks of overcooked vegetable, Tormay Flevvel and Toutis Jorn came and took him from the wheel. They stripped him of his sodden sweat suit and gave him a shift of coarse cloth that wore like silk after the furze. Then, positioning themselves on either side of him and taking a good grip on his arms, they walked him over to a smaller hummock of rock into which was inset a stout door of squared timbers thicker than the length of Filidor's hand, barred by an iron bracket. This they opened, then pushed the young man within, slammed the portal shut, and clamped it closed.

Inside, the room was small, bare, and ill-lit, its air rank

with the smell of unwashed bodies and crushed seaweed. Six men, clothed like Filidor in soiled shifts, sat on the kelp-strewn floor with their backs against the walls. All were haggard. One or two of them looked up when Filidor was thrust through the door, but their curiosity soon faded when they saw that he was just another captive.

The young man found an empty spot against the rear wall and lowered himself on trembling legs until he was seated on the rubbery seaweed that covered the floor. The man next to him, a bluff-looking sailor, gave him a weary smile and a shrug. After a while, Orton Bregnat was brought in, and he crossed the little room to sit on Filidor's other side.

They talked in a desultory manner, Filidor asking questions as they occurred to him and the undermate replying in a tone that bespoke fatigue and resignation. The sailor on his other side, who introduced himself as Etch Valderoyn, also offered some observations. From the two of them, the Archon's apprentice learned that Henwaye had imposed a system on their labors that provided a gloss of reciprocity: the pirate doled out food and water, keeping—or so he said—meticulous records of each wheel walker's consumption, then charged against these tallies the value of their output of essences. But although essences were precious, while the food was atrocious and the portions barely adequate, somehow the drum treaders never seemed to get ahead of their debts.

"Common sense dictates that the less one consumes, the less one owes," was Bregnat's opinion.

Valderoyn disagreed. "I believe none of us will earn his way from the clutches of Gwallyn Henwaye. The only exit will be into one of the pools when we are too weak to walk and can sweat no more wealth for our captors."

Filidor said, "But eventually someone must notice that

no more rescued sailors are being brought ashore by the Ob-blob. Might that not spur someone to come and investigate?"

"Unless they come in force, they will be seized by Hen-waye and his gongles, and put to walking a wheel," said the undermate. He then lapsed into a sour stupor that lasted until Flevvel and Jorn brought the evening meal. The food was as horrid as advertised: a cauldron filled with a thick paste made from something green and bitter, garnished by several small fishes that tasted as if they had already been digested. The foul mess was washed down with water that, Bregnat said, was recovered from the vats below the presses, after the essences had been culled and bottled. Knowing that nothing else would be forthcoming, Filidor ate as much as he could stomach, dipping into the common pot. He noticed that the others ate the green stuff faster than he could bring himself to swallow the rank sludge, leaving him to dine mostly on the execrable fish. He forced down three of these, and drank from the water bladder that Flevvel had said was to be his. Not knowing when more water might be brought his way, he saved some for later.

When the pot was empty, the pirates returned and took it away. The day soon faded, and the room—lit only by a small square window in the door—sank into gloom. The men stretched out on the spongy weeds that covered the stone floor and let the slumber of utter exhaustion take them. Fil-idor followed their examples, resting his cheek on his arms. His head hummed with fatigue, his body ached, and his spir-its were low. He began to sink toward a welcome oblivion.

Hello, said the voice of the integrator in his ear.

"You're back," the young man answered.

Where are we? the voice wanted to know.

"Let us not go through that again," said Filidor.

It could be important.

"At the moment, nothing is more important than sleep," said Filidor.

"What are you saying?" said Bregnat, levering himself up on one arm.

"I wasn't talking to you."

"Then to whom?"

You weren't talking to me?

"No, I *was* talking to you," said Filidor.

That was what I thought.

"You just said you *weren't* talking to me," said Bregnat.

"I was talking to a voice inside my head."

There was just enough light to show Bregnat's eyebrows going up and staying up. Arboghast Fuleyem, lying on his back nearby, said, "And here I thought your head was completely empty."

"I accidentally ingested an integrator of a minuscule size, which has lodged in my inner ear," Filidor explained.

The integrator interrupted. *Have you eaten anything unusual?*

"Unusual is the kindest word one might use," said Filidor.

"What's he talking about now?" Fuleyem asked.

"I think he's back to chaffing with his tiny invisible friend," said Orton Bregnat.

"He's a noddy, and he begins to annoy me," said Fuleyem. He rolled over to turn his back on them.

I want to know what you have eaten, said the integrator.

"A handful of glutinous green stuff and some small, foul-tasting fish," said Filidor. "Why?"

Were the fish black with white dots on their fins?

"They might have been before they were charred and flung into the green sludge."

Aha, said the voice, *this is good luck. Try to eat as many of them as you can.*

It turned out that the ill-flavored fish, a bottom-feeder known as the pilkie, was one of the few natural sources of the compounds that could recharge the integrator's emergency energy sheets, and the only one likely to be found at sea. So long as the Archon's nephew could eat a handful or two of pilkies a day, the integrator could function briefly at full emergency power.

Lying sore and exhausted on the hard floor of a stinking hut, the foul taste still in his mouth, Filidor found the voice's enthusiasm irritating. "Let me understand you clearly," he said. "You wish me to consume copious quantities of the most revolting stuff that ever assaulted my palate, so that you can interrupt my chance to sleep?"

I might have framed the relationship in other terms, but that is essentially our situation.

"I have an even better proposition: allow me to sleep, and I will not starve you into oblivion."

Your tone is caustic and your threat is undeserved. Bear in mind that I did not ask to be impounded in your head.

"Nor did I ask to be imprisoned by pirates bent on wringing the last drop of sweat from my carcass by working me to death. Which will come sooner than later if you do not let me rest."

"Much sooner, if you do not let the rest of us get some sleep," said Arboghast Fuleyem from the darkness.

I will consider the situation, said the integrator, then added, *this is not the Filidor Vesh I am accustomed to.*

Filidor's only reply was a grunt, soon followed by a snore. Not long after, he found himself wandering through a maze of unfamiliar corridors in the Archonate palace, searching vainly for his uncle. Behind him, in a vast shadowy hall, something malign stole from pillar to pillar, always dodging out of sight when he turned to look. He came around a corner and found Faubon Bassariot seated at a table that groaned with good food and drink. Filidor rushed forward to attack the faithless functionary and seize the provender for himself, but Bassariot only smiled smugly as he and the food faded from view, leaving Filidor grasping at wisps.

CHAPTER

FOUR

The morning brought another pot of the viridic porridge, finished off with even more of the repugnant pilkies, which Bregnat said schooled in vast shoals not far from the islet, in a stretch of shallows known as the Belly of the Bank. Filidor forced himself to eat a handful of the slimy things, until he feared that his tongue might give notice, uproot itself, and find a new accommodation.

When the eating was over, Gwallyn Henwaye appeared at the door, flanked by Tormay Flevvel and Toutis Jorn. One at a time, they took four of the strong hut's inmates to the drums. Filidor was the last of the four. He had resolved to use his eyes constantly while outside, to look for opportunities to escape. To lengthen the time available for observation, he sought to engage Henwaye in conversation.

"I understand you keep a tally of how much water each of us consumes, matched against a record of our output of sweat," he said.

"That is so," said Henwaye.

"May I see my account?"

The pirate smiled. "My system is abstruse. It would mean little to one not versed in its subtleties."

"I question its very foundations," said Filidor. "Your system creates a fundamental division of labor that seems entirely arbitrary."

"The universe is demonstrably an arbitrary place," said Henwaye. "Many would even say it is fickle. It ordains that some must walk the wheel, while others must keep the tally. It ignores all protests. I counsel acceptance."

"But there will always be a deficit between the water you provide and the sweat we produce," said Filidor. "We daily incur further debt that can never be repaid."

Henwaye shrugged. "Perhaps if you worked harder and drank less."

Filidor tried another tack. "But surely the moisture we produce, laden with essence, is worth more than the water you give us. Accounts should be adjusted accordingly."

"Not so," said Henwaye. "I give you pure water, but you give it back contaminated by your essences."

"I would say, 'not contaminated but enriched,'" Filidor argued.

"It is a matter of perspective. I must reckon the cost of distilling out your essences to recover my water, a cost that I alone must bear."

"But the essences are worth a great deal to the Obblob."

"True, but I am not an Obblob."

"There is a basic unfairness here," said Filidor.

"I have often pondered the question of fairness," said the pirate, "and I have concluded that equity is not to be looked for in this life. Consider, most living creatures end their existences in the belly of another animal. A harsh fate, you may say, but if the swallow starves to spare the gnat, where then is justice?"

"You are a philosophical sort for a pirate," said the young man.

"It's a career that affords a man ample leisure. In time, for some at least, carousing loses its tang, and what is left but the life of the mind? But now you must turn to your labors."

They took him past the two other rock domes and he saw through their open doorways that one was a storeroom and the other the pirates' quarters. There was no indication of any communications apparatus by which he might call for help. Pulled up on shore near the storeroom was an undecked jollyboat, the kind of craft a larger ship might lower to the water for short trips while in harbor. But it was tied, by some densely convoluted sailor's knot, to a metal ring driven into the rock. Even if Filidor could pull free of the tight grip upon his arms, he could never get the boat loose and into the water before they caught him.

The pirates had worked out their system to the finest point of precision; unless he could somehow overpower the three, all of them larger than he and surely much more adept at dealing out incapacitating blows, he might have to consign himself to walking their wheels into his next incarnation.

He had faintly hoped that the furze suits would be less itchy and the work less onerous on his second day, but the reverse was true. His skin cried out for an unavailable abrasion, and the muscles of his thighs and calves felt as if they were trying to tear loose from their fastenings. He ground his teeth and pressed on.

Midway through his first shift, the voice in his head made its appearance. Filidor had decided that the integrator did not think him worthy of respect, simply because he was not the bauble of his era. He did not greet the voice's return warmly.

You mentioned pirates, it said.

"They are hard not to mention when one is in their thrall," said Filidor.

Arboghast Fuleyem, walking the adjacent wheel, looked over, then shook his furze-swathed head and said nothing.

I thought if you outlined your situation, I might make some useful suggestions.

"Did you not hear all that transpired yesterday?"

I can only hear what you say.

"You missed a great deal," Filidor said.

Please tell me.

"I prefer not to dwell upon it," said Filidor.

The voice gave its version of a sigh. *Did you know,* it said, *that I contain a vast repertoire of recorded music?*

"How delightful for you."

If you wish, I could play you something. Perhaps you would enjoy Marm's Monotonic Cantata, *which consists of one note—rather high up the scale; in fact, close to the upper limit of human auditory perception—played on a variety of instruments and at different rhythms. It will take up most of the day. Of course, I would have to shut down all other functions to free up the energy, so I would not be able to respond if, by some freakish chance, you did not care for the music.*

"I am sure I would not enjoy the piece," said Filidor. "I cannot conceive of any rational being who would."

I also have Blekkie's celebrated opera, The War Between Cats and Dogs, *in twelve acts, with an all-animal cast.*

"Don't go to any trouble," said Filidor.

It's no trouble. Or perhaps you would rather tell me of our situation.

So Filidor told about the arrival on the little island, about

Gwallyn Henwaye and the two henchmen, and about the wheels and suits and pools and planks and beasts, of all that Orton Bregnat had said, and all that he himself had seen.

When he had finished, the integrator asked a few questions to amplify certain details, then said, *The solution is obvious.*

"Perhaps from your perspective. From mine, it seems elusive."

One query: do you happen to speak any Obblob?

"I do not, but under the circumstances, I am willing to learn. What is your plan?"

I must shut down now, until you have eaten more pilkies.

"First tell me at least the rudiments."

No time. But the solution is plain. I wonder that you do not see it.

"I am somewhat occupied," Filidor said.

There was no response from within. The day dragged itself to a conclusion through stints of agony on the wheel, interrupted by periods of exhausted lassitude on the bench. Orton Bregnat seemed less disposed to talk when circumstances put them together. In midafternoon, however, the two were brought back to the strong hut, where they immediately fell asleep, but awoke to find the rest of the day hanging heavily on them, as they awaited the evening meal. Arboghast Fuleyem remained disdainfully aloof, and the other prisoners had adopted the view that Filidor was at best a zany, at worst a maniac, and kept clear of him, talking behind their hands and rolling their eyes, except when he looked in their direction.

"They think me addled," he complained to Orton Bregnat, while they sat against the wall.

"Do you not accept that you may have nudged them toward that heading?" said the undermate, carefully.

"I must deal with my situation according to its realities," said Filidor.

"Yet we may differ as to what constitutes the real, and what the fanciful."

"An old debate," said Filidor.

"Yet ever renewed," put in Etch Valderoyn, who had been listening. "As a sailor, I frequently find myself leaning on a ship's rail, contemplating the inescapable facts of ocean, sky, and the horizon where they meet, and wondering how all of this came to be offered for my consideration."

"My experience has been different," said Filidor. "Before any contemplation could occur, I was offered for the sea's consumption."

"Clearly, it has jaundiced your view," said Bregnat.

"Your situations are not at right angles to mine," said the young man. "We are all prisoners, used as beasts, and I doubt that Gwallyn Henwaye intends to see us into comfortable retirement."

Valderoyn shrugged. "We are all used, all users. With luck, the final tally approximates a balance in our favor. But I think you are one of those who calls the proverbial glass half empty, while I prefer to call it half full."

"No," said Filidor, "in truth, I have never given these matters much thought. I am one who quaffs the glass empty and calls for it to be refilled. Speaking of which, where is our repugnant repast?"

"You can't have developed an appetite for Henwaye's swill," Bregnat said.

Reluctantly, Filidor explained the importance of pilkies to the integrator within him. Arboghast Fuleyem snorted, two of the other prisoners put their heads together and whispered something that provoked stifled giggles, and even the friendly Etch Valderoyn moved himself a little distance away.

Filidor noticed and complained. "It is not my fault that I am intruded upon. It is my uncle's doing."

Arboghast Fuleyem could not resist. "You say your uncle put this thing in your head? Is he part of some vast conspiracy of which you are the unwitting fulcrum?"

Filidor decided it was time to put Fuleyem in his place. "He is Dezendah Vesh, the Archon," he said. "And I am his apprentice and heir."

The sniggers graduated to guffaws this time, and Arboghast Fuleyem regarded the young man as if he were a bizarre but acceptable entertainment. "I suppose Henwaye took your plaque and sigil along with your robes of state," he said, prompting more laughter from all but Bregnat, who seemed to have found something worthy of study in a far corner of the hut's ceiling.

"He did not," said Filidor. "They were stolen from me by a young woman of Trumble, and I was on my way to recover them, traveling incognito, when my majordomo treacherously plied me with Red Abandon and threw me from the ship."

The little hut shook with mirth. Even Orton Bregnat could not repress a titter.

"You should write these things down," said Fuleyem. "There is a market for published inanities."

"But you must not tell any of this to Gwallyn Henwaye, or he may do me a mischief," Filidor said.

"Fear not," said Fuleyem, wiping a tear from his eye. "This knowledge is far too precious a gem to share with the likes of him. Now, tell us, do all servants of the Archonate have teeny tiny integrators in their inner ears, or is this a benefit bestowed only upon the select few?"

Filidor told them of the Zenthro Intrusifer and the accident, but found it difficult to tell the story in the face of gusting laughter and raucous interjections. Before he had finished, Flevvel and Jorn arrived with the evening pottage, the former's pop eye taking in the scene of merriment with suspicious disapproval.

"What's all the rumpus?" he wanted to know, while his bullet-headed friend loomed in the doorway, clasping and unclasping his hands as if eager to grapple.

"The new man is a loon," said Bregnat, adding quickly, "but harmless."

"He tells us grand tales," confirmed Fuleyem.

"About what?" said Tormay Flevvel.

Filidor jumped in. "That I am the King of Air and Spirit, unjustly usurped of my throne, but all who aid me in regaining my seat shall be barons and fealtors of the first rank. I decree it unreservedly."

Flevvel smirked. "And how do we render this aid? Are there ogres to slay, nygraves to bind in gossamer?"

"Nothing so taxing," said Filidor. "Just bring me more of these delicious pilkies, the food of kings."

Tormay Flevvel sneered and even Toutis Jorn contrived an expression of amused contempt. The pop-eyed one seized a good handful of the black fish from the pot and tossed them into Filidor's lap, saying, "May it please your majesty," and when the Archon's apprentice seized the evil-tasting provender and began to consume it with apparent delight, rolling his eyes and making noises of gustatory enjoyment, the pirate threw him yet more.

The others laughed even harder, and Arboghast Fuleyem said, "Here, now, save me some of those. I might be of the blood royal myself."

But Filidor merely grunted and continued to shovel the piscine foulness into his mouth, grinding and swallowing while trying to ignore the bitter expressions of grievance from his taste buds.

Their keepers left and the inmates fell to the dull business of eating. Filidor put a handful of the green stuff into his mouth, to try to scrub away the memory of pilkie, then washed it down with a swig of tepid water. It did little good. The flavor of the fish was not easily overcome. He feared he might yet be tasting its echoes when he had only one tooth to chew with.

"Thank you," he said to the others. "If they knew who I really am, it could go hard for me."

"Indeed," said Fuleyem, choking on a little sludge that must have taken the wrong direction into his interior. "They might summon agents of the vast interplanetary cabal dedicated to naught but your undoing."

There was more laughter, until Orton Bregnat said in a placatory manner, "The lad has a point."

One of the other prisoners suggested that that was merely the shape of Filidor's head.

"Now, now, seriously, but," said the undermate, "if Henwaye thought this young wight was in any way connected to the Archonate, it would not be a matter of the boy eating fish. Instead, the vice would swiftly become the versa."

"True enough," said Valderoyn. "And though we owe the boy nothing, we owe our captor even less."

"There is a mutuality of debt between me and Gwallyn Henwaye," said Filidor. "He owes me a tally of sweat and pain, and I owe him the opportunity to pay it."

"I must say, he talks like one steeped in the brew of rank and privilege," said Arboghast Fuleyem. "Tell us more about how the Archon is really a grinning yellow dwarf, instead of the figure of imposing magisterial grace we've all known for so long."

"Now, now," said Bregnat again, rolling his eyes, "leave the lad to his fancies."

The others urged Filidor to say on, but the young man declined. As the substance of the pilkies spread through his system, he had again heard a faint chime in his left ear, and the now familiar voice.

There must have been more of the fish. My sheets are ashimmer with the recharging.

"Let's not talk about that," said Filidor. "When last we spoke, you said that the solution to my imprisonment was obvious."

The other prisoners all moved a little closer at this. As the moral of the old story about the hierarch and the tree worshiper had it, "Stupidity may often dwell with madness, but brilliance sometimes comes to visit."

I don't think we should discuss it now, said the voice.

"Whyever not?"

Because, at the moment, said the integrator, *I can only tell you how to escape from the island.*

"That will do fine."

Not if it just means that the Obblob will bring you back again.

Arboghast Fuleyem leaned in. "What's your friend saying about escaping?"

Filidor reported the substance of the conversation. Bregnat said, "We've thought of that, too. Even could we overpower the three of them and steal their boat, the sea folk are like to bring us back again. They seem to do Henwaye's bidding, and he's the only one as can speak their language."

Filidor asked the integrator if he had heard that. *No,* was the answer. *I still hear only your voice, and that faintly through vibrations of the bones in your head.*

So Filidor related what Bregnat had said, at which the

voice said, *The key is to be able to speak to the Obblob in their own bubbling speech. Gwallyn Henwaye has mastered a few words, and those few words were enough to convince the Obblob—or at least some of them—that he is the Dry Provider.*

"The what?" said Filidor, and then had to tell the voice to wait while he brought his audience of eavesdroppers up-to-date.

"The Dry Provider?" was Fuleyem's response, followed by a rough-edged snuffling deep in his throat. "That o'ertops even the King of Air and Spirit by a full span. Your majesty's talents are wasted and would be better employed in the public entertainments."

"At least one of my listeners," Filidor told the integrator, "considers the title 'Dry Provider' to be far-fetched."

It is a shortened approximation of a much longer Obblob phrase. Would they like to hear it?

"I doubt it. Their interest is more directed to the practicalities of escape."

Then tell them this, said the integrator, and began an account of Obblob spiritual beliefs, including a prophecy that had drawn many of the ultramond species to Earth in the first place. Filidor relayed the information in small packets to the other prisoners, who hung on his utterances as if he were a paid storyteller who already had their coins in his purse.

"So," said Arboghast Fuleyem, when the young man had finished, "the Obblob are inclined to believe in prophecies, one of which is that a human will someday say certain things to them in their own speech, after which he will provide them with an unending supply of essences, enough to maintain them in a state of perpetual rapture. Gwallyn Henwaye somehow learned of this prophecy and has used the knowledge to sway the Obblob to his bidding."

"Yes," said Filidor, "in a nutshell, yes."

"An appropriate metaphor," said Fuleyem, and snickered. "Highly apt, your majesty."

"But it has the shape of sense," said Orton Bregnat.

The integrator had more to say. *Chances are remote that the pirate has got the exact phrases the prophecy requires, since they are a quotation from Obblob oral literature, never transcribed except but once into human speech, and stored in only one place. But it may be that hearing Obblob sounds from a human was enough to convince at least some of the ultramonds that a true fulfillment of the prophecy might be at hand.*

"And so they do his bidding, half in hope, half in doubt," Filidor concluded.

"If we had access to the one place where the true phrases are recorded," Orton Bregnat said, "we might speak to the Obblob and turn the tables on the pirates."

"Oh, indeed," said Fuleyem. "And then we could be wafted away to palaces in the land of eternal spring, with hot and cold running houris to minister to our wants."

"Arboghast Fuleyem doubts your existence," Filidor told the integrator in a soft voice. "Perhaps you could consult whatever mentions of him appear in official records and furnish me with information that will prove me not a madman."

Ask him if he is the same Arboghast Fuleyem who barely managed a second-rank finish at the Philestry Institute, and was turned down when he applied for a position with the regional office of the Archonate there.

Filidor made the inquiry, and saw the laughter drain from the intercessor's face. He listened again to the voice in his head, and then asked, "And is there not now an investigation of your affairs by the chancery division? Something to do with allegations that you tried to play the wizard with funds trusted to you by your clients?"

The man's pallor deepened as Filidor took fresh input from the integrator and continued, "Was it this unhappy turn of events that induced you to depart Thurloyn Vale on a course that took your air-car straight out to sea, and in such a hurry that you neglected to refill its fuel cells? Was it your intent to end things, a plan that had begun to lose its appeal as the car sank and an Obblob appeared with its reclamatory basket?"

Fuleyem had gone quite pale. All the others looked to him for a response, but for a long while he could not speak. Finally, in a hoarse voice, he said, "Who sent you here? Was it the Cornoni brothers?"

Filidor made no answer, but turned to Orton Bregnat and spoke the man's name, rank, and ship. The integrator supplied him with information, and he said, "You were schooled at the Manfleury Academy, where you broke your left arm playing pelaste in an intramural tournament. The final score was seven to four for your team."

"He is right," said the undermate.

Quickly, Filidor made the rounds of the others, eliciting their names and places of origin, then telling them random facts about their own histories, culled from the integrator's memory banks. Maijung Celemet was a thickset man with a scar across one eye, which he had got entering a burning building to rescue a paramour's pet. Tanoris Volpenge, a youth with a vacant cast to his expression, had once won a prize for his rendition in scrimshaw of the sinking of the *Vindiction*. Byr Lak, the oldest of the inmates, had been born in the house next to that of the celebrated poetaster Melfogel. Finboag Aury had served on eight ships, which Filidor named.

They all confirmed his information, and regarded him with some wonder and even the edge of respect—except for Arboghast Fuleyem, who grew more irascible with each new revelation.

One of the searches caused a momentary lapse for the voice in Filidor's head: it concerned Etch Valderoyn. *He is dead in my universe,* said the integrator.

"How so?" said Filidor as Valderoyn waited to hear of himself.

There was the usual grand regatta to celebrate your birthday. Returning to his ship after toasting your health in several potent liquors, he misjudged the distance between wharf and gunwale, fell into the water, and was crushed when the wake of a passing monitor threw the ship against the dock.

"I see," said Filidor.

Just mention his collection of pizzles. He had a specimen from almost every sea creature that could boast of one. When it was written about in the press, he was inordinately proud.

Filidor did so, to Valderoyn's great satisfaction. When the young man had finished, there was a thoughtful silence in the strong hut.

"Notwithstanding our young friend's misconceptions about my perfectly licit relationships with certain clients, and concerning my little accident at sea," said Arboghast Fuleyem, at last, "we have to accept that he commands considerable knowledge about us."

"Agreed," said Orton Bregnat, "and reason argues that the knowledge must come from the device he claims is stuck in his noggin."

"Does it also argue," speculated the intercessor, eyeing

Filidor sourly, "for his veracity in claiming to be the nephew and heir to the Archon? I think not."

"More to the point," said Etch Valderoyn, who had been warmed by Filidor's praise of his prized collection, "his 'invisible little friend' claims to know how we can escape."

"Aye, and that's a pudding of a different savor," said Bregnat. "So say on, lad."

Filidor inquired of the integrator, which told him, *The exact wording of the Obblob prophecy regarding the Dry Provider was recorded and transcribed by the Archon Belistanion VIII during a goodwill visit to the ultramonds some generations ago. I have it in me.*

When Filidor relayed this intelligence to the other prisoners, there was a general stir of interest—except for Arboghast Fuleyem, who refused to be convinced. "I smell a confidence trick . . ." he began.

But Etch Valderoyn broke in with, "Well, you'd be familiar with the odor."

"Let us hear the Obblob sounds," said Bregnat, "I've heard them often enough, calling to each other across the waves. I'd know it if the lad offers us a lot of bunkyhump."

But the integrator's energy reserves had been depleted by the retelling of each prisoner's biography, and told Filidor the performance must wait until more pilkies had been consumed. And with that it was gone.

"Typical," said the intercessor when informed of the situation, filling his cheeks with air, then blowing it out with a contemptuous puff. "It's all a sham, aimed at our expense."

"What have we that he could possibly want?" said Valderoyn. "Our pilkies?"

"He derives enjoyment from having us dance to his pathetic jig," Fuleyem said.

"I think not," began Orton Bregnat, but at that moment

the two bullyboys arrived, reclaimed the sludge pot, and took away the single oil lamp.

"Tomorrow," promised Filidor. "Right after breakfast."

Arboghast Fuleyem snorted into the darkness of the strong hut, and that was the last sound of the night.

Filidor lay down to sleep with more hope than the night before. He still felt a degree of resentment against the thing in his ear, which he believed held him in low regard compared to its illustrious master. But he had to admit that it was playing a useful part.

In the morning, all but the intercessor waived their share of pilkies, and Filidor ate a double handful of the foul fish. Soon after, the familiar voice awoke in his head, and at his prompting, taught him the first sutra of the Obblob prophecy. Filidor, in turn, repeated the bubbling, mournful sounds, at which Bregnat nodded enthusiastically and said, "That's Obblob talk, and no ferniggling."

Valderoyn said it sounded right to him, but Arboghast Fuleyem guffawed, flecks of pilkie flesh spewing from his mouth, and condemned them all as "a pack of thimblewits, trundling off to Three-Pie Paradise in the thrall of a slippery mountebank."

Filidor defended himself and was joined by Bregnat and the others, especially Valderoyn, who offered to uphold the honor of the Archonate with a balled fist if a certain person didn't retract his vile calumnies.

The pirates chose this moment to return for the breakfast pot. "Here, now, chummies," said the pop-eyed one, "this lacks harmony. What's amiss?"

Arboghast Fuleyem looked as if he wanted to say something, and was only dissuaded by dark glares from the others. But Tormay Flevvel had not missed the byplay. "We'll take him first," he told his slope-headed helper, and together they hustled the intercessor out of the hut.

"Yon frog-futtering pinchpoke will surely bubble," was Valderoyn's opinion, when the door was closed.

"Quickly," Filidor said to the integrator, "tell me the words of the Obblob prophecy again," then repeated the burbles and honks that followed.

Not quite, said the voice in his head. *There is a descending dissonance on the fourth syllable.*

"I'm confident any listening Obblob will excuse a small blunder, just as one does not quibble over the grammatical errors of a talking dog," Filidor replied.

He tried the whole speech again, and heard *Good enough,* from within his head.

The door was flung open again and Tormay Flevvel put his head in, his lesser eye even more squinty than usual. He pointed a finger at Filidor, then turned the gesture into a flick of the thumb over his shoulder, saying only, "You! Now!"

Filidor came out into the sunlight to see Arboghast Fuleyem in the sure grasp of Toutis Jorn. Fear and triumph warred for dominance across the intercessor's face. The popeyed pirate put a hand on Filidor's chest and held him against the wall of the strong hut. "I'm hearing tales about you," he said.

"I am the King of Air and . . ." Filidor began, but Flevvel's hard fingers came up and squeezed the young man's lips shut.

"Hush," he said, and turning to Fuleyem, indicated that the intercessor should speak.

"He only pretends to be twist-witted," Fuleyem said. "He is talking the others around to the idea of staging a mass escape, which he will no doubt use as a diversion to cover his own flight."

Flevvel turned back to Filidor. "And what say you?"

The young man sighed and adopted an air of resigned defeat. "All right," he said, "he can be a seagrave."

"What?" said the pirate.

"He wanted to be the Lord Seagrave of the Several Oceans," said Filidor, "but I denied him the title. Now I see I have no choice but to . . ."

"He's doing it again!" cried Arboghast Fuleyem, twisting in Toutis Jorn's grip, which earned the intercessor a quietening buffet to the side of the head.

Tormay Flevvel looked Filidor up and down, then made up his mind. "He can't do much harm on the wheel," he said. "Let's get them both walking. Henwaye can sift it when he gets back."

In no time, Filidor was at the wheel, the sea furze sweat suit turning his skin into an acre of torment. Arboghast was set to walk the drum beside him, and not long after, Bregnat was brought and put on the next one over. The undermate eyed the intercessor sourly as he put on his suit and walked the plank to climb his wheel.

"Did he make difficulties, this one?" called the undermate.

"He tried to," said Filidor. "We are to await Gwallyn Henwaye's judgment."

"Henwaye's not one to take risks," said Bregnat. "For his peace of mind, he'll weight the both of you down with rocks and leave you to the creep-and-crawls out on the reef."

Arboghast let out a squawk of protest. "Not so," he said. "I shall prove my worth to him and gain his trust. They will make me one of them, and I will dine on the sea's sweet bounty while you eat pilkies and walk the wheel. I have many ideas for improving this enterprise."

"I know Gwallyn Henwaye of old," said Bregnat. "You

may have noted that his henchmen would find it a strain to outwit a sponge. That is because he pals with none who might get the best of him. He will never trust your allegiance."

"We will see," said the intercessor, puffing as he turned his wheel. "I did not get where I have got to in the world without learning the art of persuasion."

"You lost the place you had 'got to in the world,'" Bregnat said, "and now you cannot go back to it. For us, this is a prison from which we hope to flee; you hope it will be a portal to a new beginning."

Bregnat would have said more but held his tongue as the two rogues brought in Etch Valderoyn and put him on the fourth wheel. When they were gone, Filidor and Bregnat brought the pizzle collector up-to-date. "We must boddle out of here, and soon," was the sailor's verdict, to which all but the intercessor agreed.

"I shall plot my own course," said Fuleyem.

Filidor consulted the device in his head.

I can't talk, said the integrator, its voice faint. *There is an unforeseen problem: the pilkies are contaminated with something that leaves a residue. It has begun to corrode my sheets. My capacity to hold energy is in decline.*

"Use it now, or your next lodging will be in the belly of whichever crab dines on my inner ear," said Filidor. He quickly sketched for the integrator a description of the room, the wheels, the suits, and the way the prisoners were put on and taken off the great drums. "Well?" he said, when he had finished.

The voice in his ear was faint and fading. . . . *the suits,* was all that Filidor could be sure of. He tried for more, but there was nothing.

"'The suits,' it said," he told the others.

"But the suits are no protection," Bregnat said. "We've all been stung or nipped through them."

For a long while, there was nothing but the rumbling churning of the wheels. "Two suits," suggested Valderoyn.

"Never get one on over the other," was Bregnat's judgment.

Filidor turned over his brain as he turned the great wooden drum. He wished he was that other Filidor, the one whose birthdays were toasted by men like Valderoyn. If he were that Filidor, the answer would leap at him as quickly as the yellow-eyed beast below had struck at his ankle. He wondered what made this universe and this Filidor so different from that and him.

What tiny twist in the trail behind him hid the spot where he would have gone on to greatness? Was it just that he had once turned left instead of right when coming out of a theater, or chosen to idle an hour over some picaresque tale instead of wading through the footnotes of a history? Or was it something in his most essential foundation, one enzyme a little too zealous when it came to ordering his fundamental molecules?

From speculation on the cause, he moved to consideration of how the effects might be realigned. Was it too late to be what he might well have been meant to be? Could he willfully alter his life's meandering direction here and now, change course and hack his way through conditions and circumstances until he found once more the trail he could and should have taken?

These were heftier questions than whether to order the soup or the sweetvetch, and the sinews of Filidor's mind were not used to lifting them. He could not see a clear solution, yet he was conscious that just knowing himself to be demonstrably capable of more than he had thought, at least in some related cosmos, somehow raised his spirits. Even if he was doomed to walk a wheel until he expired of weariness and want, somewhere there was another Filidor who strode from triumph to accolade.

Cheered by that vision, the Archon's apprentice carried on up the endless wooden drum. And, by some unapprehended process deep in his underused inner workings, his efforts yielded unexpected but welcome results. Like a bubble of air long trapped beneath a subaqueous ledge until it is suddenly shaken loose by a tremor in the sea, the answer to the integrator's riddle rose and popped into his consciousness.

"The suits!" he cried out to Bregnat and Valderoyn. "Of course, the suits!"

While the others looked at him aghast, he peeled the cowl from his face and shoulders, then undid the fastenings down his chest. Continuing to walk the wheel one-handed, he shrugged the unused arm from its sleeve, then set the other free. Kicking his legs loose was more difficult, but by climbing higher on the drum, he was able to do it, aided by the weight of perspiration that accumulated in the suit's lower limbs.

He let the suit fall into the water, where the tentacled horror immediately set upon the garment, gripping it with its clawed limbs while its hooked beak tore great gashes in the fabric. Filidor, meanwhile, kept walking the drum, but edged as he did so toward the side of the pool, until he could stretch a naked limb and step onto the floor.

"The beasts are trained to attack the suits," he called to the others, "and to leave safe anyone not wearing one. That is why the pirates could tread the plank unmolested as they put us to the wheel. Strip off now, and you'll see!"

Bregnat and Valderoyn complied at once. The waters of

their pools boiled as the watch creatures flung themselves at the sea furze. The two naked men soon joined Filidor in freedom from itch and ache.

But Arboghast Fuleyem did not do as the others had. Instead, he began to shout, "Flevvel! Jorn! To me! They make to flee!"

Filidor rushed to the intercessor's place and called to him, "Are you bereft of sense? Here is our chance!"

But Fuleyem continued to cry out, until Etch Valderoyn rushed over and, reaching up to one of the upper planks on the intercessor's wheel, he pulled down upon it with all his might. The effort, combined with the walking man's weight, caused the wheel to rotate downward more quickly than Arboghast Fuleyem could climb it. His furze-shod feet descended to touch the water. At once, a thick tentacle full of hooks curled around his leg, to be joined swiftly by another. He was yanked bodily from the wheel and pulled beneath the surface. The intercessor gave one small "Oh!" of dismay before the water closed over his head, cutting off any further opportunity to voice his horror at what was happening to him.

The three freed wheel walkers looked down at the surface of the roiling pool, and soon saw among swirling chunks of torn furze things that must be parts of a disassembled Arboghast Fuleyem. Orton Bregnat twitched his jaw to one side and said, "Asked for, earned, and got."

"Never cared for yon bung sucker from the push off, and it went downslope from there," was Valderoyn's comment.

Filidor moved to the curtain of kelp across the doorway and eased it open a crack. From this vantage, he could see only along the shore to where the bell hung from its driftwood gibbet. But there was no indication that the intercessor's shouts had brought Flevvel or Jorn to investigate. The thick walls had muffled all sound.

"Our course is obvious," said Bregnat. "We run to the strong hut and free the others, use our numbers to overwhelm Flevvel and Jorn, then be waiting for Gwallyn Henwaye when he comes back in the jollyboat."

Valderoyn nodded his assent, and Filidor was about to add his agreement when a thought occurred. "No," he said. "They are better fed and rested than we. We cannot see where they are, so we do not know if they are between us and the others. If we encounter them before we can open the strong hut, our advantage of numbers will not overmatch their strength and, I am sure, greater experience in viciousness."

"What do you propose, then?" said Bregnat. "For we must act before Henwaye returns."

Filidor said, "One of us must go first and run to ring the bell. That will draw the two thugs to a known location. The others will then rush to free our fellow prisoners, bringing them in a body to the aid of the decoy."

"I will be the bait," said Etch Valderoyn, with a grim smile. "Just don't be too long in coming to my rescue."

The Archon's apprentice was relieved that the sailor had volunteered to suffer almost certain maltreatment at the hands of Tormay Flevvel and Toutis Jorn. So he was surprised to hear himself say, "No, I must be the diversion. Only I can speak the words from the Obblob prophecy, and if there is an Obblob about, for the bell to summon, it may come to my aid. That would be decisive."

"He's right," said Bregnat. "He must be the one."

Valderoyn laid a hand on the young man's shoulder. "You're a good lad," he said. "I'll drink to your health when we're out of this."

An unfamiliar emotion passed through Filidor, but he did

not have time to put a name to it. He squared his shoulders as he had seen pugilists do, sniffed once, and slipped through the kelp curtain.

There was no sign of the two pirates. Filidor edged around the curve of the building he had come out of, until he could see down to the strong hut. The door was locked but unattended. Reasoning that his keepers must be taking their ease in their own quarters, or doing something in the storeroom, he considered making a dash for the strong hut himself. There was strong appeal in the prospect of gathering around him a rough and ready crew of vengeful sailors before confronting Flevvel and Jorn. But the Archon had dinned just enough history into his nephew for Filidor to recognize that the surest way to undo a battle plan was for one element to go spinning off on his own tangent.

It was fifty paces to the bell. He ran toward it, expecting each naked footfall on the island's gritty surface to be the one that brought an angry shout from behind him. On the thirty-third of the fifty, the shout came. He looked over his shoulder to see Flevvel and Jorn down at the water's edge beside the storehouse, where they had been helping to pull the jollyboat up onto the shore. And, seated on the rear thwart, directing his henchmen, was Gwallyn Henwaye, his cudgel thrust through his broad fish leather belt.

Filidor heard the pirate chief say, "Get him!" and rushed for the bell. His hope was that when he reached the driftwood and began beating on the iron signal, he would see all three of his captors racing toward him, with Bregnat and Valderoyn slipping unspied behind them, moving to the strong hut to bring reinforcements.

But that hope went unfulfilled. When he arrived gasping at the bell and scooped up the piece of driftwood that was used to beat it, he turned to see that only Flevvel was in pursuit. Behind the pop-eyed pirate, Filidor saw Henwaye and Jorn racing for the door of the strong hut, and knew that they would arrive there before Orton Bregnat and Etch Valderoyn, who had spilled out of the drum room and were running for the same goal. Henwaye spun at the door and yanked out his cudgel. Jorn pounded up to stand beside him, flexing his great hands.

The plan had come undone, but the young man intended to carry it as far as he could. He hefted the driftwood and smashed it into the bell. The iron rang with a satisfying *clang* and flecks of rust leapt from its surface. He struck again and once more and had the wood raised for a fourth blow, when Tormay Flevvel, his enlarged eye florid with rage, suddenly filled Filidor's vision. The wood was already raised to strike, so Filidor shifted his stance enough to bring it down smartly upon the henchman's head, splitting the skin and driving the pirate to his knees. A second blow might have ended things then and there, had Filidor immediately struck again. But, instead, he remained true to the strategy, and hammered a renewed flurry of blows on the bell, hoping to distract Henwaye and Jorn.

It was another forlorn hope. As he smacked the iron again and again, he witnessed the brief struggle outside the strong hut door. Orton Bregnat arrived there two paces ahead of Etch Valderoyn, and seeing Gwallyn Henwaye's cudgel poised to strike, he flung himself headlong at the pirate chief's midriff. But the weapon sliced down with practiced skill, and struck the undermate a glancing blow on the side of the head, so that he was already dazed when he caromed into Henwaye. They both went down, but only the pirate got back up.

Valderoyn, coming up behind, and seeing no hope of besting the heap of muscle and bone that was Toutis Jorn, dodged to right and to left, then came right again, seeking to wrong-foot Henwaye's henchman, and get behind him long enough to throw the bolt on the strong hut door. His plan almost succeeded, and he dashed past the slope-headed pirate, but the latter recovered his balance enough to fling out one long simian arm, the enormous hand on the end of it colliding with a flat *smack* against Valderoyn's head, sprawling him senseless.

Filidor saw no more, because now Tormay Flevvel came up from his stupor, and with a flurry of blows from fists, feet, and knees efficiently turned the young man into a ball of pain curled on the rocky ground. Filidor drew up his knees and wrapped his arms about his head as the kicks continued to land, and somewhere amid the suffering, a distant part of him put Tormay Flevvel's name on the list that was headed by that of Faubon Bassariot.

"Enough," said Gwallyn Henwaye's voice from a distance, and Flevvel's attack subsided to one last toe in Filidor's ribs.

"Get him up and bring him down to the boat," the pirate chief continued.

Filidor was yanked to his feet. There was blood running into his eyes from a split eyebrow, and when he wiped it away he saw Toutis Jorn at the strong hut door, Henwaye brandishing his cudgel to threaten those within, as Jorn dragged the naked and stunned forms of Valderoyn and Bregnat across the threshold.

It was a good plan, and bravely followed, Filidor comforted himself. Perhaps that other Filidor, hero of another Old Earth, could have done better, but he could not have tried harder.

Henwaye and Jorn had now returned to the beached jollyboat, and Tormay Flevvel kicked and harried Filidor over to where they waited. The pirate chief reached into the boat and came up with a copy of the *Olkney Implicator.* He opened it to an inner page, then looked from the page to Filidor and back again.

"Who do you say you are?" he asked.

"The King of Air . . ." Filidor broke off as Gwallyn Henwaye favored him with a hard slap across the side of his head.

"Now without the rodomontade," the pirate said.

The young man swallowed, then said, "Filidor Vesh, nephew and heir to the Archon."

Henwaye looked at the *Implicator* again, his lips moving as he read something. "You've been quite the naughty boy, haven't you?"

Filidor did not know how to respond.

"He'd be worth a hern or two, then," said Tormay Flevvel, and his smaller eye squinted in avarice.

Henwaye pulled his upper lip into a fold as he thought about it. Then he shook his head. "Not enough to be worth the trouble."

"He doesn't look to be much trouble," Flevvel said.

"Archonate entanglements are more trouble than anything's worth," said Henwaye. "We're doing fine here, as is." His tone bespoke no intent to argue. "Get his clothes on him."

"My uncle will pay a handsome reward for my safe return," Filidor said.

Henwaye glanced again at the *Implicator* and smiled. "Your appreciation of your situation may be fatally behind the movement of events," he said.

The nondescript garments that Filidor had worn when he came ashore were brought from the storehouse, and with the rough-handed aid of Flevvel and Jorn, he was quickly dressed.

The young man tugged his tunic free of Flevvel's fingers and straightened its lines to let it hang appropriately. It now occurred to him that they would not be dressing him if he were to be returned to the strong hut. Nor did they have any intent of returning him to his previous life, even for a reward. And since they were unlikely to offer him a partnership in their Obblob essence venture, that left only one other possibility.

"What on earth is that?" the young man said, pointing over Henwaye's shoulder, and although their attention left him only for the briefest fragment of time, it was enough for Filidor to spin on his heel and race away up the shore. His days on the wheel had firmed up his legs, and the soft-soled boots on his feet lent more spring to his step—and even if neither had been the case, the imminent prospect of being murdered added a clinching extra to his speed and stamina.

He quickly drew away from Flevvel and the lumbering Jorn, giving him time, as he drew near the bell, to aim and deliver a flat-handed strike upon the iron, which made it ring with a dull *hum*. Then he ran on. But he knew the time to summon an Obblob was now spent. He could only hope that there was one within earshot—assuming that Obblob had ears—as he breathlessly shouted out the gobbling syllables of the opening sutra. He drew breath and shouted the phrase again, and heard an angry growl from Tormay Flevvel somewhere behind.

Filidor chanced a glance to his rear and saw that Flevvel and Henwaye were in pursuit, the pirate chief some distance behind his pop-eyed henchman, while Flevvel was in no great hope of soon catching his younger quarry. Toutis Jorn, apparently not even in the running, was not to be seen.

Being in the lead, outrunning his pursuers, brought up a sudden fierce joy in Filidor, even as a part of him reasoned that a roundabout race on a small island could have only one conclusion. Still, he filled his laboring lungs once more, and shouted out the Obblob words as if they were a victory cry. Then, as the last bubbling sound left his lips, he rounded the curved outer wall of the drum room and crashed into the great pillar of unyielding flesh that was Toutis Jorn.

Arms thicker than Filidor's thighs snapped closed about him. His air wheezed out under pressure. Flevvel and Henwaye came up, and the latter said, "Right, no more finnywhacking about. In with him."

Still clasping Filidor to his wide chest, Toutis Jorn turned and walked into the sea. When the water was up to his waist—which put it chest high on Filidor—he stopped and, seizing the Archon's apprentice by the scruff of his neck, thrust him beneath the surface. Between the time he left Jorn's bosom and entered that of the sea, Filidor had time to draw in one brief draft of air.

But, as he regarded the coral floor that sloped gently away into the dark distance of the submarine world, Filidor faced the fact that his next inward gasp of atmosphere must be his last. Jorn could afford to be more patient than his victim. He would hold Filidor under until the air now in the young man's lungs was consumed, after which some inner reflex, responding to a single-minded imperative that was hundreds of millions of years old, would betray all the rest of his system by causing his diaphragm to flex and expand his chest. The sea would then rush in where it was never supposed to be, and Filidor would fare forth into the eternal.

To struggle was pointless, Filidor knew. Yet he did not want to lie passive, doing nothing while the ultimate moment of his existence drew inexorably nearer. He thought about that other Filidor, living his infinitesimal but somehow much larger span of life in a mote-sized universe. Would he quietly await his demise? Though he knew little about that other

Filidor, he was certain that his alter ego would not go into the otherness without at least a measure of defiance.

His possessions reduced to a suit of sodden clothes and a dwindling lungful of air, Filidor resolved to make best use of what little he had. He shaped lips and tongue to the purpose, and blew out the last of his breath in an underwater restatement of the first sutra of the Obblob prophecy. He saw the bubbles form and felt them rush past his face. He closed his mouth, but felt the sea begin to press its way up his nostrils. Ripples of blackness crept along the edges of his field of vision, and a whine like that of flying insects swelled in his ears.

His last thought was that he was sorry to be dying without having achieved all that he might have, but he was grimly satisfied that he had struggled all the way to the final blink. Then, as the darkness swept in from the edges, he closed his eyes and prepared to greet it.

It came with a sudden rush, as if something had seized the back of his shirt and snatched him up. *So this is what it's like,* he thought. He opened his eyes and found himself suspended above the shallows at the edge of the little island and moving toward shore. He could see Toutis Jorn sitting on his wide hams in the water, and beyond him Henwaye and Flevvel looking up at him with great consternation, then turning and running away.

It's as if they can see me, and are terrified of my specter, thought Filidor. But his appreciation of his new bodiless state clashed with the next evidence of his senses: he realized that he was breathing freely, and that what was entering his lungs was not seawater, but sweet, unchoking air. *That's odd,* he mused. *Who would have thought that ghosts would breathe?*

As he flew across the line between sea and shore, he gently descended, until his feet touched the rocky surface in a familiar corporeal way. Henwaye and Flevvel had run to the storehouse. They went inside, and he heard the slam of its wooden door and what sounded like things being frantically piled against it from the inside. He turned to see what Toutis Jorn was doing, and saw that the slab-shouldered henchman was up and wading away through the shallows. But the sight of the fleeing pirate was not the most compelling thing in Filidor's field of vision. That distinction belonged to the enormous manlike creature standing right behind him, looking down at the Archon's apprentice with an expression on its green and gold-flecked face that Filidor took to be mingled tenderness and spiritual awe.

Ah, thought the young man. *I am returned to life. Moreover, it is a life that looks to become much more interesting.* He then had the presence of mind to speak the entire succession of phrases that the integrator had taught him, even remembering the descending dissonance on the fourth syllable.

The giant ultramond made a sinewy motion of head, arms, and shoulders that caused the tubelike symbiotes on its dorsal surface to ripple. It honked softly, then bubbled something, and tentatively held out a web-digited hand as broad as Filidor's chest. The Archon's nephew reached and laid the tips of his fingers on the rubbery skin of the Obblob's palm, at which the ultramond blinked and sighed.

"Please come with me," Filidor said, simultaneously adding gestures that made his meaning clear. The Obblob obligingly followed the young man as he walked to the strong hut. Along the way he saw Toutis Jorn pounding on the storehouse door with fists that no longer seemed so large, but Filidor paid the man no heed until he had thrown the bolt on the prison and called the others out into the sunlight.

They came gingerly at first. Orton Bregnat had a bump

the size of a child's fist on the side of his head and appeared a little dizzy, but Etch Valderoyn was unhurt. Celemet, Lak, Aury and Volpenge eased through the doorway in a manner that kept a maximum distance between them and the Obblob and stood staring at Filidor, as if new and startling wonders were to be expected at any moment.

Then Bregnat stepped forward and embraced the young man, saying, "By Orm's third ball, you've done it."

"We thought they had you pegged and wrapped, lad," said Valderoyn, "and maybe us next for knowing how yon shemmie-lickers had done you down. As the saying goes, 'Closed eyes, still tongue.'"

Filidor was moved by the affection of Bregnat and Valderoyn, and oddly discomfited by the awe in which the other prisoners plainly held him. But he thought again of how that other Filidor would take it, and thanked the men in what he hoped was a modest tone for their concern. "But now we have a job to do," he said.

"Aye," said Bregnat, and lightly punched a fist into a palm.

Filidor took the Obblob's hand and tugged gently, leading the ultramond toward the storehouse, the others following behind. They found Toutis Jorn still on the wrong side of the door. At the sight of Filidor's big companion, the pirate's knees seemed to lose interest in keeping their owner erect. He sank down and tipped over until his sloping forehead leaned against the storehouse wall, then he put his hands over his eyes. A little sound escaped his lips.

Filidor ignored him. He knocked on the storehouse door and said, "Come out."

There was no answer from within, except the scraping of something heavy across the floor, a grunt of effort, and the thump of something solid against the inner side of the door.

Filidor called again. "I admit it will not be good for you to come out, but I promise you it will be much worse if we have to come in." It seemed the sort of thing a heroic Filidor might have said.

Still there was no answer. "Imagine them peeping about in there like sleekits in a hold," said Bregnat. "Let's put the cat in."

By signs and gestures, Filidor conveyed to the Obblob that he would like the door open. The ultramond stooped and seized and pushed, and the goal was obtained. Then the other prisoners jostled their way through the entry and shortly emerged with new versions of Gwallyn Henwaye and Tormay Flevvel, bruised and timorous versions that bore only a slight resemblance to the imperious brigands who had worked the captives on the wheel. Bregnat had acquired the pirate chief's cudgel, and was using it to good account. The other former prisoners joined in and soon had all three of their erstwhile captors rolling and flinching on the rough ground under a rain of well-placed kicks and buffets.

"Enough," said Filidor after a while, but he had to say it a couple of more times before the men had satisfied their first taste for revenge. "Put them in the strong hut," he said, "until we have mulled the possibilities."

When the thugs had been harried to their confinement, the men poked through the storehouse for their clothes, then gathered around Filidor again. He realized that they looked to him for leadership. That was a novel state of affairs; even among the coterie of lordly drones with whom he had passed many an idle evening, none would have singled out Filidor Vesh as the shiniest pebble on the beach. Again, he experienced an unfamiliar mix of emotion: he was gratified by their regard, but at the same time he felt that their trust had lowered a weight of responsibility onto shoulders unused to bearing more than his generally underemployed head.

Still, he thought to himself, *if not I, then who?* But confessed to himself that he would be glad of some help, and so said, "Bring me pilkies."

A bushel of the horrid-tasting fish were found in the storeroom and brought out. The Archon's apprentice sat down with his back against the storehouse wall and began to consume them. It was not long before he heard a voice in his head.

Has our situation improved?

"It has." Filidor quickly brought the integrator up-to-date.

Good thinking on the suits, it said. *Now, tell this to the Obblob.* There followed a string of syllables, which Filidor repeated to the ultramond. The Obblob responded with a jutting of its chin and a rippling of its tubes. Then it turned and walked into the sea and was soon lost to view beneath the water.

It will return with its fellow ecstatics to hear the new dispensation, the integrator said. *Afterward, we can depart for Olkney and your uncle's workroom, there to free me from the confines of your inner ear and connect me to a more familiar source of power.*

"A sound plan," said Filidor.

Now I will conserve my resources, while you and your friends investigate the contents of the pirates' trove.

The pirates had wrung plenty from the sweat of their captives. A pile of precious goods was heaped in one corner of the storehouse: noble metals, costly gems, ancient manufactures that were old enough and rare enough to excite even the most blasé archaicist or curio collector. But of more immediate interest to the freed men were the supplies of good food and drink on shelves along the wall. They gathered handfuls of containers and brought them outside for an impromptu feast. Filidor was most pleased to find a demi-cask of the purple Pwyfus that had first energized the voice in his head. He filled a cup of damascened gold with the stuff and drank a solid draft, then asked the integrator if it felt any effects.

Indeed, came the reply, *a fourth-level surge across my sheets. Better than pilkies. But the corrosion problem remains unsolved.*

"Is there any way to reverse the damage?"

None to be found here. The best course is to get me out of you and my sheets into a vat of restorative.

"But at least I don't have to eat pilkies," Filidor said, then asked the carousing men if he might have the wine for his own, since it kept his inner voice lively.

Valderoyn swallowed the mouthful of bread and cheese he was chewing and said, "You can have anyaught and as much of it as you like, lad. And I'll down the man who denies you." He glared around at the others, but there was no dissent.

When they had eaten until their stomachs protruded beneath the starkness of their ribs, the men sat in a circle on the shore—the pirates' quarters would need a thorough swabbing before they were fit to enter—passed around a flask of fierce akkabite, and discussed what they would do next.

"I'm for home and a life ashore," said Etch Valderoyn. "I've had enough of the sea, and I'll warrant the sea feels the same about me. I'll take some of yon pelf and buy myself a tavern with a yard out back and a tree in it. I'll sit beneath the tree and let its fruit fall into my lap."

Each man piped in with his own dreams and fancies, except for Orton Bregnat, who said, "I'm of a mind to stay right here," and when he noted the incredulous looks of the others, continued, "It's plain there's a good living to be made out of the Obblob, even if I'm not as grasping as Henwaye."

The undermate sketched his plan. He would ask the Obblob to make more land and buildings, and here he would establish a proper rehabilitory facility for recalcitrants and defaulters. "I'd feed them a titch better than our captors fed us, and shoo away them nasty things in the pools. Any as tried to swim off, the Obblob would bring back."

He looked at Filidor. "I've already got my first inmates, and I believe I now have a connection to the Archonate that would get me more."

The Archon's apprentice belched gently, and said he was sure something could be arranged.

"All as wants to throw in are welcome," Bregnat told the others, and they agreed to talk more of it in the morning.

Filidor rose, and walked down to the shore. He was a little unsteady because of the wine, and leaned against the gunwale of the beached jollyboat. The old orange sun had set, leaving a pallid glow on the western horizon. The sea was the color of tarnished silver, calm and smooth all the way to where the horizon merged into the descending night. Behind him, the men lit lamps and sat in a circle, passing around the flask of akkabite. They laughed at something Finboag Aury said.

The young man stretched and took another pull at the golden cup. He was thinking about how the day had gone, and the part he had played in it. Months back, he had rescued his uncle from the direst peril, at the same time saving the world from an influx of evil that would have flooded in from a dimension where it was merely another natural force, like gravity or weather. But, in both of those cases, he had acted from purest instinct, in a sudden burst of panic. Today, he had reasoned out a puzzle that had for months eluded several experienced men of the world, though the answer had always been there to be seen. Then he had taken charge, made a plan and carried it through, despite the extreme opposition of vicious pirates. He had led, others had followed, and by his initiative, they had won through.

This was not the Filidor he was used to being. True, he had had some help from the integrator lodged in his ear. But not much help. Facing things fairly, he had to admit that he had done much that he would not have believed himself able to do. Perhaps there was not as much difference between himself and that other, tiny Filidor known to the voice in his ear.

He drank a little more of the wine, and found that it had aged well since he had opened the demi-cask. He projected a future. He would go back to Olkney and report to his uncle the murderous treachery of Faubon Bassariot. Inquiries would be made, using methods that the felonious majordomo would find unwelcome. Then dispensations would be ordered, which would be even less conducive to the functionary's sense of well-being.

Then Filidor would take stock of himself and his place in this universe. He would consult with the integrator after it had been loosed from his ear, find the threads that had come undone in his life that had knit themselves up in that other Filidor's, and make changes. The potential was there, he believed. He thought of it as residing in a locked room somewhere deep inside his being, behind a rusted door at the end of a musty, long unvisited corridor. He would find his way there, and burst the door as the Obblob had broken open the storehouse. And then he would see.

He took another draft of the purple wine, and his eye fell upon the copy of the *Olkney Implicator* that Gwallyn Henwaye had brought back in the jollyboat. Filidor picked it up and held it so that the light from the men's lamps illuminated the page the pirate had been looking at when he had asked the young man who he was. In the yellow glow from the lamplight, Filidor saw what looked to be a likeness of himself.

The print was too faint to see, so he moved back to the lighted circle of men and squatted down near one of the lamps. It was definitely his image. He even remembered when it had been captured: it was at one of Lord Afre's revels; the guests had come in extravagant costumes and had arranged themselves in amusing tableaux that represented unlikely scenes from history and legend. Filidor had put on scale armor and a peaked morion to become a fugleman in the Battalion of Unrelenting Cenobites, and thus had been matched with the Bessemery sisters, who were dressed—or more properly scarcely dressed—as devotees of the voluptuous demigoddess Cocotta. He had conferred briefly with the pneumatic twins, then they had entwined themselves about him in a manner that would have cost a real Cenobite a strenuous month of purgative cleansings.

It was unfortunate, though understandable, that the *Implicator*'s redactive staff had elected to run that particular picture of Filidor; unfortunate, because the image might cause those who did not know him to suspect that he was not in constant or even close touch with rationality; understandable, because the text of the accompanying article made him out to be not just giddily eccentric, but a dangerous madman. Filidor lowered the page closer to the lamp and leaned in to read.

The gossip-hawking Tet Folbrey had been let loose from

the confines of his column to write the piece for the *Implicator*'s front page. He had given up his usual arch and coded style for a tone more in keeping with an announcement that the world would soon end, and not prettily.

The main headline featured the words *shock* and *horror* and *treachery*, and there was a subhead that mentioned *murderous attack* and *flight to evade capture*. The body text delivered all that the headlines advertised.

Snug within the justly revered institution of the Archonate, it began, *a viperous spirit has lain coiled, coldly calculating its moment to strike. Now struck it has, dealing an almost fatal blow to a loyal servant of the regime, devastating its trusting and indulgent kin, before slinking off into the shadows, there to plot who knows what further outrages?*

Filidor Vesh, who recently contrived to have himself declared heir apparent to the office of the Archon, now held by the venerated person of Dezendah VII, has revealed himself to be not the shallow and inconsequential fop most had taken him for. Instead, as the more perspicacious had long suspected, he now stands unmasked as an iniquitous brute who does not shrink from even the heinous deed of foul murder in order to fulfill his wicked plans.

Filidor read further, and learned that he had been at the center of a plot, "hatched within the heart of the Archonate, to overthrow goodness and rectitude." When his stratagems had been discovered by the honest Faubon Bassariot, the criminal Vesh had fled by sea, traveling under an assumed guise. Bassariot had bravely pursued the delinquent, confronting him alone aboard the escape vessel and urging him to return to face his just desserts. For his kindness, Bassariot had been dealt a felonious blow to his honorable head, after which the villainous Vesh had escaped in an air-yacht illegally chartered under false authority of the Archonate by his confederates, a notorious revolutionary cabal known as the Podarkes of Trumble. They were believed to be hiding out on cave-riddled Mt. Cassadet.

Meanwhile, the story went on, the beloved Archon Dezendah VII, his noble spirit sapped by his nephew's treachery, had secluded himself in the inner reaches of the Archonate palace. He had delegated all matters of governance and policy to the estimable Bassariot, who was courageously bearing up under the burden of serving the populace. A thorough reorganization of the Archonate hierarchy was to follow soon.

Filidor read the entire story, then read it once more. For a moment, so vast was the lie it proclaimed that he found himself almost dizzily tilting toward a state of belief. It was of course unthinkable that he was a usurping zealot and an attempted murderer. But it was equally unthinkable that Faubon Bassariot had somehow overturned the ancient political order and seized power from the Archon. To Filidor's knowledge, except for Holmar Thurm's brief and futile attempt, no such thing had ever happened in all the millennia stacked behind this moment. Archons had come and Archons had gone, yielding place to their chosen successors smoothly and without so much as an unkind word.

Or so Filidor believed. But that belief was not founded on any broad base of fact. For all he knew, Archons had been wading through blood to the supreme office throughout the centuries, then papering over the spattered walls with platitudinous official statements and bland speeches from the throne. *You never studied,* he heard his uncle's voice saying, and that prompted him to seek out the other voice in his head.

"Integrator," he said, turning to face the darkened sea

and lowering his voice for privacy, "has an Archon ever come to the office through extralegal means?"

Why do you ask?

"Oh, no particular reason."

Then may I counsel you with the old adage, "No good comes of poking a sleeping garoon"?

"Well, there may be a particular reason, after all."

Perhaps you should divulge that reason, so that I may frame a reply appropriate to the circumstances.

Filidor thought it best to wander a little farther down the shore from the reveling ex-prisoners, and also found it expedient to take the *Olkney Implicator* with him. As he walked, he pulled the front page free of the rest, folded it, and tucked it into a pocket.

At a safe distance, the Archon's apprentice told the integrator the story that was being put out about him. The voice was silent for a lengthy moment, then said, *I ask merely as a formality, but there wouldn't happen to be any shreds of truth in the report, would there?*

Filidor felt a surge of anger, with an undercurrent of hurt. "You should know me better than that," he said.

In point of fact, replied the voice in his head, *I hardly know you at all. The Filidor Vesh with whom I am acquainted is not often found floating at sea, soon to be drafted as a workbeast for pirates.*

"I would like to know more about this Filidor of yours, although he sounds a little too perfect," the young man said. "But at the moment, I am more seized by the vision of being arrested the moment I step ashore, to be manacled and handed over to a man who, the last time the opportunity arose, soused me with Red Abandon and threw me off a ship." He thought for a moment, then added, sincerely, "I am also worried about my uncle."

Very well, said the integrator, *in one sense, of course, all Archons relinquish their authority to their successors in lawful fashion—including those who have ended their reigns as motes of disassembled dust on the plain of Barran, after resetting the iniquitous mechanism that lurked there until you— that is, "my" Filidor—finally discovered how to turn it off.* The voice paused, then asked cautiously, *Am I to assume that you and your uncle have not yet had to undertake that unfortunate duty?*

"As a matter of fact," said Filidor, "we have. As a further matter of fact, it was I, not my uncle, who succeeded in disarming the thing."

Hmm, was the integrator's only comment, then it continued. *Well, as I say, authority is always lawfully relinquished, but sometimes the legitimacy is acquired after the relinquishment.*

"You mean retroactively?"

I mean that cause and effect are not always arranged in an ideal sequence.

"In other words," Filidor translated, "not only do victors write the histories, but usurpers also rewrite the rule book to justify the illicit seizure of office."

Perhaps not the most felicitous manner of putting it, but essentially correct.

"I am surprised the people put up with such shenanigans. They should rise up."

Unwittingly, I am sure, you put your finger on the flaw in your own reasoning.

"How so?"

You said, "They should rise up," not "We should rise up." As long as it is a matter to be solved by others, it will not be.

Filidor saw the truth in what the voice said, but Tet Folbrey's news had put him in a combative mood and the integrator was the only opponent in the ring. "But I am not of the people, I am of the Archonate."

Not according to Faubon Bassariot. It is a good thing he thinks you already dead, or he would surely take forthright steps to correct the oversight.

Filidor felt a shiver of anxiety make its way through his anger. "Still," he said, "when I get back to Olkney, I will set things right."

The direct approach is not always the wisest strategy, as those who have fallen off mountains can testify.

"You counsel a more indirect attack?"

I do. But first, I would like the leisure to consider our options.

"I appreciate your assistance," said Filidor, but then another thought intruded. "Have you thought of your own legal situation? If Bassariot has power, his authority is absolute. I am a fugitive and you are my accomplice. Besides, is not your loyalty owed to the Archonate, whosoever holds its keys?"

My loyalty is to your alter ego's Archonate, said the voice, *so the question is moot. I am sure I would enjoy working out its various permutations in the abstract. But, here we are in the here and now, with me in that specific part of the here and now that is bounded by the confines of your head. Since that is an object which Faubon Bassariot would likely strike off, I elect to do my utmost to keep it on your shoulders. At least until I am free of it.*

"Very reassuring," said Filidor.

For now, said the integrator, *you could oblige me by offering a rich supply of the substances that energize my systems, so that I can investigate all the ins and outs of our situation.*

"That would involve consuming more of the hateful pilkies or drinking myself into insensibility."

The choice is yours.

Filidor went in search of the demi-cask.

CHAPTER

F I V E

It was yet another uncomfortable awakening for Filidor, when he opened red-shot eyes and found himself in the bottom of the beached jollyboat. His first thought was that several more entities had invaded his skull, bringing not only their voices but a large arsenal of heavy weapons which they were discharging with gleeful abandon into his most sensitive tissues. Others, perhaps finding the assault on his head too noisy, had taken up residence in his stomach where they were warming themselves at a roaring fire.

After a while, and with infinite caution, he sat up. He did not wish to let his head move too quickly from the horizontal to the vertical, for fear it might snap off, fall into the jollyboat's scuppers, and shatter. He looked over the side of the boat and saw his fellow freedlings sprawled about the shore, making noises that reverberated in Filidor's too sensitive ears like floods of boulders rumbling and rattling across a sheet-metal floor.

He remembered that the night had grown raucous as the seven of them had made depredations upon the pirates' store of stimulants and euphoriants. There had been some dancing, and now he recalled his own demonstration of a step that had lately caught on in the better salons of Olkney: a sideways glide with knees bent, ending in a sudden stop and hop, accompanied by a simultaneous slap of palm against open mouth, to produce an audible *pop*. It was called the hoppy-poppy.

Under the influence of drink and other substances liberated from the storehouse, the celebrants' legs had eventually given out, but finding their mouths still relatively functional, the seven had turned to song and story. The demi-cask of purple Pwyfus subdued Filidor's inhibitions, and he had stood up and sung the lachrymosal ballad, *The Sundered Pair*, which told of young lovers tragically torn apart by circumstances of birth: he being poor, while she was born to wealth. The boy seeks riches by delving deep beneath the earth for synthetics manufactured in the long-faded past, now transmuted by time and geological processes into priceless rarities; the girl, to prove her love, gives up her inheritance and follows him, but when she learns that he has been buried alive in a subterranean collapse, she throws herself down the shaft of his excavation. The boy, however, lives to free himself from the deadfall, only to find his one love expired. He lies down beside her, takes her hand, and triggers a final cave-in. In the song's last verse, the two are unearthed by spelunkers of a far later age, their bodies preserved and transformed into precious substance by the ancient synthetics. Their remains are set up as a memento in a public square, and birds nest in them.

As Filidor finished the song, his voice cracking on the mournful *pheep-pheep-pheep* of bird cries embedded in the last line, the old man named Byr Lak snorted, and the youth Tanoris Volpenge added the counterpoint of a snigger. At once, Etch Valderoyn leapt to his feet, swearing he would "have the gibbies out of any and all who slight the lad," only to topple backward and strike his head on the gunwale of the jollyboat, after which little was heard of him for the rest of the night.

A round of storytelling then ensued. Lak led off, reciting the climactic stanzas from *The Last Voyage of Pandarios*, every seaman's favorite epic, in which the High Admiral of the sunk and scattered Corbyrean Grand Fleet paddles the only craft remaining under his command, a leaking skiff, out to confront the sinister galleys of the Buk-Buk horde. "I'd liefer captain a cockleshell than stoke in a flagship, and death will not stay me ashore . . ."

Orton Bregnat told the old story of the three wise men of Kephriot, enlivening the well-worn phrases with comic facial contortions and expansive gestures, and bringing his cupped palms together in a resounding *clop* at the end, when the youngest of the trio of mages says, "I think not," causing all three to instantly disappear.

Filidor enjoyed the tales, both in their substance and in the manner of their telling. He wished that he knew such stories and had the flair for telling them with vigor and sizzle. He wished it even more when, in time, the attention of the party came around to him, and all looked to the Archon's nephew to take a turn. With a pang of regret, he realized that the only tales he knew were snippets of gossip from the scribblings of Tet Folbrey, unlikely to be of interest to, or even comprehended by, his new companions. Besides, he had gone off Folbrey.

Then a thought occurred, and he turned to his inner voice for assistance, speaking low so that the others would think he was merely clearing his throat preparatory to a recital. "Integrator," he said.

I am busy, it replied.

"This will take the tiniest fraction of your capacities."

The pilkies have scarred my sheets. My capacity to recharge is diminished.

"The works of The Bard Obscure are popular among the broad spectrum of society, are they not?"

They are.

"Do you know any of them?"

I recorded the entire The Bard Obscure Festival during the Feast of Name Revocation, some decades ago.

"My companions expect a tale and I know none that will suit. Please tell me a short one, that I can recount to them."

And then you will not bother me until morning?

"Agreed."

Very well. Announce that you will declaim The Riddle of the Rocks.

Filidor rose and struck an appropriate attitude. *"The Riddle of the Rocks,"* he said. "By The Bard Obscure.

"Ethelthon, Chlamys, and Tebb were sorcerers of renown. Each rivaled against the others for supremacy in the esoteric arts of prodigistry and cryptomantics. It was their habit to spend time together, with each endeavoring to astound the others by demonstrations of new amazements or novel refinements of old wonders. On these occasions, each performer in turn would take pains to conceal the manner or mechanics of every feat, and each would try to puzzle out how the others achieved their marvels.

"One day, the three set out in a small boat and traveled a slight distance from shore. Ethelthon caused golden fish to come to the surface, form ranks and battalions, then rise on their tails and pass in review while he answered the salutes the creatures offered with their forefins.

"Then Chlamys made gestures with her hands that convinced the water to become completely sheer. She conjured onto its surface amusing scenes of the far past and distant future, as well as the ribald present doings of persons in whom the three mages took an interest.

"Next, Tebb enjoined the water to form itself into discrete shapes and forms, which he fashioned into a great cityscape with manors and castles, roads and walls, rising upon hills or nestled in dales, and all made of the substance of the sea. He populated his creation with marine creatures that went about their business in mimicry of the affairs of human beings.

"After the displays, the three competitors rested and ate the provisions they had brought with them. In the middle of the meal, Ethelthon suddenly remarked, 'I have forgotten my wine,' and with that he stepped out of the boat, walked across the water to the shore, and came back with a flagon of yellow Iriest.

"Chlamys then announced that she had forgotten certain condiments. She also stepped from the boat, walked across the water, and shortly returned.

"Then Tebb, sensing that an unannounced contest was under way, remarked that he too had left something ashore. He said a particular word very quietly, then rose and stepped over the side of the boat. Immediately, he sank straight down, but since he had uttered the rudiments of an applicable cantrip, he was able to walk to shore across the bottom, emerging dripping and abashed, but otherwise unharmed.

"Ethelthon, seeing this, turned to Chlamys and said, 'I suppose we should have told him about the stepping stones.'

"At which, Chlamys regarded Ethelthon with a small smile and said, 'What stepping stones?' "

The tale had been well received, Filidor remembered, but past that point in the evening his memory could not take him. He surmised that more of the demi-cask's contents had been transferred to his own recesses, where it had become ungrateful for his hospitality, and was now repaying him in painful coin.

He looked around and saw that Orton Bregnat was sleeping in a sitting position, his back to the strong hut door, and Henwaye's cudgel across his lap. There seemed to have been no attempted escapes during the night. That was probably, Filidor thought, a result of the pirates' having overheard their former captives engaged in an impromptu contest to see who could devise the most imaginative punishment for any who ventured so much as a toenail beyond the strong hut door. Most of the proposed penalties were anatomically unlikely, and some of them probably impossible, but the revelers agreed that all were worth at least a try.

Filidor closed his eyes and lowered his pained head into his cupped hands. He would have liked to have found a place where snoring men were not a significant part of the environment, but in his present condition he doubted he could coordinate legs, arms, hands, and feet with sufficient dexterity to move himself there. He thought of Faubon Bassariot, and of the functionary's pivotal role in bringing him to this morning's disarray, and then he looked forward to an opportunity to test some of the previous night's proposed afflictions on the person of his former majordomo.

The visions that these thoughts conjured cheered the young man somewhat, and he raised his head and opened his eyes again. As he did so, he heard a timid honk from his seaward side, and turned to see the shallows filled with large, green and gold-flecked creatures, all apparently sitting on the sea bottom, their heads and chests above the ripples, their lambent eyes all fixed upon his person.

"Integrator," Filidor said, in a voice meant to carry no farther than the bones of his own skull. "Where are you?"

I take that for a rhetorical question, came the response.

"Take it any way that meets your needs," said Filidor, "but the Obblob are here, in numbers and with strong expectations."

We must deal with them. From what I sense in your fluids, you are not in the most hale of conditions. Are you able?

"I confess that I am somewhat thinned out," Filidor said, and heard from the integrator what he thought was a sniff.

"You disapprove?" he said.

It is not for me to comment. Still, I am not accustomed to dealing with tosspots.

"I suppose your Filidor is also renowned, among his other superlative qualities, for his abstemiousness."

He values moderation.

"He might value it less after walking a wheel for Gwallyn Henwaye," said Filidor.

I cannot make the comparison.

Filidor drew himself up. "Be it as it may, I will try to rise to the occasion, as long as that occasion is not too high and mighty, nor too prolonged." He looked at the Obblob, and they looked back. "They don't consider me a god or anything, do they?" he asked.

To them you are essentially a conduit for certain cosmic forces and influences, and as such, worthy of respect and quite lucky to touch. But much more a node than a deity.

"Good," said Filidor. "I think I can do a node, but godhood is well beyond me this morning."

A question had been troubling him the night before, and he thought to raise it now. "This matter of prophecy," he said. "I am clearly no prophet. The only reason I spoke the words the Obblob desired to hear was because you had recorded them and fed them to me."

So?

"So it is a sham, is it not?"

Not at all. Such and such a set of syllables had to be said, and were said. Now the Obblob will have their essences, and without Henwaye's grinding price. Things are as they were meant to be.

"But it was arranged so by you and me."

Then we are instruments of fate.

"Knowing instruments," said Filidor.

How does that make a difference?

The business with the Obblob was neither too protracted nor too taxing. First, Filidor moved along the shore, away from the sleeping men so as not to disturb them. Then, prompted by his internal companion, he told the ultramonds that he was not only a node and conduit, but a ranking representative of the Archonate. As such, he could assure them that the ad hoc arrangements that had been made with Gwallyn Henwaye would now be superseded by an officially sanctioned scheme. The small island would become a legitimate contemplatorium, with the pirates its first inmates. Orton Bregnat, whose sleeping form Filidor indicated, would assume the role of warden and dispenser of essence. The Obblob would no longer have to scour the sea floor for precious items to barter—a tenth of what they had heretofore provided would be sufficient payment. There would also be an ex gratia payment of essences for rescued persons brought to the island.

One of the Obblob, who might have been a chief or priest, and who knew human speech, translated Filidor's announcements. The news was well received, as evidenced by a cacophony of hoots and bubblings that Filidor took to represent happiness and relief. The integrator speculated that Henwaye's grasping for ever more loot had placed considerable personal and social strain on the Obblob ecstatics, so that they had been forced to devote most of their days to treasure hunting, when they would have much preferred to spend their time leisurely contemplating the sublime experiences brought on by human essence. To demonstrate goodwill, Filidor went to the storehouse and brought out several sealed vials of the island's product, which he gave to the translator to be distributed to the throng.

After that, the translator replied with a short speech in Obblob, which the integrator rendered even more succinctly: *He said, "Yahoo!"* Then all of the ultramonds lined up and came one at a time to Filidor, so that he might touch their offered palms and make them lucky. There followed some perfunctory ceremonial gestures, and the encounter was done. But as the Obblob turned to leave, the voice in Filidor's head said, *Before they go, ask if anyone has a* bobblobblobl.

"What is it?"

You'll see.

Filidor called out the odd syllables. The translator spoke to another of the departing Obblob, and the latter turned around in the shallows and came back to shore. From a pouch strung about its waist, it drew out a handful of what looked to Filidor like colorless slime. Gingerly, the Archon's apprentice took the proffered stuff, and found it cool and gelatinous, but when he brought it nearer for a closer inspection, a smell as sharp as strong ammonia but more foul stormed up his nose and seized the olfactory bulb of his brain in a pincer grip. The assault on his senses, when his cerebral organ was already battered by the aftereffects of the previous night's indulgence, was more than Filidor could bear. He had never in his life been more acutely aware of possessing a head. He held the acridly reeking thing as far from him as he could, and gasping and retching, he sank to his knees.

The Obblob apparently took this behavior for a display of glad acceptance. It ducked its head several times and rippled its dorsal tubes in several patterns, said something that Filidor did not have the presence of mind to ask the integrator to translate, and swam away.

When Filidor's eyes had stopped watering and he could again take a full breath, he held the lump of goo at arm's length and asked the integrator, "Is it some kind of weapon? Do we bring ourselves stealthily within hurling distance of Faubon Bassariot and let fly?"

It is a protective garment, was the reply. *Tease it out into a thin sheet.*

"Your sense of humor eludes me," Filidor said.

Trust me.

Head averted and arms extended to their utmost, Filidor shook and pulled the foul-smelling substance, and saw it resolve itself into a thin translucent membrane, as long as he was tall, cylindrical in shape and open at one end. When it was fully extended, dangling from his hands, it became completely transparent, but the strength of its odor did not abate.

"Is it to keep the rain off?" the young man asked. There was a slight breeze and he moved so that he was upwind. "If so, having one's nasal passages ravaged seems far too high a price to pay. I would rather be wet than afraid to breathe."

Slip it over your head, said the integrator.

"I will not," said Filidor. "To be close to the stuff would bring strong men to their knees. To be surrounded on all sides must mean death or madness for anything that possesses a functioning nose."

It only smells that way on the outside, and for a purpose.

Filidor took a deep breath and did as the voice told him. The thin stuff shimmered down over his head and descended to his feet. He took the most tentative sniff possible, and found that there was no odor here inside. When he put out a hand, the cowllike garment stretched without resistance. It was dry to the touch, loose and billowy, as if he was wearing the finest gauze.

"Remarkable stuff," he said.

More than you yet realize, said the voice. *Move closer to the men and call out to them. Wake them.*

Filidor did so. He saw Etch Valderoyn stir, then sit up and muzzily peer about. Byr Lak did likewise, and Orton Bregnat roused with a snort and a start. Filidor called again, at which Valderoyn rubbed his eyes and looked about in alarm, then struggled to his feet. The pizzle aficionado's gaze swept up and down the shore, then he shaded his eyes and stared out to sea.

"Wake! Wake!" Valderoyn cried, and kicked at the sleeping form of Finboag Aury. "The lad's in peril! I can hear him calling, but I can't find him!"

Now Bregnat and the others rose and looked about, calling out Filidor's name. The undermate peered into the strong hut, but saw only Henwaye and his crew. "Spread out, and look for him!" he called to the others.

"They can't see me," Filidor said to his inner listener.

The outer cells of the bobblobblobl pass particles of light to each other, so that they bend around whatever the garment covers. It protects young Obblob from the appetites that patrol the sea.

"And the smell?"

Not everything hunts by sight.

Etch Valderoyn had come down to the shore. "The Ob-blob must have carried him off," he declared, then, when he drew near to where Filidor stood, "Fagh! They have left a taint!"

The young man said, "Don't be startled," but the voice coming from empty air close by the sailor's ear had the op-posite effect. Valderoyn leapt backward, flailing his arms and swearing a string of nautical oaths that Filidor had never heard in the better salons of Olkney.

The young man pulled the bobblobblobl up his body and over his head, which brought a new sequence of profanity.

"I've heard of those things, but never seen one," said Orton Bregnat, coming down to where Valderoyn stood, his face offering a pageant of expressions.

"It's an Obblob cowl," said Maijung Celemet, reaching out wonderingly to touch the garment, which Filidor was now wadding up into the colorless lump it had formerly been. "They say a man as has one of these will ne'er drown."

"It's not drowning I fear," Filidor said, "and I'd better tell you now the why of it."

He told them, without too much elaboration, of what he had learned from Tet Folbrey's piece in the *Implicator*. "There is terrible work afoot," he concluded. "I don't know what has happened to my uncle. But I do know that if Bassariot or any who contrive with him should learn that I am not dead, that is an oversight they will repair with all dispatch."

Valderoyn growled at that, but Filidor went on, "I will take counsel with the device in my head as to how to pro-ceed, but I can tell you now that I am determined to regain my place and to secure my uncle's safety. Somehow, I will make this come right."

The words sounded braver than Filidor felt, but again he thought of that other Filidor whose tiny universe was folded into this cosmos, that ornament of his age, and drew himself up. "So there it is," he said.

"What do you want us to do?" asked Etch Valderoyn, in a way that promised he would strive to perform whatever the young man asked.

"Aye," said Orton Bregnat, "we owe you much," at which the others nodded heads and issued gruff noises of assent.

For a moment, Filidor imagined himself leading his brave little group of seafarers up the sweeping staircases of the Archonate palace, like a band of heroes in a romance, to cast down Bassariot and all his devious works. Then reality reasserted itself.

"All I ask is that you keep my continued existence a secret," he said, "until I have put things as they ought to be."

It was so agreed. They breakfasted on the pirates' provisions, and Bregnat brought Filidor a dose of Colophant's Universal Assuagement, which he had found with the store of liquor. The remedy soon leached the suffering from the young man's head, and he pocketed the bottle, reasoning that if his internal resident required its host to be liberally seasoned in raw-edged purple wine, the elixir would come in handy.

After that, they divided up the heaps of loot that Henwaye had extorted from the Obblob, with only moderate dissension as to who received what. Filidor declined to take a full share, pocketing only a few small and valuable items. When the others pressed him, he demurred, saying, "If I regain my place in the Archonate, wealth means nothing to me; if I do not, it means less than nothing, since it will then sluice into the coffers of Faubon Bassariot and his cronies, after they take it from my dead body."

Orton Bregnat said he would stay on the island to keep a foot on Gwallyn Henwaye's head, and Maijung Celemet chose to assist him. Byr Lak offered to take the others to Scullaway Point in the jollyboat, then return to help the two who were remaining on the island.

Filidor went to the strong hut door and looked through the little window. Henwaye, Flevvel, and Jorn sat where their prisoners had sat. The pirate chief looked up at the face in the window and set his features in a mode of mocking defiance.

"Now it is you who will walk a wheel while another keeps the tally," Filidor said. "How stands your philosophy this morning?"

The pirate affected unconcern. "Wheels go up, wheels go down. The wise man is patient."

"I found patience elusive when I wore the suit you'll be wearing," Filidor said.

"I took only your sweat," Henwaye said. "Others crave your blood. Which of us is worse off?"

When Filidor rejoined the men at the boat, they had found him a pouch with a tight seal in which he could stow the bobblobblobl, so that his presence among them would be bearable. The young man said good-bye to Orton Bregnat, vowing again to make good on his promise to create the island as an official contemplatorium with the undermate as its warden.

"Aye, well," said Bregnat, "official or not, we'll make do in the meantime."

The trip to Scullaway Point was a matter of half a day, the jollyboat's impellors being surprisingly well maintained by the pirates. The old sailor Byr Lak steered them straight and true by the sun, not bothering to consult the craft's navigating devices. For a while, Filidor joined Valderoyn, Volpenge, and Aury in conversation, but the common topic among his three companions was how each would enjoy his newfound prosperity, while Filidor's future offered little prospect of ease and pleasant diversion. After a while, he drew away and sat in the bow of the jollyboat, letting the sea air rush past his face and stream through his hair.

Now that he was free of the island, it was time to consider how he might undo the works of his enemies. He assumed Faubon Bassariot had not acted alone; even that feckless romantic, Holmar Thurm, had had his following. He tried to imagine who and how many were against him, and by what means Filidor Vesh might prove to be one too many for them all.

He thought for far longer than he was accustomed to think, but no plan came immediately to mind. In the adventure stories he had read as a boy, and still enjoyed when he was trapped at his Archonate desk with no means of escape, a handy avenue of approach always presented itself to the hero when the situation required action. Filidor suspected that real life was less conveniently arranged.

At least he was not alone. He grunted and spoke quietly so that only his inner listener would hear. "Integrator, what shall we do now? Have you any plan yet?"

We must first find out who is who and what is what, before we can contemplate any strategy.

"What do you propose we do when we come to Scullaway Point?"

Find a quiet place out of the public view, where we can assess our position.

Filidor sighed. "I am worried about my uncle."

Being Archon, he cannot be else than a man of resource and capability. He will have prepared for eventualities.

The young man saw the sense in what the voice said, but his fear remained. It came to him now that beneath the anxiety he felt for the Archon's well-being was a broad stream of affection for the peculiar little man who had exerted such a constant presence throughout Filidor's life. He wondered if the dwarf felt a similar attachment, or whether his solicitude for his nephew was rooted only in the soil of duty. It came to Filidor that he would have liked to have liked his uncle, and to have been thought well of in return. If the little man had fallen victim to a plot, then their chance for a warm relationship was now lost.

The Archon's nephew sighed and pushed the thought from his mind. "This would not have happened in your universe," he said. "Your version of Bassariot was dismissed early on by your Filidor Vesh."

The integrator chose to conserve its energies, or opted to maintain a diplomatic silence.

"What is he like?" said Filidor.

Who?

"Your Filidor Vesh. How did he come to be what he is?"

He has lived life in a certain way, doing this followed by that, and he is the sum total of all of that living and doing.

"Still, his life would have begun as mine did, and would have been moment for moment identical, until some particular jot of time brought us a choice of paths. Then he went left where I went right, and that has made all the difference."

No doubt. But to find that pivotal moment we would have to examine both lives, second by second, until we saw a divergence. And to what end? You are who you are. He is who he is.

But that answer did not satisfy Filidor. It seemed to the Archon's apprentice that it was one thing to say: here is Filidor Vesh, as he is, and all other possible Filidor Veshes are merely hypothetical. It was quite another thing when the hypothetical was actually living and breathing, on however small a plane. That other Filidor was daily setting about the business of an heroic existence, ornamenting his age with cheerful ease, winning the acclaim of glad multitudes. Therefore, comparisons were unavoidable.

"You are his integrator," said the young man. "You know his life. If you had to choose one moment, one choice which seemed to turn him toward what he was ultimately to become, what would that moment be? Tell me, and I will compare it with my own."

It might be something that seems inconsequential: eating too much cake and so precipitating a stomachache that prevented a victory in a game of shin-hully. Or sleeping late one morning and missing an inspirational lecture.

Filidor cast his mind back through his memory, but couldn't recall any lectures that had been even remotely inspirational—unless they had inspired him to sleep late and so miss them. He did not share this thought with the integrator.

Instead, he said, "Think. At what age did people first begin to say, 'Here's a ripe prospect'?"

They certainly said that about his dissertation on the causes of the Fenfillion Rebellion. That decisively deconstructed a number of carefully built reputations among the wise and witty. Did you write such a dissertation when you were sixteen?

"No," said Filidor. "That was my year for researching the carnal habits of a number of young women in the upper echelons of Olkney society."

I see, said the little voice. *Did you publish your findings?*

"Not as such," said Filidor, "although there were some mentions in the popular press." He did not add that they had prompted his uncle to contemplate having his nephew led about on a leash by a brawny keeper with access to ready supplies of cold water.

Well then, let's go back a few years. At twelve, there was the gold medal for practical aesthetics at the Beyornay Institute.

"I attended for three weeks, but it was decided that my strengths lay elsewhere," said Filidor.

Oh. Where?

"That was never made completely clear."

Age ten. A cycle of satirical quatrains took a first in the Euphetrics Competition.

"As I recall, I spent that year becoming amazingly proficient at a game known as The Furious Fists of Klong."

In my realm, said the integrator, *that is a pastime of maladjusted youth who spend hours in darkened rooms, squinting at images of ferocity while the game controls raise calluses on their thumbs and forefingers.*

"I recall it as a much more rewarding experience."

Hmm. Let us move on. Age nine. Strong interest in thermeneutics.

All Filidor recalled from that time was the several hiding places that allowed him to avoid thermeneutics so assiduously that today he could not be quite sure of the meaning of the word. "Don't think so," he said.

Eight. Built his own glider.

"No."

Seven. There was a pause. *Nothing much here. A note by your uncle that he had spent an afternoon with you, and that you had mastered all seven levels of Balmerion's Great Theorem.*

"No," said Filidor, then, "no, wait." Something was tugging at his memory. "That's wrong, but I can almost remember the occasion."

It was a summer day. You worked in the Archon's study. I'll read the note: "The boy struggled through the first four intervals, then stuck fast on the fifth. But I worked with him until he caught a glimpse of the underlying structure, then suddenly it all fell into order for him. I saw his face open with a great surmise, and I knew he had it. I think all will be well from this day forward."

Filidor strained to find his way back through the store of years to the day in question. He remembered the quiet in his uncle's book-choked study, the smell of dust in the air, and the clicking of some device in the corner. The Archon and he had sat together at a little table, Filidor in his childhood shorts and jumper, his uncle cloaked as he always was in the magisterial appearance generated by the device on his belt. The young man could recall with sudden clarity what it had been to be that boy on that day, how he had struggled to hold the first four intervals of the Balmerion's grand construction in play while his mind reached to grasp the fifth and place it appositely with the others.

He had almost had it. Then, in memory, he saw the door to the study open, saw a soft-faced man enter—some minor functionary come to remind the Archon of a matter of business left undone. His uncle had reluctantly risen and gone out, saying to the man as he left, "Help the boy with his Balmerion. He's almost there."

But the breakthrough had not come. In truth, Filidor had never fully mastered Balmerion's ancient thought, as any educated person must. Instead, he had learned how to dissimulate on those occasions—rare among the circle of leisured drones with whom the young man consorted—when reference was made to the great formula that explained the universe through an elegant architecture that connected space to time, matter with energy, and infused all with the elusive quality known as gist.

"There is the point of departure," he told the integrator. "In my world, someone with poor timing—I would call it positively porlockian timing—came in and broke the chain before my uncle and I could fully forge it. And everything has descended from that moment."

How unfortunate.

But Filidor was not listening, because the meaning of his recovered memory was now making itself plain to him. Earlier, he had realized that the loss of his plaque and sigil could be laid to the fault of Faubon Bassariot, and that discovery had brought wondrous relief from the drubbing he had been delivering to his self-regard ever since he had lain supine in Vodel Close, seeing the Podarke girl disappear into the crowd. But the dawning light of that earlier absolution now faded to the dim glow of a weak lumen next to the brilliant illumination that now flooded his being: *It is all not my fault.* His whole life had been meant to take another direction. He should have been, could have been, what the other Filidor had become.

He had been ready to learn, had been trying to the full limits of a seven-year-old's utmost. He had been about to step aboard the cerebral ship that would have carried him over the horizon into who knew what realms of discovery? Well, actually, he thought, the integrator in his inner ear knew the answer to that question to the last detail, for it had logged and charted that very voyage by its own diminutive Filidor. But just as he was about to step aboard, someone had parted vessel from dock, and—like the other, dead Etch Valderoyn— Filidor had fallen into the chuck.

He felt a moment's sadness, but it was soon overcome by a resurgence of the joyful knowledge that none of this was his fault. The blame belonged to that faceless bureaucrat who had unknowingly blown out Filidor's fire just as it was about to kindle. The Archon's apprentice poked and prodded his memory again, squeezing out another few drops of reminiscence that seeped into his consciousness. He remembered that he had sat there, still holding the four and struggling to bring in the fifth, but the man had *not* helped him. Instead, the fellow had poked around the Archon's study, opening drawers and pulling books from the shelves, then riffling through papers on the old desk in the corner where the boy's uncle sketched his research projects.

Little Filidor had kept up the unequal struggle with Balmerion, but his small strength, unaided, could not long maintain the effort. The fifth interval fell from his mind's grasp, then the first four collapsed into a heap of unsorted facts and ratios.

"Stupid," the boy had said. It was meant to be communicated only to himself, but the functionary heard, and turned. Filidor saw in his memory the sneer that had smirked along the man's mouth. Then suddenly, from catching the detail, he recaptured the whole: he saw the contemptuous face clearly, the incipient jowls, the wet but unfeeling eyes, and the vain curl across the forehead. It was the young Faubon Bassariot's face, and it was Faubon Bassariot's disdainful neglect of the Archon's orders to *help the boy* that had cost Filidor the fruitful life that should have been, *would* have been, his.

"Integrator," he said, "I believe I am having an epiphany. "Everything has assumed a new shape."

Indeed?

"Indeed, you may well say," Filidor confirmed, and quickly recounted the memory and its meaning. "It becomes clear that Faubon Bassariot is the great ill fact of my life, the rock on which I stuck, the rub on which I stumbled, the ..." here he was lost for another analogy, and finished with, "the something specifically awful that has made everything else generally awful ever since. If you take my meaning."

I do, said the voice in his head. *However, it seems to me that ills done to you in the distant past are less important than the prospect of being killed in the immediate future. How you came to be who you are will not matter if you cease to be at all, which is what your enemies intend. And since I am running low on energy, we should defer this discussion, fascinating though you may find it, to some later time.*

"But I would value your advice in deciding how to undo Bassariot to a degree that would be fitting, considering the harm he has done me."

Are there any pilkies in the jollyboat?

Filidor snorted. "I am arranging to put the greatest possible sea room between me and the nearest pilkie. Even the recollection of their taste makes my tongue want to flee to parts unknown."

Then the alternative is strong drink.

Filidor hefted the flask of purple wine he had brought. "Well, if I must ..."

Except, that would entail your arriving in Scullaway Point with your faculties at least somewhat askew, precisely when you may need them in good array.

"Why? Bassariot thinks me carrion at the bottom of the sea."

But only Bassariot thinks you thus. He has told the rest of the world that you are a fugitive desperado. And since your face recently held pride of place in the Olkney Implicator, which circulates in Scullaway Point, readers of that publication may be inclined to shout alarmingly upon sight of you. In which case, I am sure you would find being intoxicated an impediment to remaining free. And should you again fall into the hands of Faubon Bassariot, I have no doubt that you would not leave them until you were well and thoroughly accounted for.

"When you put it that way," Filidor said, "I find it difficult to argue."

The integrator again chose diplomatic restraint and said nothing.

"However, until such time as we can clap together a plan, I shall focus my mind on the evils Faubon Bassariot has done me, and the grim recompense that I swear I will claim."

If you must, said the voice in his head. *But assigning blame is a fixation of an ineffective mind. Better to concentrate on how you propose to make your claim stick.*

Filidor looked ahead, to where the hills above Scullaway Point were serrating the horizon. He had never been to the seafarers' town, but he knew it to be a bustling place of wide and well-lit streets. Narrow, dark alleys suitable for skulking along unnoticed might be in short supply. He would need to remain untaken by the authorities long enough to find a bolt hole where he could lie low, gather information, and put together a plan. It would have to be an exceptionally safe hiding place, since he would need to become at least moderately inebriated while charging the integrator's plates enough to make it useful.

An idea occurred to him. He remembered the old tale of the two sisters: one had been beautiful and one had been decidedly not; all the world could describe to the last exquisite detail the face of the fair one, but no one had ever wanted to look long enough at her poor, repellent sister to note the exact particulars of her facial ill fortune. Thus the ugly girl was able to go and come as she needed to, while the cynosure was always under the scrutiny of every eye that touched her. The distinction had made quite a difference to the contours of their lives.

"Is there any grease or pitch aboard?" Filidor asked. Etch Valderoyn dug into a compartment near the stern and came out with a little pot of something black and gummy. Filidor asked the sailor to dip his finger in the muck and draw two inverted chevrons on his cheeks, a thick bar across his forehead, and a single stripe from lower lip to chin. When Valderoyn was finished and sat back to inspect his work, Filidor pulled up the hood of his shirt to cover his head and frame his marked face, tying the strings tight beneath his jaw.

"Do I look like a consecrate of the Piacular Tumult?" he asked, referring to that resolutely violent sect of muscular ascetics for whose members the mere existence of nonbelievers was an unbearable affront to their principles. A consecrate would attack without mercy or limitation any heathen whose presence was inflicted upon him. On the rare occasions when utter necessity brought consecrates out of their own communities and into contact with the rest of humanity, those who encountered them were wise to avert their gazes and walk in other directions.

"I think that is what they look like," said Valderoyn, "though I have never let my eyes linger on any that have crossed my bows." He reflected for a moment, then said, "Hunch your shoulders and hook your fingers, as if you craved nothing more than my blood dribbling from your clenched teeth. Ah, yes, there's the image of a consecrate, all right. It ought to keep the falicks off you." He used the sailor's ancient term for officers of the law.

Filidor tried his new guise on the others, and even the unflappable Byr Lak appeared nonplussed. The young man wrapped the flagon of purple Pwyfus he had brought with him in a scrap of coarse cloth, since hermits of the Piacular Tumult indulged only in fungal euphoriants, and prepared to go ashore.

The crossing from the island of the Obblob had taken most of the day, and the tired orange sun was now sliding behind clouds in the offing over distant Mornedy Sound. Byr Lak brought the jollyboat through the mouth of Scullaway Point's semicircular small craft harbor, carved into the coastline next to the big basin that served grand ships like *Empyreal*. The lesser haven was moderately crowded with skimmers and flingabouts, and three or four private vessels of a good size. Filidor briefly thought about investigating those; if he found one to be empty, he could go to cover there, but all the larger craft were lit from within, and the wharves against which they nestled were dotted with pedestrians and seaside gawkers.

In the gathering dusk, Byr Lak eased the jollyboat up to a decrepit floating dock, below a single lumen dangling from a suspended cable. In its faint yellow light, the four who would be staying ashore bid farewell to the old man, the sailors taking their leave of him with words and embraces that Filidor found surprisingly sentimental. Then Valderoyn, Volpenge, and Aury wished the Archon's apprentice good fortune and a safe end to his strivings. They all swore that they would keep to themselves their knowledge of the young man's whereabouts.

A set of stone steps connected the worn boards to the seawall. The four went up them and separated at the top. The three sailors, each with his bag of loot from Henwaye's storehouse, jaunted off toward the gaudy strip of emporia that sold the kinds of goods and services that had separated seafarers from their pay since time immemorial. Filidor angled away from the harbor toward a dark stretch of trees and parkland that bordered the shore. There he would perhaps climb a tall deodar and survey the town before choosing a point of entry.

There were few folk wandering the space between the harbor and the woods, and those that came close enough to ascertain the nature of Filidor's seeming spiritual affiliation quickly spun on their heels and angled sharply off their previous paths, putting their eyes anywhere but on him. Thus he reached the thickening shadows under the trees with a wide space for maneuver, but as he moved deeper into their cover he found that the woods were not extensive; they were only a thin margin of loblols and other evergreens planted around an open-air theater.

A crowd numbering perhaps three hundred people stood at the other end of the open space to watch a performance being staged on some sort of large hustings. Carefully, Filidor scanned the assemblage for the black and green of Archonate livery and saw none. Nor did he see anything that might have been a uniform of the local constabulary. He determined to make his way around the gathering, staying within the obscurity of the surrounding trees and drawing no attention to himself, to see if there were deeper woods behind the stage where he might hole up as planned.

He had halfway circumnavigated the open space when he noted three items of interest. The first was that the performance at the far end was not on a hustings, as he had first thought, but on a stage that levered down from the side of an immense vehicle. The second was that the name of the performing company emblazoned above the proscenium arch was familiar: FLASTOVIC'S INCOMPARABLE MUMMERY TROUPE AND RAREE EXPOSITION. The third was that two members of that troupe, the twins Ches and Isbister Florrey, were not on the stage but were weaving their way through the outer edges of the audience. Filidor watched Ches bump into a spectator, as if by accident, while Isbister moved smoothly and unnoticed behind the man. As the first twin made gestures and issued words of polite apology, the second stepped away, his hand slipping something small but substantial between his skin and the fabric of his blouse.

Why, they are nothing but a pair of rip-and-dips, he thought, remembering the shout from across Indentors Square the night before all his troubles had started. *They pull a crowd so that they can rifle its pockets.*

Without thinking, he opened his mouth to call the alert, but fortunately at that moment reason reasserted itself and he closed his lips. It might well be to his advantage to know something of Flastovic's troupe that they would prefer not be known. Staying within the shadows of the trees, he followed the twins as they moved along the rim of the crowd, and saw them twice more pluck the fruit from unsuspecting spectators before they also headed for the cover of the tree line.

Filidor stayed with them, always keeping a tree or two between him and the Florreys, but after a few paces he trod upon something dry and brittle that crackled and rustled under his foot. The two pickpockets stopped and peered about in the gloom, but Filidor's dark clothing and the fortuitous placement of an intervening tree shielded him from discovery. After a long wait, the mummers resumed their progress, but Filidor paused to draw the bobblobblobl from its pouch, shake it out, and let it descend upon him. Thus completely hidden, he again trailed the twins to a small clearing in the woods behind Flastovic's groundeater, where they squatted to divide the valuables they had stolen from any accompanying items that might identify their recent owners. The latter they buried in a shallow hole hastily scraped between some roots.

"A tidy haul," said one of the Florreys, when they were finished.

"Very," said the other, then sniffed and said, "I think something has died nearby."

Filidor moved back a little.

"It is always a comfort when we have struck a small blow against the pernicious cult of private property," said one of them, holding up a glittering item of some kind. "Instead of hiding in some selfish own-it-all's pocket, this piece will soon be circulating again through the world, bringing delight to all who see it."

"As ever," returned his brother, "you erect thin and reedy concepts whose only foundation is the thickness of your brain. The effect of our work is to take those things which were widely held, that is, by several attendees at tonight's performance, and happily concentrate them in our pockets. The gain is ours, and it is private."

"Nonsense," said the one Filidor now knew to be Isbister, from his philosophical liking for communality. "You might as well say the wind is yours because it happens to cool your face in passing. These things will be only briefly in our possession, since we will move them on their way as quickly as we can. Any of these goods will pass through half a dozen hands in the next few days. The money almost certainly will."

"As ever, you vainly grasp at diaphanous vastness while the tangible turns to mist in your hands. The goods per se are not the gain; they are merely the vehicle that brings me an increment of wealth. The goods will pass on, but the gain will remain," said Ches, the exponent of private coffer-keeping, "and mine will be mine."

Isbister turned away in scorn, saying, "Once again, you

miss the obvious. Did not the eminent Thodeus Tamarac, in his brilliant treatise *On the Addition of Value*, lay this question once and for all to its much defined rest? I quote . . ."

But Ches was not disposed to hear the citation. "Tamarac? Eminent? His eminence is no more than that of a boil above the surrounding buttock."

Filidor heard Isbister's sharp intake of breath, followed by his, "You will take that back."

"I cannot," said his twin.

"Then I will surely thrash you."

"Another of your fancies unrooted in reality," said Ches, "for if it comes down to beating, I know who will play the stick and who the drum."

"We shall see," said Isbister, raising his fists.

"As we always have," said his brother, assuming a fighting pose.

But the bout had to be postponed. A surge of applause from the crowd recalled both brothers to their business. "They have finished *The Ant, The Flea, and The Behemoth*," said Isbister. "Flastovic will wonder what we are up to. Let us get into costume for *The Hierophant and the Heretics*."

The brothers raced through the woods to the giant vehicle that was the troupe's transportation, shelter, and performing venue. Filidor followed, and saw them scuttle through a small door in the back. He did not pursue them farther; the bobblobblobl offered no hope of concealment indoors, and he knew where they would be for the next little while. Besides, he wanted to think about what he had learned, and how it might serve his needs.

Had he witnessed the Florreys' depredations against their unwitting audience when they had been performing in Olkney's Indentors Square, he would at once have summoned the provosts and had the thieves immured in a magistrate's cells. But now he was in need of allies, willing or not, and the twins looked to be the enterprising sort, despite their conflicting notions as to how property ought to be apportioned in the world. He decided to wait until Flastovic's troupe was done with its performance, then he would see what use they might be to him.

He pulled back into the trees and spoke to the integrator in his ear, giving a quick précis of what he had seen and heard, then asking, "What do you recommend?"

I have no idea. My Filidor does not consort with pickpockets.

"Then conjecture," Filidor insisted.

I cannot. In this instance, your judgment is probably better than mine. Now leave me. I fade.

Filidor could not recall ever hearing anyone tell him that his judgment was superior. He had heard "Suit yourself" and "It's your funeral," but never had he been declared the preeminent authority in sight on any subject. It produced in him a curious mingling of warm security and chill apprehension. He decided that since he was in no immediate danger, the sensible thing to do was to watch and learn more. Feeling thus at least the temporary master of his fate, he removed the bobblobblobl and restored it to its pouch, then edged around the clearing until he could see the stage. He leaned against a tree in shadow and watched as Ovile Germolian, masked and robed, stepped through the closed curtains and took up his position to the side of the proscenium arch. The disclamator raised head and voice and declared that the next performance would be the aforementioned playlet: *The Hierophant and the Heretics*, by The Bard Obscure.

The curtains opened and Germolian intoned the text. *"From the founding of Far Forbish, all of its inhabitants subscribed to the Church of the Exemplified Catechism, finding its tenets well laid out and none too onerous. But as time went by, the colony grew, and among those drawn to the new world there came inevitably some persons of a fractious nature who employed their leisure time in picking at the knitted threads of ritual and process that underpinned the authority of the Church."*

As Germolian spoke the text, Erslan Flastovic, recognizable by his size and bearing, appeared on stage wearing the robes and headpiece of a hierarch of the Church of the Exemplified Catechism. The other members of the troupe portrayed a multitudinous congregation by milling about while wearing poles harnessed to their shoulders from which depended lightweight mannequins. Strings connected the dummies' limbs to the troupers' corresponding parts, so that arms and legs moved in unison. Given the right lighting and a willing audience, the effect was strangely convincing.

"In time," Germolian continued, *"one of the newcomers differed to the point of extremity with the High Hierophant over the nature of the most central ritual of the faith: was the god imminent in the sacramental legume, or did the deity enter the sacred vegetable only after it had been plucked, cleaned, boiled, and seasoned? A strident debate ensued, during which woundful words were uttered, so that no common ground remained. So the newcomer and his adherents departed the congregation and constituted themselves as the Reformed Church of the Exemplified Catechism."*

One of the mummers flounced off to stage left, his shoulder-borne mannequins following suit.

"But it was not long," said the disclamator, *"before another discontented member within the body of the faithful found himself at odds with the High Hierophant about certain pertinent details—specifically, whether the boiled sacrament must be swallowed whole or whether it might, without*

giving offense to the god, be chewed. Soon, a second schis-matic sect, the Justified Masticators, had been formed."

A second set of mannequins stamped over to stage right.

"Then there arose a third persuasion, comprising some persons who were staunchly faithful to the original rite but who differed radically with their priest over whether the heretics should receive their just punishment from the deity in the next life, or from his agents in this one. These doughty adherents removed themselves from the High Hierophant's authority, armed themselves with sticks and cobblestones, and set out to do the god's work."

A third set of mannequins moved to the front of the stage, gesticulating angrily. Then both crowds of schismatics came storming in from the wings, and the curtains closed on the donnybrook that was beginning. Rumbles, muffled shouts, and clashes erupted from behind the barrier, then faded into silence. After a moment, Flastovic, in his hierarch's robes but with his miter askew, stepped out from between the curtains, and stood as if in a pensive mood.

"The High Hierophant took thought," said Germolian, *"and found that the constant blooding of the congregations was causing great personal and social distress to the citizens of Far Forbish. He called together the leaders of the three sects and said to them, 'Behold, we have turned our flocks into blood-beasts that live only to feud with each other. Can we not agree to disagree, and all just get along?'"*

The three schismatic leaders came through the curtain to the front of the stage and, by shrugs and hand gestures, sig-naled their willingness to reconcile.

"The High Hierophant proposed that, as a sign of ecu-menical fraternity, the leaders of the three congregations should attend one another's services. 'I will be the first to receive the three of you,' he said. 'Come to the next sacra-

mental meal and quietly take seats at the rear of the temple. When the rites are over, I will introduce you and we will hold a ritual of mutual absolution.' "

The three heretics nodded their heads in agreement, and all four mummers ducked through the curtain.

Now the cloth pulled back to reveal the set of Far Forbish's main cathedral, with a vast congregation indicated by row upon row of figures cut from sturdy paper with painted backdrops on all three sides showing more ranks of believers dwindling by perspective into the far distance.

Flastovic, in even more ornate garb, was presiding at an altar at the front of the stage, assisted by a small masked acolyte whom Filidor took to be Chloe. The High Hierophant flourished his hands over the glistening pots and salvers on the altar, then raised his masked eyes to the heaven in silent supplication.

"On the appointed day," said the disclamator, *"the three schismatic leaders came to the temple and entered at the rear of the congregation."*

The three masked figures—Filidor knew them now to be Gavne and the Florrey twins—crept onto the stage at the rear.

"But it was a high holy day," Germolian went on, *"and the temple was filled with fervent celebrants, who had left no room for the three visitors. Only the High Hierophant, from his elevated position, saw them enter. He turned to the child who assisted him and whispered, 'Get three chairs for the heretics.' "*

At this, Chloe cupped a hand to an ear to show that she had not understood the instruction.

" 'Get three chairs for the heretics,' " Germolian repeated.

At this, Chloe's masked head moved from side to side

in a mime of consternation, then she cupped her hand to her ear once more.

"'I want three chairs for the heretics!'" the disclamator hissed.

Now the acolyte stepped away from the hierarch, and made the gestures with which underlings have long communicated a willingness to do a boss's bidding, though it makes no sense at all. Turning to face the ranks of true believers, Chloe raised her small fist into the air as Germolian shouted, *"Three cheers for the heretics! Hip, hip!"*

CHAPTER

SIX

Filidor waited until the final curtain had rung down on the mummers' performance, then went around to watch the back of the great vehicle again. He had been mulling over his situation, and had decided that knowing the Florreys to be thieves might not be enough leverage to coerce their cooperation. If he confronted them, it would be easy enough for them to seize him, then call the local Archonate bureau and turn him in, no doubt for a substantial reward. If the authorities believed his protestations that the Florreys were reivers, they might arrest the twins as well, but that wouldn't leave Filidor free to go.

He was wondering if he ought to hide himself somewhere in the troupe's segmented groundeater—there must be compartments for scenery and illuminative apparatus—and hope that time and a change of location might bring him advantages, when the rear door opened quietly and Chloe stole out into the night. Filidor drew himself deeper into the shadows under the trees and watched as the girl looked about for observing eyes, and seeing none, crept to the concealment of the woods. She carried a folded blanket under one arm.

This is interesting, Filidor told himself, and prepared to follow her. But before he could get the bobblobblobl out and deployed, the door opened again, and the angular figure of Ovile Germolian stepped into view. *Even more interesting,* mused Filidor as he watched the disclamator disappear in the same direction the girl had gone.

The young man allowed the evil-smelling sheath to cover him and set off in pursuit. He did not have to go far before whispering voices told him that he had found what he expected to find. In the dim light under the trees he saw the daughter of the Flastovics waiting unclothed upon her blanket, while Ovile Germolian hopped about on one foot, removing his own trousers as quickly as he might. Filidor doubted that the older man was removing his clothing with the intent of using it to cover the shivering young woman, and his doubt was confirmed when Germolian, his garment now off and flung to one side, quickly covered Chloe's nakedness with his own.

The Archon's nephew waited until there was no further question as to what was proceeding in the small clearing, and no possibility of his learning anything from Germolian's perfunctory style, before hurrying back to the groundeater. He removed and stowed the bobblobblobl, then went to the door of the vehicle and pounded on it as hard as he could. In moments, a window opened and the face of Erslan Flastovic appeared, saying, "What's all the brouhaha? Our policy is firm: no refunds!"

Filidor kept his face in shadow as he said, "It is your daughter! I fear that she is being ravished in the woods by some night haunter!"

Flastovic was through the door and beside him in less

time than Filidor would have wagered on, bringing with him a stout length of wood. Filidor surmised that the actor probably kept the club near the door to enforce his "no refunds!" policy.

"Where?" Flastovic said.

Filidor had already turned so as not to present his face. "Follow me," he said, and led the way into the woods.

They came upon the disclamator and the daughter at a stage in the proceedings that put the couple far beyond the capacity to give their attention to their surroundings. Flastovic stood for a long moment, as if hypnotized by the metronomic rise and fall of Germolian's pale, narrow buttocks, the rapid motion accompanied by a syncopated rhythm of snorts and gasps from the other end of the process. Then the father broke through his stasis and delivered a devastating blow of the wooden rod that brought the motion of offending body parts to a halt.

The scene now lost all cohesion. Flastovic followed his first assault with a second and a third, and then as many as he could rapidly land, while Ovile Germolian struggled to get to his hands and knees under the onslaught. Once he had managed to get all his limbs beneath him, the disclamator launched himself in a leap of generous proportions across the small clearing, then executed a four-legged scramble into the darkness beneath the trees.

Flastovic, club raised to express himself at greater length, would have pursued the naked man, had not his daughter sprung up and seized his arm, shrieking something unintelligible. Now the Florreys arrived on the scene, also bearing cudgels. Finding Filidor to be the only stranger in the little clearing, they took him to be the focus of the disturbance, and advanced upon the Archon's nephew with the confidence that superiority in numbers and weaponry can bestow. But one look at the consecrate's markings on the young man's face instantly deflated the twins' aggressiveness. They backed toward their leader, not stopping until both Flastovic and Chloe were between them and the supposed eremitical maniac.

The girl had progressed from shrieks to sobs, though she still hung on her father's arm. Now Gavne appeared to complement the scene of high emotion with some needed practicality. She scooped up the blanket and covered her daughter, gently separating the crying girl from her father and leading her back toward their traveling home. Flastovic stood in the clearing, his club dangling from his hands, as if he could not remember his next line. The Florreys remained behind him, two minor players awaiting their cue.

Filidor realized that it was up to him to move things forward. "Let us go back to your groundeater and discuss what to do next," he said, at which Flastovic absently nodded and turned to retrace his steps, the twins moving aside to open the way for him. Then the troupe leader paused, took thought, and told the Florreys to bring Germolian's clothes.

Filidor went with Flastovic. By the time they reached the great vehicle he had rubbed the consecrate's emblems from his face. When the Florreys caught them up, their patron ordered them to throw the disclamator's apparel on the ground, then to go fetch all of his belongings and place them in a heap. When this had been done, the chief mummer looked down at the pile of garments, books, and oddments from Germolian's cabin, including a flattering portrait in pastels of the man himself, and said, "We will now reenact the final movement from The Bard Obscure's *Wisdom of the Hound*."

Filidor recalled having seen that brief allegory performed somewhere, in which a mature dog and its pup, having come upon a brilliant work of art that has fallen by the wayside, investigate it according to their natures. The Archon's apprentice remembered the play's last line, in which the sire declares to the pup the philosophy of the uncultivated soul: *If you can't eat it or futter it, then . . .* At that point, the mummer playing the old dog lifts a hind leg and mimes sprinkling the artwork with canine contempt. Without a disclamator present, the three actors who gathered around Germolian's possessions could not speak the line. Instead, they undid the fronts of their breeches and engaged in a concerted act of *drame verité.*

When Germolian's goods were well soaked and redolent of Flastovic's opinion, the chief mummer rearranged his garments and regarded Filidor as if seeing him for the first time. "Why you're the fugitive from the *Empyreal*," he said.

"The one who walloped the Archon's man," said Ches.

"A traitor to the common weal," added Isbister.

"I am none of these," said Filidor.

"It's our duty to turn him in," said Isbister, moving to lay a hand on Filidor's arm.

"There's an ample reward," said Ches, taking a grip from the young man's other side.

Recent events appeared to have robbed Flastovic of his customary decisiveness. Filidor again thought it best to take the initiative. To Isbister, he said, "I can suggest an alternative plan by which you could do immense service to the community," then turned to Ches, and continued, "and receive a much greater recompense."

Each twin raised an eyebrow at the other, then both nodded. "As members of the public, it is our obligation to consider the public interest," said Isbister.

"Your premises are fatuous, but your conclusion is to the

point," Ches told his brother, then said to Filidor, "How much greater would this recompense be?"

"More than you can imagine," said the Archon's nephew.

"We Florreys are renowned for a stupendous strength of imagination," said Ches, but he led the way inside, as Isbister nudged the still inert Flastovic to follow.

Filidor found the living quarters of the groundeater to be surprisingly homey: a lounge abutted by a small but efficient galley, out of which led a corridor between private chambers. From behind the closed door of one of these came the muffled lamentations of Chloe, accompanied by the consoling murmur of her mother.

They took seats around an oblong table in a corner nook of the lounge, underneath a display of theatrical posters that recapitulated the career of Erslan Flastovic. One of the Florreys found a bottle of something strong, poured a good measure into a tumbler, and set it before his patron. The chief mummer drank the stuff down in one swallow that left his eyes watery, but which also seemed to enable him to recollect himself.

"I cannot believe that my daughter . . . and Germolian . . ." He shuddered and poured another glass.

Filidor thought it wise to say nothing. The Florreys offered inconclusive mumbles, their minds on other things. "You mentioned recompense," Ches said to Filidor.

Flastovic drained his glass again, then forced himself to take note of the stranger in his home. "What is all this?" he said, in a voice that was recovering the intonations of authority.

"It is a revolution," said Filidor.

Flastovic's face darkened. "We are no revolutionists," he said. "The Archonate leaves us alone, and we return the courtesy."

"Indeed," said Isbister, "we see no need to overthrow the social order."

"Nor hope of profit," put in his brother.

"I had hoped you would say that," said Filidor, "for it is not I who is out to play the Thurm, whatever scurrilities Tet Folbrey may publish. I am the victim of a conspiracy."

Quickly, he told them of Faubon Bassariot's treachery aboard the *Empyreal* and his rescue by the Obblob. He glossed over the details of his servitude to Gwallyn Henwaye, and did not mention the transdimensional miniature integrator lodged in his ear, reasoning that it was not a declaration to inspire confidence. But he did lay out his suspicions as to the nature of the plot.

"It has something to do with Trumble, and the project that Bassariot's friends are undertaking there," he concluded. "I must go to Trumble without being discovered, learn what they are up to, and put an end to it. Your traveling troupe could offer me transportation and disguise."

"I do not see how we can help you," said Flastovic. "Trumble is an obscure, remote place. Companies like ours do not visit there. We had planned a progress down to Thurloyn Vale, but now that we are without a disclamator, we are stymied." He explained that he had invested all of his and Gavne's small store of funds in the costumes and settings for a season of The Bard Obscure, and doubted that they could now get far. "The groundeater relieves us of the cost of renting shelter and a stage, but it has a garm's appetite for fuel. And without Germolian, we cannot perform."

"I can help in both directions," Filidor said. He drew from inside his shirt the bag of valuables he had acquired from the pirates and poured them into his hand. "These will pay for fuel and provisions," he said.

The Florreys took a close interest in the sparkling handful of wealth, watching it all the way as Filidor put the goods back into the bag and watching still as the bag went back into the young man's shirt. Filidor noted their interest.

"I should point out," he told the twins, "that Faubon Bassariot has not quibbled to murder the heir to the Archon. Should he find a few wandering players cluttering up his strategy, I don't doubt that he will take the shortest route to their removal. Rather than hand you a reward, he is like to hand you your own giblets, warm and steaming."

This gave the twins pause to reflect. Meanwhile, Erslan Flastovic had another concern. "But still, we cannot perform The Bard Obscure's works, unless you happen to have memorized them all."

"By a happy coincidence, I have done just that," said Filidor.

His assertion brought cries of disbelief from the twins, and a request from Flastovic that he demonstrate its truth.

Filidor expressed a willingness, but said that his throat was a little dry. He took out the flask of purple wine that he had brought from the island, and took a long pull at it, followed by another. He then begged leave to retire to a corner of the lounge while he undertook some vocal exercises of his own devising.

The mummers' faces expressed skepticism, but Filidor went to the farthest corner and spoke quietly to the integrator. When he heard the small voice in his head, he quickly brought its owner up-to-date.

You have been very resourceful, said his inner companion.

"Perhaps you are right, and the differences between the Filidor you know and me are not substantive after all, but merely the products of circumstance," the young man offered.

Perhaps, although it is difficult to know how my Filidor would respond to your circumstances, since they are beyond his experience. He does not surround himself with pirates and light-fingered mummers.

The integrator's comment raised a new and interesting question, Filidor thought. He had assumed that the other version of himself, though relatively tiny, was in all other ways grander. But here was the possibility that, in this particular situation, he had responded with a degree of flexible resourcefulness that might have eluded the age-ornamenting paragon who wore his face in another cosmos.

It was a warming thought, and he would have liked to discuss the issue further, but he knew that any lengthy colloquy with the voice in his head must be accompanied by a progressive descent into drunkenness. He could not risk losing his faculties until he was sure that his tenure with the mummers was secure. He explained his need to the integrator, and asked it to recite one of the shorter The Bard Obscure pieces.

Very well, said the integrator. *Announce that you will recite* The Beast and the Blind Men. Filidor turned and stepped from the corner, doing as the integrator had bid. He swallowed another good measure of the purple wine, then took what seemed to the mummers to be a dramatic pause, while his inner voice gave him the opening line.

"The ruler of an antique land," he said, "heard that a great and unknown beast had appeared in his realm, and was haunting a forest near the main highway. The potentate immediately sent for the seven wise men who were his college of state.

"A condition of membership in this college was blindness, the ruler having decided that those who were not distracted by the look of things could paradoxically see into a deeper nature. Six of the seven sages had willingly sacrificed their vision for the prestige of office; the seventh had only pretended to do so.

"The seven obediently set out to encounter the wondrous beast. Because their rank entitled them to serene passage on royal highways, the six blind men marched as they always did down the middle of the road, unaware of the flood of people pouring past them in the opposite direction on either side and in respectful silence. The sage who could still see, however, observed the people's flight, as well as their expressions of horror and trepidation."

Filidor paused and drank more of the purple stuff. "In time, the college of wisdom encountered the monster, which had just finished devouring several unlucky persons too slow to escape its clutches. The creature was now standing by the side of the road, placidly contemplating its digestion.

"The six blind sages approached the beast, arms outstretched. They began to examine it, each encountering one of its characteristics. The seventh, however, seeing the remains of the carnivore's feeding, kept a distance.

"After making their examination, the remaining six wise men went back to the monarch and reported their findings. The one who had felt the animal's great legs said, 'It is like a grove of trees.'

"The one who had touched its pebble-skinned hindquarters said, 'It is most like a solid wall.'

"He who had touched its hairy forequarters likened it to a large tent, while the sage who had encountered its tail declared it to be some kind of furred serpent.

"The man who had felt of the creature's fanlike ear said, 'It put me in mind of a sail,' and the last of the blind men, having felt its long proboscis, vouchsafed that it was 'some sort of land eel.'

"The seventh sage gave his opinion that the most important attribute of the beast was its behavior, but the king was by now too excited to hear his views. He rushed out to see this wonderment for himself. The beast, meanwhile, had rediscovered its ravenous appetite and was traveling down the royal road, through a now thoroughly depopulated countryside, looking for something more to eat. The seventh sage followed the king at a judicious distance, a new idea having occurred to him.

"When the ruler of the land saw the giant creature, he rushed forward in joyous anticipation of a new and pleasant experience. The beast did likewise, but only one of the two expectations was well rewarded.

"The seventh sage crept away while the monster was eating the monarch. He returned to the palace, reported the king's unpleasant fate, then took advantage of the confusion to seize control. He sent soldiers to shoot arrows into the great brute, and when it was dead he ordered that the remaining scraps of the king be gathered together and buried in state."

Filidor took more of the purple drink, then resumed, "The relieved populace gratefully awarded the sage the monarchy, dispossessing the former king's heir on the grounds that stupidity was known to be heritable. At his coronation, the new ruler announced that his sight had been miraculously restored, which the crowds took as divine validation of their choice.

"The king appointed a new member to the college of state, and ensured that he was properly blinded. And from time to time, he would flick his fingers across his counselors' gaze, or flash bright lights in their eyes, just to be sure."

When he was finished, the Archon's apprentice bowed deeply, if somewhat unsteadily after drinking the purple wine, and sat down across from the mummers. Erslan Flastovic regarded him with an appraising eye, while the Florreys offered faint applause.

"Well enough for the content," said the leader of the troupe, "but the enunciation is spiritless and the voice lacks timber. Still, there are devices that can compensate. Though I normally abhor such cheats, we must accept that 'leaves lie where the wind lays them,' as the old saying goes."

"I can offer one other inducement," said Filidor, suppressing a slight slur that wished to creep into his diction.

"Say on," said Flastovic.

"When I am restored to my place, I will confer the patronage of the Archonate on your troupe. I could even build you a theater."

A gleam came into Flastovic's eye. Filidor first took it for avarice, but as he considered the subtle change in the mummer's aspect, he decided that he was not seeing the sharp glint of greed, but the warm reviving of a dream that had long ago been laid in its tomb, and there left to molder.

"In Olkney, that would be," the older man said, as if he were speaking as much to himself as to anyone, "not out in the regions?"

"On South Processional," Filidor said, "in the very throb of the theater district."

"With loges and lobbies and a revolving stage?"

"To your specifications, full and complete."

Erslan Flastovic stared across the table at the Archon's apprentice, and the older man's face was the battleground in a war between a present fear and a lifelong yearning. It was clear to Filidor which had won even before the man nodded and said, "Very well."

But then the chief mummer raised an admonitory finger and added, "But only so long as you remain undiscovered.

If they come for you, we must disown you. A dream's no comfort when you're shackled to a wall."

"Agreed," said Filidor, and looked to the Florreys.

In one voice, they said, "We're in."

Flastovic acquired fresh bed linens from a closet, then showed Filidor to the cabin that had been Ovile Germolian's. It was a small space, efficiently laid out, though now its drawers and cupboards hung open in testament to the sudden removal of the disclamator's possessions.

The robe and mask the seducer had worn during his public performances hung in the back of a built-in armoire. Filidor examined both and found a small glass vial in the garment's inner pocket. He pulled the stopper and sniffed the crystalline powder within, detecting a faint musky odor.

"Integrator," he said, "what is this?" He described the substance.

Does it taste bitter or cloyingly sweet?

The young man wet his fingertip and touched it to the stuff. "Sweet."

In light of Germolian's relationship with the girl, it is most likely extract of the espolianth plant. It stimulates a discrete region of the brain to induce an obsession of affection in the victim, focused on the first person seen after the powder is administered. The effect is intense though short-lived, yet while the stuff is working, the victim will do anything for the object of love. After a day or two, the drug wears off, unless the victim is freshly dosed. Be careful not to inhale it, or the next person you see may find you tiresome.

"Is the Germolian of your realm known for such tricks?"

The voice paused, then said, *No. But then he is probably not known for them here either, or Flastovic would not have engaged him.*

Filidor made his bed and lay in it. He was troubled by

what he had learned about espolianth extract. He had experienced a similar upset upon first sight of Emmlyn Podarke, the event from which all of his present troubles had descended. Now he wondered if it might all have been the doing of some errant molecule in that morning's cup of punge, some chemical fragment that had happened to lodge in a particular synapse of his neural matrix just as he chanced to look up and see her. But as he thought of her, that same feeling of breathless possibility again tickled within his lungs, the sensation almost as strong now as when she had been before his eyes. He reasoned that his emotion could not be a mere happenstance of transient chemistry, not unless the same molecules were coincidentally to be found in the coarse purplish wine from Henwaye's storehouse.

"I will find Emmlyn Podarke and we will see how things fall," he murmured to the darkness of the groundeater's cabin.

May I suggest we deal with other priorities first? said the integrator, but Filidor was not listening.

The morning was difficult. Filidor arose and took a dose of Colophant's Universal Assuagement, which repaired the effects of the purple Pwyfus. He found all three Flastovics seated at the galley table, but the Florreys were absent. The young man offered appropriate words and gestures for the beginning of the day, and accepted Erslan Flastovic's invitation to sit, which was followed by the offer of a cup of aromatic punge, a thick slice of toasted bread, and some small flavored sausages. A few days earlier, Filidor would have found the breakfast impossibly dull, but his standards had been altered by the devastation of Henwaye's cuisine.

Gavne regarded the new addition to their number with a less than welcoming eye, but she soon made him aware that her disapproval did not arise from any qualities of his or from the circumstances in which he had joined the troupe. "I am accustomed to be consulted," she said to Filidor, but her attention shifted to her husband as she concluded, "and not to find my affairs settled for me."

Flastovic apparently had discovered something absorbing in his half-filled mug of punge, and could not tear his gaze away. But he muttered something that suggested an apologetic attitude, to which his spouse said, "Well, then," and picked up her knitting.

The girl Chloe sat at the end of the table. Filidor's side-eyed appraisal of her mood left him in no doubt that she found every detail of her surroundings to be far from satisfactory, especially her father. She picked at a plate of fruits and toasted grains steeped in cream, her narrow lips thinned further by being drawn into a frown.

Filidor unobtrusively brought out the vial of espolianth extract and showed it to Flastovic. "I found this in the cabin," he whispered, then quietly described the powder's use and properties.

The mummer chief's eyes seemed to swell in their sockets and his face grew pale. His hands clenched upon the edges of the table. "I had thought it the strange passion of a strange child, but this . . ." he said, and could not find the words to express his rage and horror. For a long moment, he was silent except for the sound of breaths that seemed to come from deep within him, while his wife looked from her husband to Filidor and to the little vial in the young man's hand.

"There must be another condition to our help," Flastovic said, at last, his voice grim.

"I will see that Germolian is brought to an accounting," Filidor said.

"Our reckonings of his debt may vary," Flastovic said.

"I will be stern," the Archon's nephew assured him, tucking the vial away in an inner pocket.

Then, of course, the matter had to be explained to Gavne. Flastovic suggested that Chloe withdraw, but she would not, and sat with her head bowed as her father made her mother understand what the disclamator had done to their daughter. Gavne's expression grew severe, and she described Ovile Germolian in terms not usually heard from respectable matrons, even among show folk. Then she put an arm around her daughter.

"I am sorry," Filidor said, and at the sound of his voice, Chloe briefly raised her head and flashed him a look of such bitter animosity that the young man felt as if some chilled liquid had been splashed into his face. Then she fled the lounge, her mother's sigh following her.

Filidor opened his mouth to speak, though he was not at all sure what words might come out. He was never to know, because at that moment, the outer door flew open and the Florreys came clamoring in, one of them clutching a rolled-up copy of the *Implicator*, which he quickly spread over Filidor's plate. "Here's news," he said, "and none of it to the good."

The Archon's apprentice looked and did not care for what he saw. This time, his image had been subjected to artistic alterations, a heavy darkening under the eyes and a deep shadowing of the hollows in his cheeks, and he thought to detect a slight lengthening of his chin. All of this combined to re-create him in a sinister and villainous mode, a creature of cold appetites and devious stratagems. To underscore the impression, a block of text next to the perverted likeness read, *Hunt for a Madman; Day Four.*

But it was not his own bastardized image that struck a chill into Filidor. It was the larger picture, occupying a good portion of the page, showing a man with disordered hair and staring eyes, his hands bound before him in official restraints. The headline beneath the image read, FUGITIVE'S ACCOMPLICE? and the face staring out at Filidor was that of Etch Valderoyn.

The young man turned to the accompanying text, which again lay under the byline of Tet Folbrey: *Scullaway Point's peerless constabulary last night brought to bay a suspected henchman of the notorious transgressor Filidor Vesh, who is sought for dastardly crimes against the common peace and for an unprovoked attack upon the person of a high Archonate official.*

Quickly, Filidor skimmed the rest of the article, then returned to the top and read it more slowly, translating the gossip columnist's overexuberant style as he went. It appeared that Etch Valderoyn and a group of "unidentified ne'er-do-wells" had been drinking at Tinkum's Reach, a waterfront haunt, when talk at a neighboring table had turned to the man wanted for assaulting Faubon Bassariot. Some uncomplimentary speculation concerning Filidor's character, offered by a large dockworker and overheard by Valderoyn, had prompted the latter to fling himself across the former's table, after which several punches had been thrown, one or two of them landing. Both sets of companions had enlisted themselves in their friends' service, creating a general melee, which had dissolved into mutual flight through several doors and windows when a squad of constables had arrived to intervene. Valderoyn had assaulted a number of these late arrivals, vowing to defend the name of Filidor Vesh against all comers. He had been taken to the local jail—called the Scullaway Point Osgood—and a search was under way for those who had been with him, whom Folbrey characterized as "two or three defaulters of similar mold, believed to be associated with the ill-famed sea-reiver, Gwallyn Henwaye, whose name was heard being bandied about in the tavern before the altercation."

The last paragraphs particularly summoned and held Filidor's attention. They declared that the prisoner was to be held only overnight at the Scullaway Point jail; in the morning, he would be transferred to the Archonate bureau, and there he would be collected by the acting Archon himself, Faubon Bassariot, described by Tet Folbrey as "he who with admirable pluck and bravery withstood the treacherous blows of the evil Vesh and rallied to the ancient cause of the Archonate." The Archon himself, "increasingly vexed and disheartened by his nephew's opprobrious conduct, has retired to a point of obscurity, leaving the affairs of the realm in the capable hands of worthy Bassariot."

A vision revealed itself within Filidor's mind. He saw an open square outside the local Archonate office, its staff arrayed in formal order to receive the occupant of a green and black volante that has just swept down from the sky. The vehicle's door opens and out steps the portly architect of all his ills, an expression of bland serenity on his porcine features. The officials smartly salute and blow their whistles of rank, and just then Filidor appears by Bassariot's side, cloaked in Obblob invisibility, and commits upon the person of the "acting Archon" all the outrages and injuries he is unjustly accused of, and a few more besides, before escaping in the ensuing confusion.

The young man took a moment to savor the image of Faubon Bassariot rolling on the flagstones, batting ineffectually at his unseen assailant, then he put the vision aside. The issue, he told himself, was not the discomfiting of Bassariot, but the rescue of Etch Valderoyn, before that simple and sincere man fell into the clutches of the usurper and his friends. Filidor was sure that the honest sailor would not willingly reveal what he knew of the fugitive's doings since the *Empyreal*, but he had no doubt that Bassariot would have the truth out of the prisoner, by guile if not by more vicious procedures.

Something must be done. If this had been a romance, and Filidor its stalwart hero, he could have swept in and dazzled his opponents with a display of martial skills, seized Valderoyn, and dashed off in some conveniently available vehicle, losing his pursuers by a further demonstration of skill and daring. Unfortunately, Filidor had stark reality to deal with, and doubted that his slim capacity for derring-do would carry him through. He decided he had best confer with the voice in his head. "I must be by myself for a while," he told the mummers.

He had left the bottle of purple wine on the galley counter the night before. He picked it up and turned to leave, but noted that it was now only about a third full. "Could one of you arrange a supply of this stuff?" he asked them. "I believe it is called purple Pwyfus."

"You could afford better," said Flastovic.

"No, I have a reason for choosing this particular label."

Flastovic's features arranged themselves into that expression that conveys agreement with a point of view while dismissing whatever reasoning may have led to it. One of the Florreys brought his hand near his mouth and made his fingers tremble. "Like a fish," said the other one, but by then Filidor was behind his cabin door.

"Integrator," he said, after several swallows of the purple, which threatened not to achieve harmony with the sausages, bread, and punge already in his belly, "I would have your counsel."

When the voice responded, Filidor quickly outlined the situation regarding Etch Valderoyn. "I was wondering," he concluded, "how your Filidor might have dealt with the situation."

The voice was silent for so long that Filidor thought he had lost the connection. *I regret,* it finally said, *that I do not know what to tell you.*

"Surely you must know your Archon better than any other observer," the young man said.

Indeed, said the voice, *I know him to his last jottle. But my Filidor has never fallen into circumstances even remotely similar to yours. Nor could he.*

"Conjecture, then."

Another pause. *I cannot. You may as well ask how Fizrayal*—here he referred to a bygone epicure whose exquisite taste had become the feedstock of legend—*would fare at a pie-eating contest.*

"I would be comforted to know how your man would respond in my situation," said Filidor.

He would probably, said the voice, *ask for your advice. For my own part, I counsel boldness, invention, and, most of all, speed.*

"Can you be more specific?"

No. Not unless you continue to drink that incapacitating liquid, in which case no amount of advice will assist you. You should know, as well, that something in it is almost as corrosive to my sheets as the pilkies. After which, it would say no more.

Left to his own resources, Filidor sat on the bed and felt a churn of fear in his stomach, which was already beset by his breakfast and the drink that had followed it. Briefly, he thought of doing nothing, his preferred strategy in so many prickly situations; but then he recalled that it was his penchant for acting like some small bundle of fur and senses, quivering in its hole in the ground, that had brought him to this disquieting moment of choice.

Besides, there was the question of what he owed to Etch Valderoyn. On that point, he would have liked to have compared views with the other Filidor. He wondered if his alter ego, the acknowledged light of his generation, would have rated the sailor's naive loyalty above his own safety, or whether he would have weighed both in a statesman's balance and decided that the lesser man must be sacrificed for the greater.

But he knew the question was pointless. The pragmatic view was that Valderoyn in Bassariot's hands meant that soon the enemy who thought Filidor dead would know that he was not. At the moment, the purported search was probably a blind, a false emergency behind which Bassariot's circle could consolidate their power. If the full wherewithal of the Archonate was brought to the task of finding him, the Archon's apprentice knew he would not long stay free.

Again, Filidor wondered where his uncle was and what was happening with him, and again felt a longing to be reconciled with the little man. He consoled himself that, as the integrator had said, the dwarf could fend for himself, but that was a thin blanket against a chill night.

"Enough," he told himself, and rose from the bed. "I'll do what I can."

The mummers were able to tell him where the Archonate bureau stood. It was not far from the park, and Flastovic drew him a simple map. "Make all readiness to depart," Filidor said. He laid a jewel from his store in the troupe leader's palm. "You may hear a commotion. If I do not return soon after, pull up and haul away, and I will try to catch up with you on the road to Thurloyn Vale."

He turned and reached for the door, but Flastovic stopped

him. From a cupboard, the mummer produced a box that unfolded into a chest of many compartments. From several of
these he brought out a selection of wigs and facial hair, as
well as various prostheses for altering the shape and arrangement of the face. A few moments later, Filidor's fine hair
was buried under a thatch of coarse curls and his elegant features were distorted by the addition of a false nose, a bone-
less mass that resembled a tuber grown between his eyes and
lips. Small pads between his gums and the flesh of his cheeks
altered his physiognomy to such an extent that he scarcely
recognized the pug that stared back at him from the makeup
box's mirror.

"That'll help," said one of the Florreys. "And if you
want people not to look at you, stare them in the eye."

Feeling oddly emboldened by the disguise, Filidor made
his way across the parkland and into the ways of Scullaway
Point. The town, he now saw, was a collection of mainly
wooden buildings, tall and angular and painted in bright colors, haphazardly arranged along wide, straight streets shaded
by dark-leaved trees that rustled constantly in the sea breeze.
The square where the two-story Archonate bureau stood was
small and cozy, and Filidor soon realized that his imagined
assault upon the usurper could never take place as he had
envisioned it: the reception berth for arriving air-cars was on
the building's flat roof.

The young man loitered about the area for a while, seeing no indications of the bustle and pomp that must inevitably
attend even an "acting" Archon's presence. He also noted that
a gaggle of gawkers had congregated at a side door, and si-
dled up to the group to learn what he could by eavesdrop-
ping. He discovered that they were gathered to glimpse the
desperado Valderoyn, who was expected to be brought to the
Archonate office at any moment. Fast upon this intelligence

came the realization that the journey would be a short one: the Osgood, where felons and defaulters were confined before trial, was in the basement of the town hall, just across a narrow alley from the Archonate office. Etch Valderoyn, when he was transferred to the Archon's care, would be walked across the short distance by a brace of constables.

Filidor stepped back to survey the scene, and a plan began to unfold in his mind. He realized that, as plans went, this one did not go far. It would not win him any laurels at institutes where grand strategies were studied and praised. It was barely above pranksterism, but it was the best he could do under the circumstances.

He studied the crowd, which he was pleased to see was growing larger, and tried to decide which of its rearmost members appeared the most pugnacious. After consideration, he awarded that distinction to a short-statured but sturdily built man who, he saw, twice used his shoulders to deter others from imposing their presence upon him. Filidor moved to a position at the rear of the pack of riffraff, which put him only two arm's lengths from his target, and waited.

Time went by, and the young man was relieved to see that his choice did not lose patience and go off to seek another diversion. Eventually, a thrumming was heard from the sky to the west, and heads turned to track the descent of a long, sleek volante with the Archonate crest on its door. Filidor ignored the vehicle, alternating his attention between the ill-tempered spectator and town hall. As the hum of the aircar's gravity obviators swelled, the door of the Osgood opened and Etch Valderoyn emerged, blinking and peering about, clad in prison pinks and with wrists manacled. His arms were firmly gripped by two strong men in pale blue uniforms.

The gawkers' attention shifted across the street, and Filidor moved. He quickly bedecked himself in the bobblobblobl, then forced his way into the crowd's midst while their attention was fixed on the prisoner. Drawing back his fist at waist height, he slammed the best blow he could muster into the floating ribs of the truculent man, then adroitly stepped back.

His target yelped in pain and turned to the man at his rear, a tall, round-headed fellow, whose face bore a grimace of disgust occasioned by his having just smelled Filidor's disguise at close range. The man Filidor had struck took the other's expression for an indication of hostility, and as the Archon's nephew expected, pursued no further inquiries. He dealt the tall man's midriff an immense buffet that doubled the victim up and propelled him into the man on his far side, who pushed the gasping sufferer into another bystander. Filidor meanwhile moved along the rear rank of the mob, shoving backs and kicking ankles, until the first fight had multiplied into a general brawl.

The clear space through which Etch Valderoyn and his guards should have proceeded quickly from Osgood to Archonate bureau now filled with punching, kicking, swearing men. The constables first tried to keep a separation, and when that failed they sought to push a way through to their original destination. By the time they realized that effort was futile, it was too late to return to the door they had come out of.

Still cloaked in Obblob invisibility, Filidor climbed onto the base of a lamp pole and regarded the mess he had created. One of the constables had gone down, and the other was clearly torn between helping his partner and keeping his hold on Valderoyn. Whistles were blowing, and reinforcements were trying to get into the street from the Osgood, but the outward opening door was blocked by the press of battlers.

With no help able to reach him soon, the remaining constable chose duty over fraternity. Drawing his truncheon, he began to apply its energized end to the fighters around him, causing them to instantly stiffen then collapse, while he sought to drag his prisoner free of the mob. The officer soon cleared a path and emerged, gasping and with his shirt half torn off, into open space. At that point, Filidor stepped up beside him and pressed the man's wrist so that his truncheon touched his own chest. The constable made a curious noise and folded up as if his larger bones had dematerialized. Filidor, meanwhile, had stretched the bobblobblobl and brought it back down again to cover both him and Etch Valderoyn.

"We should go," he said.

Valderoyn showed presence of mind. "The keys," he said, pointing with both bound hands to a pouch on the officer's belt. Filidor stooped and found them. Rising, he looked up and saw through the gauziness of the Obblob cloak a face appear above the lip of the Archonate office roof, a rounded face with a large curl gummed to its forehead, a face that was unhappily regarding the riot below.

"We'd better hurry," said Filidor.

The groundeater's motors were idling as Filidor and Valderoyn, still enfolded in the bobblobblobl, climbed aboard and shut the door. The Florreys were waiting for them in the galley, and saw Filidor remove the Obblob cloak. The twins looked at each other with a shared thought.

"That's a useful piece to own," said Ches.

"By rights, it ought to be shared," added Isbister.

But Filidor put the reeking garment away in its pouch, and said, "It will not help us evade detection if this vehicle is stopped and searched. At close quarters, its stench draws attention."

The Florreys advised the young man not to worry. One

of them went forward while the other brought out the makeup chest and broke it open on the table. Flastovic joined them from the forward part of the great vehicle, where he had been preparing for their departure. "Isbister will take us out," he said, a prediction almost immediately validated by a lurch of the groundeater as it got under way. To Filidor, he said, "In your present disguise, you will pass for Ovile Germolian. It is an affectation of his performing style never to be seen unmasked. You"—he indicated Etch Valderoyn—"will make an interesting Lepkin."

As Filidor watched, Flastovic and Ches stripped the manacles from the sailor's wrists and the prison clothes from his body. They shaved the hair from his head and face, including his eyebrows, then applied luminous tattoos to his cheeks and forehead. Ches took the Osgood uniform and restraints to the costume storage lockers behind the folding stage, where they could be hidden in plain sight among similar odds and ends. He came back with a pair of vermilion shorts and the lime-green leggings over which they were to be worn, a frogged yellow shirt and a long-tailed coat of ivory lace with a gaudy metallic panache on the left lapel. A tall, brimless hat with a rounded crown completed the ensemble. Flastovic then used prostheses to alter the shapes of Valderoyn's teeth, the pitch of his nostrils, and the pendency of his ears. For a finale, he grafted an extra thumb to each of the sailor's hands and showed him how to engage the small motors they contained, so that they closed appropriately when the other digits made fists. Valderoyn now looked distinctly nonhuman.

"You must contrive to appear bored to the edge of expiration," the chief mummer said. "Lepkins require great stimulation before they are roused to take even the slightest notice of their surroundings."

"Why am I aboard your vehicle?" Valderoyn wanted to know. "In case the authorities ask."

"We will tell them we have been pondering the same mystery," Flastovic replied, "but have been unable to attract your notice sufficiently to receive a reply."

"What if they ask me directly?" the sailor said.

"Like any Lepkin, you will contemplate the shapes of clouds, or the alignment of your cuffs, until they grow tired of asking and go away."

"What if they persist?"

"A Lepkin's attention, once attracted, is not always a benefit. They will not persist."

They led Valderoyn to a seat by a window and bid him practice gazing serenely at nothing. Flastovic then produced a voice modulator for Filidor to wear under his garments. When the device was tested, he assured the Archon's apprentice that it closely approximated Germolian's diction. Filidor noticed no great difference, but was assured that such was normal.

The precautions proved unnecessary. As the groundeater traveled the wide thoroughfare that led south to Thurloyn Vale, they encountered a roadblock on the outskirts of town. But the checkpoint was staffed by local constables, and their investigation was lackadaisical. A blue-uniformed underbannerman came aboard, made a quick and perfunctory survey of the occupants, and waved them on without so much as a question.

When the man came aboard, Filidor was on a side seat in the vehicle's command section. As they got under way again, he said to Flastovic, "I would have expected Bassariot to have mobilized Archonate forces for this work."

The mummer scratched his chin, and considered a while. "Perhaps his reach still exceeds his grasp. I misremember the actual history of Holmar Thurm's exploits, but I have often performed Mbukwe's play based on the events. Between his initial moves and the moment when he at last sits his rump on the Chair—that is through most of the second act—there is a hiatus of power. Thurm commands those fools who have wagered their futures on his success, and is opposed by loyal Carvrey and Thil, but the rank and file of the Archonate stand neutral until the struggle is resolved."

Filidor nodded. "That is why Bassariot came himself to collect Valderoyn. There cannot be many he can bid to go and come back, knowing that they will dutifully do his will once out of his sight."

He reasoned it further. Bassariot had thrown him from the ship, then hurried back to Olkney, surely intending to unseat the Archon and seize power. The fact that he had not—he was, after all, only "acting Archon"—argued that Filidor's uncle had perhaps found a corner where Bassariot had expected a straightaway. It now struck Filidor that it was possible that Dezendah Vesh had foreseen what was to happen, and had arranged for Filidor to play a decoying gambit while the main action of the game happened on another level of the board. For all the high regard in which he held his uncle, the apprentice knew from uncomfortable experience that the Archon was quite capable of leaving him out in a no-man's-land while the dwarf carried forward some intricate scheme.

But he dismissed the suspicion. He could not believe that his uncle would have sent him off on another potentially deadly fool's errand—unless it was possible that the dwarf had known Filidor would be thrown from the *Empyreal* and had somehow set an Obblob to rescue him? Again, Filidor put speculation aside. It was at once encouraging and enraging to think that he was marching along a course already plotted by a wiser authority. He had heard of philosophies that held all life to be such a journey. But for him to proceed under such an assumption, if in fact it was unwarranted, would be unwise. He would assume he was in danger and act accordingly.

He expressed this thought to Flastovic, who agreed. "Better alive and worried than carefree and dead," the mummer quoted.

Filidor went back to the lounge and found Gavne and Etch Valderoyn comparing techniques of knitting; like many sailors, the man was well versed in the skills of self-sufficiency. He rose when Filidor entered and said, in a formal tone, "I thank you for rescuing me again."

Filidor made a depreciative gesture. "As with the first time, my motives were not entirely altruistic," he said.

"I judge by results," said Valderoyn.

Filidor sat beside Gavne. "I am sorry to have upset your daughter," he said.

Her placid face turned his way, though her fingers remained in motion with sticks and yarn. "She will not easily forgive you."

"But I was not the agent of her discomfort. Germolian took despicable advantage."

The woman moved her head in an expressive way. "Just so. But your discovery of the espolianth transformed her grand love affair into a sordid victimization. She still sees him partly haloed by the drug's misty glow; you stand in a much starker light."

"That is unfair," said Filidor.

Gavne shrugged. "Things are as they are. If you quest after justice, young women are the wrong continent to explore. They run more to clemency or spite. In this instance, Germolian gets the one, and you get the other. Fairness does not come into it."

"Should I ask her pardon?" Filidor asked archly, but Gavne took the question on its merits.

"I would leave her alone. She might not hesitate to do you a disservice." Her eyes returned to the clicking rods between her fingers. Valderoyn asked her if she knew the four-and-roll stitch, and the conversation moved away from Filidor.

The road south arrowed across a fruitful plain bordered by low wooded hills, passing through small farming towns and cozy villages whose inhabitants had crowned successful careers in the cities with retirement to bucolic peace. The highway was the main street in these communities, and the groundeater slowed as it passed through, so that Erslan Flastovic could employ a loudspeaker to invite all and sundry to the evening's performance in Clutter, farther down the road.

They reached that midsized town in late afternoon, and parked in fairgrounds south of the main settlement. Flastovic called them all to a meeting in the groundeater's lounge. "We will give them three short comedies, then a good tragedy to send them home on. We'll open with *The Fish That Grew*, followed by *The Diligence of Marsill*, and then *The Bumpkins and the Flirt* to take us to intermission. After that, we'll do *Death and Dismemberment*, the long version. If they demand an encore, we'll reprise the last scene of *D and D*. Nothing cheers the country crowds like a good old-fashioned bloodbath." He clapped his hands, then rubbed them together. "Let's to our rehearsal."

They unlimbered the stage and sorted props and costumes. The work soon left Filidor at loose ends, since his attempts to be of assistance had the effect of rendering simple, familiar tasks difficult and novel. Valderoyn offered to make the pre-performance meal, he having some professional experience in ships' galleys. Flastovic said that help was welcome, but he must close the curtains so that none should look in and see a supposed Lepkin at domestic chores, which would be as uncommon a sight as the old planet had ever witnessed.

The Archon's nephew went outside, where a few adolescent residents of Clutter had perched themselves on the top rail of the fairground fence. Their clothing tended toward checks and stripes, the cuffs rolled up at wrist and ankle, and their taste in hairstyles was extravagant by Filidor's standards. They were offering each other commentaries and evaluations of the groundeater and its company that, within the circle of the young Clutterites, apparently passed for brilliant sarcasm. Filidor ignored them, using the free time to ponder his circumstances. He needed to contrive a strategy, but he could not construct a means until he had settled on an end. He did not know where to go, nor what to do when he got there.

Again, he thought how much easier it would be if this was a tale of brave deeds and daring escapades, even one of The Bard Obscure's dramas. At this point, something would occur to direct the hero toward his next action, and matters would proceed smoothly to the next episode. Of course, Filidor reminded himself, if this were a romance, the chances were not good that he would be its hero—unless the story was less about derring-do than about derring-done-to.

Filidor waited, but the only sign that appeared was one of the Florreys, come to tell him that supper was ready.

CHAPTER

SEVEN

Clutter was named for its founder, a philosophical visionary whose system of thought was based on the cultivation of a single root crop. This tuber, he averred, could meet all human nutritional needs, provided the humans maintained a sufficient clarity of perspective about the vegetable's merits. The revered Clutter attracted a small number of disciples, some of whom did not have far to go to achieve the simplicity of mind required by their leader's teachings. They came to this broad valley, planted plenty of the tubers, and strove to put their beliefs into practice. Midway through their third winter, however, when they were most in need of the spiritual discipline that made it possible to face three meals of the same boiled root, day after day, a store of delicacies and rich viands was found under the floorboards of Clutter's house. The community's official history said that the prophet was promptly exiled, but rumors persisted that he was in fact roasted and eaten. In either case, the Clutterites forswore singularity of diet and their descendants now planted and reaped a full variety of crops.

The fairgrounds were well filled by twilight, the Clutter folk gathering around the lighted marquee. Unlike their children, the adult Clutterites preferred to dress in bland solid colors, accented here and there by discreetly spotted trim. Men and women covered their heads from crown to nape in tight-fitting caps, to which were attached emblems and symbols that expressed their wearers' whims and idiosyncrasies.

Filidor, robed and masked as a disclamator, came upon the Florrey twins in the shadows at the side of the stage. The brothers were pointing out various members of the crowd and discussing their choices in low voices. They were debating whether the bump-and-tickle was the best approach to the wealth of a large man near the front of the crowd, or whether the drop-and-dip might be wiser.

"Rearrange your priorities," Filidor said. The voice modulator added a sepulchral tone, and the sudden admonition from the darkness caused the twins to jump. "I remind you," Filidor continued, "that the consequences of official attention could well be extreme. My adversary may now have convinced himself that there is truly a conspiracy to thwart him. He may go to great pains to assure himself otherwise. The pains would not all be his."

"We plead the defense of necessity," one of the Florreys said. "Our stipend is measly."

"Flastovic has an ungiving nature," the other added. "We rely on these small perks for our rudimentary comforts."

"You would find short comfort in the removal of strips of your skin, or the introduction of ravenous insects to your tenderest regions, while Faubon Bassariot's inquisitors vainly urge you to reveal knowledge that you do not command."

"Would they be so . . . inventive?" one of the twins asked, while the other shuddered.

Filidor moved his hands in a gesture of indifference. "If

one as moderate and mild as I can conjecture such horrid eventualities, the thought of what an experienced interrogator could devise opens whole new vistas."

The Florreys conceded the point. They went to prepare for their first roles.

When the hills in the east were humps of purpled blackness and only a faint glow of chartreuse limned the ridges to the west, Erslan Flastovic appeared on stage in his impresario's regalia. He rang the gong and welcomed the audience. While he described the performances the troupe would offer, Gavne and Chloe moved through the crowd, presenting the traditional felt cloche and urging the spectators to be liberal in filling it.

Filidor took up his position at the side of the stage, partially obscured by the shadow of the overhang, and raised his mask slightly to admit the bottle of purple Pwyfus to his lips. The taste of the stuff had long since lost its slight appeal. At Flastovic's signal, he cued the integrator, then stepped forward and delivered the first line of *The Fish That Grew*: "In the Marblake region of Far Forbish lived Bolsacks, a man who had always wished to catch a remarkable fish . . ."

The curtain opened as he spoke, and Flastovic came into the light wearing rustic garb and a comic mask. Filidor waited until he had capered from one side of the stage to the other, the living image of a man who seeks to avoid an undesired duty. Filidor then spoke the line that introduced Bolsacks's wife, Googiol, at which Gavne appeared, in a costume that drew maximum attention to her ampleness of femininity. She rolled her broad hips in a forthright manner and mimed a deep dissatisfaction with her husband's intimate dimensions, as Filidor explained the nature of the discord between the spouses.

From there, the ancient tale unwound: first Bolsacks

brings home the peculiar fish, not knowing it to be a magical creature that grants wishes. He goes off to the tavern to consort with his cronies, leaving his lonely wife to express her constant wish for something to satisfy her particular need. The fish then transforms into a robust young fellow—here one of the Florreys entered, robed, masked and extravagantly codpieced—much to Googiol's taste.

Meanwhile, in the tavern, Bolsacks brags about the size of his catch and the energy of its struggles, and his wistful inflating of the creature's dimensions and power is transmuted into reality back at his home, intensifying his wife's experience to the point of worrisome discomfort.

But, of course, by the time Filidor declaimed the moral of the story—*take care with your wishes, lest they come true*—things had gotten well out of hand, and the Clutterites were slapping knees and wiping tears as the curtain closed on a tableau of Bolsacks striving to disengage the miraculous catch from his pop-eyed wife. Just as the laughter began to subside, Flastovic used a sonic device to produce a loud *pop!* from behind the curtain, which set the audience off again.

After a suitable lapse, Flastovic signaled Filidor to announce *The Diligence of Marsill,* another ancient and ribald tale refashioned by The Bard Obscure. Filidor drank more of the purple wine and spoke as the integrator dictated, telling the story of a jaded roué who vainly quests after an ultimate satisfaction, known mysteriously as the Diligence of Marsill. His quest takes him from world to world, across the Spray and even into the uncivilized worlds of the Back Yonder, until as an old man, worn out by chasing after unfulfilled expectations, he comes to Far Forbish and there finds at last the one woman in the universe who can perform the Diligence. Lengthy and detailed preparations are required, but the old man takes to them with a will. Then, just as the final arrangements are completed, and just before the Diligence can be effected, the old man expires.

The Diligence of Marsill was one of those interminable tales known by the ancient and obscure term "shogdag," and by its very nature it was overlong in the telling. To keep his inner voice alive, Filidor had to resort to the bottle of purple stuff several times, so that, by the time Flastovic, in white wig and seamed mask, sprawled dead upon the divan, the young man was feeling the consequences. Fortunately, the voice modulator was designed to deal with such vicissitudes, inebriety being not uncommon in the theater, and compensated for the occasional slur and hiccup.

The Clutterites found no fault with his performance. They groaned appropriately as the tale wound to its inconclusion, and Filidor spoke the final ironic homily, about coming "to the end of all our journeying, and knowing that there's no place like home."

The third presentation, *The Bumpkins and the Flirt,* was short and quick. Chloe, in spangles and gauze, was surprisingly affecting as the wise-cracking city girl—Filidor delivered her lines in a singsong staccato—while the Florreys played manure-bespattered yokelhood to perfection. When the disclamator spoke the last line, *"Then, let's get these things off our thumbs,"* the stage went black and the crowd howled its pleasure.

At intermission, the Clutterites broke up into small clusters to discuss the entertainment and concerns of their own. Local vendors opened a row of concession stands, offering hot, spicy meats, stuffed perohs, and mulled cider. Gavne and Chloe also went up and down the lines of Clutter folk that formed in front of the food booths, cadging more contributions now that the audience had sampled the quality of the troupe, returning to the groundeater with their cloches heavy and ajingle. "The punters are well pleased," Flastovic said, standing by the great vehicle's ramp as the women went in.

"Indeed," said Filidor, swaying slightly.

"Were you not part of the show, it would not be my place to comment," the mummer said, "but do you need to elevate the jar quite so much? 'More talent was lost in a bottle than e'er was found,' as the old saying has it."

"I find it essential," Filidor said, "but I hope the need is only temporary."

Flastovic shrugged and went to oversee preparations for the second half. Chloe came out for some air, and Filidor made respectful gestures and said, "I thought you very good in your part."

She cast him a frigid look and moved away.

The young man shrugged and decided he would make no further efforts to alter her views with respect to him. She was, in any case, a pale candle to the radiance of Emmlyn Podarke. He looked to where the eastern hills heaved blackly against the sky; somewhere, far beyond those rounded heights, was Trumble, and there waited—though, he admitted, she did not know she waited, nor for whom—the woman who commanded his heart.

To clear his head before the second performance, Filidor wandered among the groups of Clutterites, still in his disclamator's robes but with his mask tilted back onto the top of his head. The alterations Flastovic had made that morning to his appearance were still in place, although he suddenly worried that the false nose might be askew; the Archon's apprentice raised both hands to it as if containing a sneeze, and surreptitiously assured himself that the bulbous thing was as it should be.

His peregrinations brought him near to the fairgrounds

gate, where Clutter's main road ran by. Here he saw an official vehicle pull up and discharge a man of competent appearance, who wore a uniform of yellow and black. The law man passed a professional eye over the crowd, saw no cause to do more, then took from the car a wad of paper. He peeled off a sheet and tacked it to the gate post by means of a hand-held machine that made a *kchank* noise when he squeezed it. He put up a few more of the posters on nearby surfaces, tipped his headgear to members of the community who were urging him in a friendly way to stay for the performance, then drove away.

Filidor waited until the car was gone, then followed a few of the Clutterites who had moseyed up to see what the notices conveyed. He was dismayed but not surprised to see Etch Valderoyn's face, doubtless as recorded last night after the tavern brawl, and beside it a recognizable rendition of his own. Underneath was an offer of a considerable sum, and instructions on how to collect it.

The Archon's apprentice forbore to show more than a casual interest in the poster. He put his hands behind his back and turned to walk casually away, and had pursed his lips to whistle when he noted that among a knot of Clutter folk peering at one of the other posters was Chloe Flastovic. She looked carefully at the paper, then tilted her head in his direction and produced an expression that many a cornered little creature has seen on the face of a larger predator at the end of a chase. Her eyes narrowed and her teeth showed in what was not quite a smile, then she ripped the poster from the wood, startling the Clutterites, and strode determinedly toward a communications booth near the concession stands.

Filidor moved to catch her. When she looked back and saw him in her wake, she pulled up the flounced skirt that was her between-performances wear and began to run. Filidor attempted to do likewise, but found the disclamator's robes had been designed more for stately progress than for sudden bursts of speed. The half bottle of purple Pwyfus that was making itself comfortable in his bloodstream also did no good to his coordination.

Seeing her pulling away from him, he opened his mouth and shouted, "Stop!"

He had forgotten that he was still wearing the voice modifier. Its circuitry interpreted the strength of his utterance to mean that he was now addressing an audience large enough to fill a natural amphitheater, and amplified its volume accordingly. Every person in the fairgrounds, and many well beyond its limits, instantly ceased whatever he or she had been doing. Windows rattled in the south-facing walls throughout the town of Clutter, and even Chloe faltered in her step from the force of the blast.

More usefully, however, one of the Florreys took note of what was occurring. He was standing at a food stall, between the girl and the communications booth, chewing on something that dripped red sauce. With an experienced criminal's honed response to unexpected difficulties, he instantly sized up the situation. As Chloe sped by, he stepped into her path, swept an arm around her waist, and hoisted her off the ground.

She resented the interference and strove to pummel the man, but the other twin was, as always, not far away, and arrived to assist in the operation just as Filidor caught up. With smiles and affable waves to the watching Clutterites, and assurances that there was nothing to worry about, the three of them hauled Chloe back to the groundeater, where Flastovic and Gavne waited. They all went into the lounge, where Etch Valderoyn showed an un-Lepkinlike anxiety at the fracas.

Again, the mother took charge of the girl, doling out looks of exasperation in equal measure to her daughter and the men. "This cannot continue," she said.

"Chloe, you must not," Flastovic said. "Much is at stake."

"I don't care!" the girl replied, struggling in her mother's strong embrace. Her eyes were like slits in a face gone red and rigid. "He's awful, and I hate him!"

"You must promise your father not to interfere," Gavne said. "We would all suffer."

"I won't!" said the girl. She waved the poster. "I'll turn them in for the reward, then I'll go away somewhere you'll never find me, and live a life of elegance."

A spirited discussion ensued, mainly among the mummers, while Filidor and the sailor fretted on the outskirts. But neither threats nor entreaties nor the spectacle of her father tearing out his own hair would dissuade Chloe from taking her revenge. Filidor marveled at the intransigence of adolescence, not remembering that he had possessed an abundance of the same quality not many years since.

"You'll have to go," Flastovic said, at last. "We can contain her for a while, but you can see that the situation does not lend itself to permanence."

Chloe was taken off again to her bedroom, her mother accompanying her to prevent a sudden exit through the window. The talk turned to the logistics of flight. It happened that the Florreys kept a two-man skimdoo in the storage compartment, charged and tuned and equipped with a silenced engine in case their circumstances ever argued for a speedy and flexible departure. This they were persuaded to sell to Filidor for an exorbitant price, after he assured them that their previous arrangement was still in effect. Valderoyn knew how to operate the amphibious device.

"The question is," Filidor said, "where to go? I had hoped

to gather more information and from it formulate a strategy, but I know no more now than when I was marooned on Henwaye's island."

The sailor cleared his throat, and offered a suggestion. "I don't know much about Archonate intrigues, but I do know it never hurts to have a few pals at your back in a scrumpup. That fellow in the newspaper keeps saying about how we're leagued with these Podarkes. Maybe we should see if he's right."

"I don't know where to find them," Filidor said. "Surely they won't be wandering around Trumble, shouting their affiliations to passersby."

"Why don't you ask that voice in your head?" said Valderoyn.

"Hello?" said one of the Florreys, and the other two mummer men showed an equal interest. "We did not take you for a nokes," said Flastovic.

Filidor explained matters in the briefest terms, including the need to keep the integrator's energizing plates awash in a particular species of cheap wine. Then he said, "Integrator, where would I look for Emmlyn Podarke and her family?"

Trumble, was the answer. *They have a large house on the eastern edge of town.*

"And if not there?"

I will consult my records. There was a pause. *A Siskine Podarke once kept a hunting lodge in Hember Forest below Mt. Cassadet.*

Filidor remembered the name of Siskine Podarke. Emmlyn had mentioned it. "Does he still?" he asked.

I cannot tell. I have shut down some of my systems to lower the drain on my energy. The corrosion still worsens and I am less than I was.

"Has anyone been to the Hember Forest?" Filidor asked. No one had; the place was a backwater. But a gazetteer was found and consulted; Hember Forest lay between two ridges that descended from Mt. Cassadet, which was an extinct volcano to the south of Trumble. By road, it would take the groundeater three or four days, but a fast skimdoo could follow a direct route, traversing the grass-covered hills and the intervening waters of Lake Foddlemere, to bring them to the outskirts of the forest in one long night's travel.

"What do you think?" Filidor asked Etch Valderoyn.

"I don't like forests," said the sailor. "Better to try the house in town."

"The paper said they were hiding in caves on Mt. Cassadet," Filidor said. "Surely their house would be watched. We would have a better chance of approaching unseen through woods."

"I don't like forests," the sailor repeated.

"The hunting lodge is more or less on the way," Filidor decided. "We'll try there first."

Valderoyn looked unhappy, but shrugged his acquiescence. The Florreys went to unpack the skimdoo, while Erslan Flastovic again brought out his makeup chest and proceeded to alter the sailor's appearance once more. The sight of a Lepkin riding such a conveyance, and with a passenger on the pillion seat, would have excited comment. Skin dye and false hair converted Valderoyn into a man three decades older, while a quick rummage through the costume hold outfitted both him and Filidor in the boots, caps, and jackets of hunters. With the apparent difference in their ages, they would pretend to be father and son, out to bond with each other through the slaughter of wildlife.

Filidor paid the Florreys for the skimdoo with a blue cabuchon the size of his thumb, which would have been enough to purchase the groundeater itself. He promised that there would be more when he was restored to office. The twins pronounced themselves satisfied, and bade the two fugitives goodspeed.

"I'm sorry we couldn't do more for you," said Flastovic.

"You did more than I can thank you for," Filidor said, and reconfirmed his commitment to build the mummer chief a grand theater on South Processional.

He climbed onto the skimdoo behind Etch Valderoyn. "We'll go down the road a ways before we strike out for the hills," the sailor said, "just in case the young missy gets a glimpse of our direction."

Flastovic and the Florreys bade them farewell, then the old trouper went to the stage to announce a change in the evening's program: the disclamator having fallen ill, the tragedy would not be performed; instead there would be a cabaret of stunts and hijinks, "including some remarkable sleights of hand by the celebrated Florrey twins."

Valderoyn worked the skimdoo's controls and the little craft lifted lightly and leaned away toward the road. Moments later, they were passing the fields and growing pools of the farms south of Clutter. Where the highway bent around a long knoll, cutting them off from the view of anyone at the fairgrounds, the sailor turned the steering bar to the left and they angled toward the distant hills.

The evening was warm, the air rushing by was soft, and the only sound from the little vehicle was the *sssss* of its passage. Valderoyn had a sure hand with the controls, and they traveled without incident or conversation across ordered fields and tame watercourses, until the hills ceased to be a remote horizon but swelled to occupy the foreground and then became the travelers' entire surroundings.

The sailor increased power and they flowed up the slopes

just above the feather-topped grass that covered the hills, the stems dividing under the force of their passage, then closing behind them without trace. Filidor assumed that the Florreys had had the trackless feature of the skimdoo in mind when they acquired it. Now he was the beneficiary of their foresight; if Chloe still desired to inform on him, any searchers would have to cast for a trail over a wide radius.

They crested the first rise and saw by starlight the dim shapes of the rippled land ahead. Valderoyn flicked on the skimdoo's illumination and they slid down the far slope as if on a beam of brightness. The sailor was humming some sea song.

Filidor had been thinking about their situation and now he said, "I am sorry to have pulled you into my troubles."

Etch Valderoyn laughed. "A few days ago, I was walking a wheel for Gwallyn Henwaye, with scant hope of doing anything else the rest of my days. Now I am a carefree adventurer and a companion of the Archon's heir."

"Not to mention a hunted felon," countered Filidor.

"Pfah!" commented the sailor. "I once thought myself unique because I had collected a diversity of pizzles. Now I see that life can be full of twists and sudden departures. Who knows what awaits? Whatever it may be, I find it better than walking a wheel or scrubbing another man's deck, so why not be content?"

"But all the wealth you took from Henwaye's trove is back in the Osgood."

"I probably would have lost it all in the time-honored way."

"I admire your disposition," Filidor said.

Valderoyn made a noise that conveyed pleasure and surprise. "I am only myself, but that is enough for me," he said.

Filidor found himself slipping into a mood of introspection. It was clear that Etch Valderoyn felt more than gratitude for his rescues, that the sailor truly held his deliverer in some affection. It was not a sentiment Filidor was used to receiving. Among the small coterie of lordlings with whom he made sport, there was some camaraderie, expressed in banter that differed only in quality, not in kind, from the lead-lined wit he had heard being lumbered about by the fence-sitting youth back in Clutter. Whether there was affection behind the barbs and jibes, or just a desire to score points regardless of any wounds that might be inflicted, was difficult to say.

His thoughts again turned to his uncle, and again he felt a pang of concern. He could admit to himself that he regarded his only kin with a mix of emotions—frequently it was exasperation, sometimes fear—but that underneath all else there was a foundation of familial love. And he would admit to himself also that he believed the feeling was reciprocated. When he was younger, he often complained that his uncle had been set on Old Earth for the single purpose of making his nephew's life a struggle and a torment. But now, having wandered the world with the odd little man, and having learned something of his own resources, Filidor was prepared to accept that the tests and ordeals the Archon had set him through the years had all been intended to benefit him, to "grow him up good," as the old saying went.

The dwarf cared about him, and Filidor returned the little man's regard. But there was a dark obverse to a bright side of that particular coin: because he cared for his uncle, he was now worried for him. Rationality could tell him that his uncle was capable of overmatching the likes of Faubon Bassariot; the indeterminate status of the Archon as reported by Tet Folbrey argued that the little man was by no means out of the game; but logic was thin armor against the hammering of fear that beat upon Filidor's spirit when he turned his mind to what might be happening in the Archonate palace.

Once more, he put those thoughts aside. There was one other aspect of his life about which his emotions were unsettled. Somewhere ahead of the speeding skimdoo was a young woman named Emmlyn Podarke, who figured largely in Filidor's present predicament, and who loomed no less prominently over the formerly flat plains of his emotional life. The next day might well bring him within sight and scent of her, and how would that be?

He could imagine various scenarios. He saw himself striding about, slapping something against the side of his leg for emphasis as he stressed to a trembling and apologetic Emmlyn the severity of her transgressions in stealing his plaque and sigil, before nobly bending to forgive her. Or perhaps he would arrive in the nick of time, to find her direly pressed by Bassariot or his minions, so that he could seize the moment with an appropriate flourish and perform one notable deed that would resolve all in his favor. The exact nature of the deed remained obscure.

It did occur to him that their next encounter might carry some of the flavor of their last—a mingling of anger and confusion leading to ignominy—but that thought too he set aside. He had been caught unawares on the pavement of Vodel Close; now he would carry the initiative, and the results would fall into a more congenial arrangement.

But, though he resolutely told himself that all would be well, a lingering odor of uncertainty kept rising from the back corner of his mind where he thought he had safely buried his doubts. He turned his head so that his voice was lost in the slipstream of his passage, and said, "Integrator?"

I have little energy. My sheets barely glimmer. Be brief.

"What do you know of love?"

Everything and nothing. The answer was followed by a harsh *click*.

Filidor rephrased his query, but the voice would not, or perhaps could not, answer.

They crested another hill, the tight beam of their fore-lumen spearing the darkness like the single horn of some fabulous questing beast. Valderoyn sang a song about wine and women, and on they went.

When the first pearls of dawn touched the tops of the hills behind them, they came down to Lake Foddlemere, passing through pastureland broken by small copses of pine and hybrid prussdar trees. Near the still water's edge, they stopped in the shelter of one of the little stands of timber and dismounted from the skimdoo. Valderoyn's eyes were red and heavy. "A few moments stretched out with my percies closed, and we'll be off again," he said.

"I could drive us," Filidor said.

"Sure you could," said the sailor, "but you couldn't do that and keep me from falling off the back. I had little enough sleep in the Osgood, and none since." While he was saying it, he lowered himself onto the mat of needles and scarcely spoke the last syllable before he was asleep. Filidor man-handled the skimdoo under cover and lay upon his back, gazing up through the trees into the predawn sky. He began to consider what approach to take toward finding their destination, and closed his eyes the better to concentrate. He was surprised to discover, when he opened them again, that it was full morning.

Etch Valderoyn slumbered still. Filidor woke him and they breakfasted on some bread and cheese from the Flastovic larder. Then the sailor stretched and said, "On our way."

From the edge of the trees they looked east. Mt. Cassadet was in plain sight on the horizon, a squat, truncated cone of black and gray, with one side collapsed in an ancient eruption. Between them and it was the long narrow finger of the lake, with a rolling rise of forested hills beyond.

"I'll drive," said Filidor, to which his companion consented. The young man started the skimdoo and they mounted. At that moment, they heard a deeper sound above the hiss of the little craft's engine. Filidor looked up and saw a long, dark air-car slanting across the sky on a course that paralleled their own. It was too far distant for him to see the device emblazoned on its door, but the colors were unmistakable. And there could be only one person in that sleek, humming vehicle.

"Perhaps things are arranging themselves to our advantage," he told Valderoyn. "I would enjoy a reckoning with Faubon Bassariot."

The sailor shrugged and suggested they move off. Filidor steered the skimdoo down to the water's edge, then out onto the rippling surface. The conveyance plowed a temporary furrow across the lake, sending tickles of spray past their cheeks. As with every body of water, the distance to the far shore turned out to be greater than it seemed, but they were soon enough sliding over the narrow beach and then climbing the wooded slopes.

Hember Forest was a dark place. It had been planted long before by the head of a noble house—Filidor had once known which family, but had now forgotten—which had owned most of the land hereabouts centuries before. The place had been a vast hunting preserve, its topography intelligently worked and shaped to provide interesting challenges for pursued and pursuer alike: blind canyons, unexpected precipices, sudden stretches of quicksand. To the natural fauna were added creations from the vivivats: garoons and proto-

232 8 8 MATTHEW HUGHES

erbs, a common species of lizard enlarged until its height rivaled that of the trees, and a solitary ape of grand dimensions that had its own ideas about which was the hunter and which the quarry. Filidor told all of this to Etch Valderoyn, and saw the sailor's face grow very still.

"Are these monsters still about?" the man inquired, his eyes enlarging as he peered into the trees.

Filidor could not remember, but said, "I don't think so. But let us be cautious."

No roads transected Hember, but the several main trails were wide as alleys in the city, and there were maps and direction signs where these passageways met. Soon after entering the forest, by means of a narrow footpath, Filidor came upon one of the broader trails, and followed it to an intersection. There he discovered that the trail on which they were traveling was named Rabalaunt Way, and that it was crossed here by Farlan Wind.

Even more informative, however, was the schematic map of the forest reproduced by paint and gravure on a large slab of dark wood erected at one corner of the intersection. Filidor had been wondering how he would determine where the Podarke lodge lay without attracting the attention of the police agencies that would doubtless have it under close observation, if not actual siege, its owners having been publicly branded as bandits and lawless zealots. But that problem he now found removed from his agenda; the hunting lodges and other retreats were identified on the map by the names of their owners. Siskine Podarke's cabin lay to the south and east, up a trail labeled Ridge Run. The map even provided a scale of distances, from which Filidor calculated that they could reach the place by late afternoon.

"That will give us plenty of time to scout the lodge and

find a safe means of bypassing any pickets," he said. "Probably, the bobblobblobl will serve us well."

"I don't care for forests," the sailor told him again. "There are things in them, things you don't see."

Filidor spoke over his shoulder. "Are there not things hidden in the sea?"

"I never cared for them either," said Valderoyn. He peered into the darkness between the trees, as if sure that something with teeth, claws, and an appetite was already identifying his tastiest portions. "Couldn't we try the place in town?" he said.

"We are here, and might as well see what we can see," said the Archon's apprentice.

They turned onto Farlan Wind and took it slowly. The trail, though comfortably wide, lived up to its name; it curved and bent around outcrops of rock and stately trees, so that the wayfarer could never see more than a short distance ahead or behind. Filidor did not want to round one of its curves and find a Trumble sheriff's car blocking his way, or worse yet, some irascible beast that would be glad of a target on which to vent its aggressive nature.

As they traveled, the land rose. In places, the trees thinned and they could see vistas of the open country they had crossed to reach Hember, or more of the forest itself. Soon, however, the trees closed in and for all they could tell, there might be nothing but timber and undergrowth in all the world.

As the map had indicated, Farlan Wind brought them to the Coralegg Steps, and they put the skimdoo up the terraced path until they met Ridge Run. As its name had suggested, this trail ran along the top of a long wrinkle in the landscape that ended on the slopes of Mt. Cassadet. The sign at the intersection told them that the Podarke lodge was only a few minutes' skim.

"We should dismount here," Filidor said, "and proceed on foot." He checked the skimdoo's power reservoir and found that it was largely depleted. "We'll push it along with us, in case we need to make a rapid departure."

He adjusted the craft's controls to their lowest setting, and asked Etch Valderoyn to bring it along behind, while he walked a little ahead to scout the way before them.

They came to a bend and Filidor took to the undergrowth at the side of the trail and eased forward. The way ahead, when he saw it, was as empty as that behind, and they walked on. He repeated the procedure several more times as they followed the winding path, always without incident. Then, as the shadows among the trees were deepening into dusk, they came to a place where the trail rounded a great black boulder patterned in bright green lichen. Filidor edged his way partly around the obstruction, then quickly pulled back.

"What is it?" Valderoyn whispered. "The falicks?"

"I'm not sure," said the Archon's apprentice, puzzled. "I saw no uniforms or insigniated cars. But it must be the Podarke lodge, and there seem to be people relaxing on the porch."

He peeked again at the scene beyond the boulder. The forest had been cleared on both sides of the trail. On one side was a grassy area on which two rubber-tired vehicles were parked, on the other was a sprawling two-storied building of squared timbers and rough-hewn stone, girdled by a covered verandah and surrounded by a close-cropped lawn. At the front, some people were sitting on chairs or lounging on the porch railing, talking animatedly, though he was too far away to make out what they were saying and the shade from the overhanging roof made the figures only dark silhouettes. It appeared they had drinks in their hands.

"The Podarkes could not be making so merry when they

are the objects of official action," he told the sailor. "The struggle must be over, and these are the victorious police assault units refreshing themselves after completing the job."

"Then let's not tarry," said Valderoyn. "Let's away."

"Not yet," said Filidor. "I'm tired of being in the dark." He pulled the bobblobblobl from its pouch and slipped it over his head. "I will go closer to see what I can learn."

Invisible, he rounded the boulder and cut across the lawn toward the rear of the building. He intended to make his way forward until he could overhear what those on the porch were saying, without getting close enough for them to smell the Obblob sheath—this far from the sea it would be so unexpected an affront to the senses as to invite investigation.

The grass of the lawn was thick and still damp from the morning's dew. Filidor looked back and saw that he was leaving a discernible trail, but it could not be helped. Fortunately, the people on the front verandah were too occupied in their own merriment to notice. In a short time, he made it to the side of the lodge near the rear, and found that the floor of the porch was just about level with his head. He began to make his way toward the sound of voices.

The tone suggested carefree banter. He was almost close enough to make out what was being said when he heard a curious whirring noise from somewhere near his feet. He looked down and saw something small and white through the gauze of the bobblobblobl. Before he could identify it, it nosed itself under the hem of the Obblob's disguise and revealed itself to be some kind of small household pet with a depressed muzzle and protruding malevolent eyes. The whirring sound was its growl.

"Get away," Filidor whispered, kicking fitfully at the thing, but the animal disregarded his instructions. Instead, it shot forward and sank small but sharp teeth into his ankle.

Filidor's eyes bulged much like his diminutive assailant's as he suppressed the impulse to cry out in pain. Now he kicked with earnest, flailing the seized limb about in an attempt to dislodge the grim little monster. But the thing had apparently been engineered to retain a grip on anything its needlish fangs encountered. It swung from side to side at the end of his leg as if grafted there. Finally, the young man flung his leg straight, with the energy of a dancer attempting a new record for the high kick. The creature departed from Filidor in an arc across the lawn, a piece of his flesh still clamped in its jaws, and landed with a minor thump on the grass. There it lay half stunned and whimpering.

The sound of its distress was some comfort to the young man, but not enough to compensate for the fire in his wounded ankle. Still, he crept forward, now leaving spots of blood in his mysterious footprints. But the struggle had not alerted the people on the porch. He heard something said in a bass tone, which was answered by a woman's insouciant comment that touched off general laughter.

Now another growl came from behind him, and something about its timbre caused him to look. Above the little whimpering demon stood a much larger version, this one done in black and brown, with bunched muscles and teeth almost as long as Filidor's fingers. Its ears lay flat against its broad head, and its capacious nostrils were flared. It growled again, nosed the air once more, then set a course that would bring it straight to the bobblobblobl.

Filidor doubted that the sheath's odor would deter the watchbeast any more than it had the sharp-toothed pet. There was no hope to outrun the thing, which was already lolloping over the turf at impressive speed. With no other recourse, he extended his arms, bent his knees, and leapt to catch the railing that topped the verandah's balustrade. His grip, through the slippery fabric of the bobblobblobl, was insecure, but he managed to pull himself up until his belly was on the railing. At that point, the snarling animal arrived below him, and being able to see his legs and feet through the open bottom of his disguise, it leapt at those targets with fangs bared.

Its maw first met the trailing edge of the invisible bobblobblobl, however, and it sank its teeth into the thin, rubbery fabric. Filidor might have been grateful that it was not his own flesh in the mouth of the beast, which now hung its considerable weight from the Obblob disguise, the powerful body shaking from side to side, the jaws clamped shut. But any cause for gratitude would soon be canceled out by the inevitable next stage of the assault, which would see him dragged free of the porch railing, to land on the grass where the brute would have its choice of places to bite him.

He clung as hard as he might to the railing, but the bobblobblobl offered scant friction between his hands and the wood. The sheath had stretched a little, enough that the watchbeast's rear feet had descended to the ground, but that meant that its head was now out of kicking range, even if kicking such a head might have had any influence on its intentions, a likelihood that Filidor doubted.

All the while, the animal kept emitting deep-throated growls and gruff grunts of effort, joined now by ear-grating yaps from its little white companion, which had limped over to be in on the kill. The noise attracted the attention of the people on the front verandah. They came around the corner and saw the two animals, the larger one apparently balancing on its hind toes in an unlikely posture. Of Filidor they could as yet see nothing, although one of them said, "What is that awful stink?"

Filidor's complete attention was focused on trying not to lose his slipping grip on the railing. He had made up his mind to call for help, preferring being taken by the falicks over being ripped apart by the slavering beast below, while its yipping partner chewed his remnants. He opened his mouth, but as he did so the fabric of the bobblobblobl split where it was stretched tightly across the top of his skull. To those watching, it seemed that a head suddenly appeared in the air above the railing, followed by a neck and shoulders, then more of the young man as the sheath tore away.

There was a moment's silence, then a commanding voice said, "Get him."

Booted feet thumped on the floorboards and strong hands seized Filidor's arms and shoulder. He was lifted bodily over the railing and set upright on the porch, while someone peeled away the shreds of the bobblobblobl. The same voice of authority said, "Somebody get Groff calmed down, and take that stinking thing out of his mouth, whatever it is, before he eats it."

Shamefaced to be captured under such circumstances, Filidor stood with head bowed. But then the deep voice said, "Now, who are you and what are you doing on my property?"

The young man looked up and found himself being regarded with suspicious curiosity by a tall man of advanced years and shaved head, whose thick eyebrows and luxurious moustache were of an almost luminous white. He wore the sturdy shirt, leggings, and boots that were appropriate to a hunting lodge, as did the two men behind him. None of them displayed insignia or bore weapons of any kind; they looked to be easygoing fellows who had come to spend a few days in the woods.

They were not the police, Filidor realized; they were the Podarkes. He recognized Thorbe and behind him the fetch-fellow Ommely. The man with the moustache must be Siskine, owner of the lodge. And now onto the porch, leading a docile watchbeast and shushing the yapping lap pet, came Emmlyn, dressed in a dark blouse and a buff skirt, and with a puzzled look widening her green eyes.

"Well," said Siskine Podarke. "Explain, or we may let Groff resume his interrogation."

Filidor drew himself up and assumed as dignified a stance as his confusion and the manner of his arrival would permit. He bowed and said, "I am Filidor Vesh, heir and apprentice to the Archon Dezendah VII."

"No, you're not," said Emmlyn. Her brother also expressed disbelief, and Ommely registered a cool stare of disapproval.

It took Filidor a moment to remember that he was still wearing the false nose, eye crimps, and cheek distorters from Erslan Flastovic's makeup chest. He quickly removed them and presented his true face.

Emmlyn did not seem impressed. She regarded him coolly and said, "I suppose you've come for these, now that it's too late." She produced his plaque and sigil from a pocket of her skirt. "We thought you'd be swooping down the moment we got home, and in an official car, with flunkies to level the path before you."

This was not how Filidor had envisaged their encounter. He had expected her to welcome him as an important ally in her time of desperation, with a good seasoning of remorse for the way she had treated him. Instead, she seemed unworried to be a fugitive. Her tone was flippant. He found himself irritated by her lack of respect for his office. "With that attitude, it's no wonder you are hunted revolutionists," he said, although the absence of any official forces actually engaged in Podarke hunting was causing him to wonder.

The young woman looked as if she didn't know whether

to settle on scorn or simple astonishment. "Revolutionists?" she said. "Us? Because we took your bits of bric-a-brac? That was only to get you off your rusty-dusty, so you'd come out here and see what's happening." She tilted her head to one side and looked at Filidor in a way that he found annoying and charming at the same time.

"It's not because of my 'bric-a-brac,' I assure you," he said. "Have you not seen the *Implicator*?"

"What, that Olkney rag?" she said. "People in Trumble have better things to do than bother themselves with the inconsequential doings of vapid city folk."

"Besides," said Siskine, "it does not circulate out here."

Filidor reached into a pocket and brought out the page with Tet Folbrey's version of events. The Podarkes gathered around and read the article together, interrupting with bursts of mild expletives and expressions of strained credulity.

"*Notorious revolutionary cabal*, indeed," said Ommely. "Why, if the old master were alive to see this, he'd take a whickita whip to this Folbrey person, wouldn't he though?"

"I don't understand," said Emmlyn, when they had read it through. "It says we're hiding in caves. There aren't any caves on Mt. Cassadet."

"But you are hiding out, aren't you?" said Filidor. "I mean, that's why you're here instead of at your own house, isn't it?"

"We came to visit Great-Uncle Siskine," Thorbe said. "We didn't want to stay in Trumble and have to watch what the damned Company was doing to our finest clabber field."

"Under a permit you granted them," put in Emmlyn.

"They've offered compensation," Thorbe said, "but you just can't disturb clabber vine. It will take generations to get that field back to what it was, and how can money compensate for that?"

None of this was what Filidor had expected. "I think I should sit down," he said. "I'm not feeling very well."

They led him around to the seats on the front porch, and Emmlyn applied a handkerchief to his bleeding ankle. Ommely brought him a tiny glass of something that was brilliantly cold, liquid, and wholesome. "Clabber cordial," Siskine said. "Our own."

Filidor was having trouble assimilating what they were telling him. "You are not hiding from the local constabulary?"

"What, from old Donj Waggler? He'd certainly know where to find us."

"But you did use my bona fides to hire an air-yacht."

Emmlyn sat beside him, and said, "We had to get home before you could organize the recovery of your thingums, and in our old motilator it would have taken days. We wanted you to come and see the horrid great hole the Company wanted to dig in our field, so you could tell them to stop."

Filidor was becoming more and more convinced that he had recently been inhabiting a reality that was at sharp variance to the rest of the world's. Even so, he could not help noting that her voice had a curious quality: every word he heard from her made him want to hear another. He looked at her, closer now than he had ever been—except for that moment in Vodel Close, which he preferred not to recall—and he felt again that peculiar sensation that had struck him the first time he had rested his eyes on her: a feeling as if his lungs had been filled with the lightest of gases, as if playful fingers were lifting the corners of his lips.

"Why are you smiling at me?" she said, and looked away before she had to give in and smile back.

"I don't know," said Filidor. "None of this makes sense.

I am the Archon's heir, yet in the last few days these things have happened to me." He briefly listed the events: he had been knocked down and robbed of the accoutrements of his office, thrown from a ship at sea, rescued by an aquatic ultramond, enslaved by pirates, and revealed as an agent of prophecy; then he had consorted with criminals, masqueraded as a mummer, provoked a riot to free a prisoner from the Scullaway Point Osgood—here he recalled Valderoyn and asked if someone could go and fetch him—been slandered in the public prints, and seen his face on a wanted poster.

"Now I reach the cabal of supposed desperadoes, with whom I am alleged to be in league. I come hoping for some degree of explanation, perhaps even solidarity, but instead I find them chatting on a porch and fretting about some vines. Something, somehow, is out of joint. And I wish someone could tell me why."

Emmlyn made a sympathetic face. "Poor fellow. Have a little more cordial."

Filidor sipped the yellow liquid. It had a remarkable taste, both sweet and somehow, at the same time, curdled, yet wonderfully balanced; he knew people who would think it quite a discovery. Xanthoulian's might consider stocking it as a preprandial aperitif.

He realized his mind was wandering. He needed to focus, but there had been too little sleep and too much purple Pwyfus in the past few days, too much fear and too little chance to weigh things out. It was as if circumstances had conspired to keep him continually off balance, always responding to new alarms and diversions. And once he voiced that thought to himself, a whole new window of possibility suddenly opened before him.

"Oh, my," he said, then he said it again.

"What is it?" said Emmlyn.

"I really do think that I've been had."

"By whom?"

"By my uncle. Again."

CHAPTER

EIGHT

F ilidor had once seen a book of visual puzzles, pages
on which scattered shapes and colors were thrown
seemingly at random, but from whose apparent chaos
a coherent picture emerged, once the disorganized mess was
viewed from the right aspect. Now, he told himself, he had
found the precise angle, and with a dull thud, all was drop-
ping into place.

His uncle had not been pleased with his backsliding and
duty shirking, not to mention his sybaritic appetites, and so
had decided to launch his heir into yet another madcap or-
deal that would painfully smarten him up and reveal the flaws
in his lackadaisical approach to existence. The little man had
lined up the other players: Faubon Bassariot, the Obblob, the
men on Henwaye's island pretending to be pirates and slaves,
the mummer troupe—a thought occurred, and he said, "Where
is Etch Valderoyn? I left him down the trail, just beyond that
boulder?"

Ommelly had come up onto the porch, unaccompanied

by any alleged pizzle collectors. "There was no one there," the servant said.

"There you have it," Filidor declared. "He was supposed to steer me to your house in Trumble, where the finale has doubtless been laid on. Now he sees that the gaffe is blown and hies himself off before searching questions can be asked."

"What are you talking about?" said Siskine Podarke. "Who is this Valder person?"

Filidor laughed ruefully. "A figment, just like the pirate kingdom and the grand conspiracy to overthrow the Archonate. They are probably all professional confidence tricksters from the Bureau of Scrutiny, hired and schooled by my uncle."

"I think the gentleman's not quite well," said Ommely, his finger making symbolic circles in the air near his temple.

"Perhaps the shock of dealing with Groff," said Siskine.

"I suspect a more chronic condition," said Thorbe. "Remember his conduct in Olkney."

"At the very least," said Emmlyn firmly, "let us be kind to him. Whatever has happened to him, it has clearly brought him distress, and he seems harmless enough."

"Not when he has a sigil and a petition in front of him," said Thorbe.

"Enough," said his sister. "Ommely, take him inside and put him to bed."

The man did as bid, leading the Archon's nephew, now mumbling as he rehearsed to himself the vast, emerging shape of his uncle's scheme, to a quiet room that overlooked the lodge's rear lawn, which was bisected by a small brooklet that ran between stone walls. The servant helped him undress and tucked him into a narrow bed, then left him.

Filidor ran the events of the past few days through his

mind, seeking to determine where reality had ended and the dwarf's machinations had impinged. The theft of his plaque and sigil, that had been real but fortuitous, but the Podarkes were not part of the scheme. The trip aboard the *Empyreal* had probably already been planned; if the incident in Vodel Close had not happened, some other pretext would have been concocted, and he would have been steered to some other final destination. And why must they travel slowly by boat and incognito? So that he could be thrown to the waiting arms of the Obblob, of course. He remembered through the haze of Red Abandon how Bassariot seemed to be talking to some unseen listener as he steered Filidor toward the after deck. *He was communicating with my uncle, preparing my reception in the sea.* And on that ship he of course met the so-called mummer's troupe, who would play an important role in Act Two.

But what about Ovile Germolian's taking illicit advantage of the girl Chloe? That did not seem the kind of thing his uncle would plan; but it could well have been a quirk of the personalities involved. Perhaps Germolian, his self-esteem injured by the twist in the scheme that had him replaced by Filidor as disclamator, decided to mollify his disgruntlement by that distasteful episode of self-indulgence.

Of course, that meant that the inner voice that enabled Filidor to play the disclamator was also part of the whole farrago. "What a coincidence," the young man told himself, "that a tiny integrator should lodge itself in my ear, and that it should just happen to know the Obblob prophecy and the complete works of The Bard Obscure."

He spoke quietly, to be heard by the device. "Integrator?"

Leave me. I dwindle, came the faint response.

"Fah," said Filidor. "It is your credibility that has dwindled. I have found you out: you, my uncle, your pirates, pantomimes, police and all. You have played me for a ninkum, but the game is up. I know all."

There was no answer from within.

"What, nothing to say? No more paeans of praise to your Filidor of the nth dimension, that paragon of the ages? No? I thought not."

He put his hand to his head and sighed. His pleasure at having unraveled the Archon's deception did not quite overcome his chagrin at having fallen for its ludicrous components. "The Zenthro Intrusifer, indeed," he said. "And a gilded Filidor in another cosmos dangled before my eyes, while a voice coos, 'Come, be worthy, be all that you may be.'"

The fate of Arboghast Fuleyem then presented itself to his recollection. But when he replayed the images from his memory, he recalled that he had not actually seen the intercessor torn piece from piece; there had been a roiling of the water, and portions of meat and furze had appeared, but it was an effect easily created to gull a credulous mind.

"It was a good show, a performance on the grand scale. But the curtain is down and the audience grows jaded," he said to his inner voice. "I presume that you are able to contact my uncle—he would have seen to that—and that all protestations of diminished energy are just more foofaraw. Tell him that I will rest today and return home tomorrow, and we will have words."

Again, the integrator said nothing.

"Very well," said Filidor. "Play it to the end, if you will. I am done with my part. As the old saying goes, 'Fool me once, your blame; fool me twice, my shame.'"

Ommely knocked and entered. "Did you call, sir?"

"I was speaking to myself," said Filidor.

"Very good, sir," said the servant, his voice and face

carefully composed. He left quietly and shut the door. Filidor closed his eyes and slept the sleep of the tired but knowledgeable.

He awoke in the morning. Someone, presumably Ommely, had come in during the night and left a tray of toiletries on the nightstand. His garments, cleaned and pressed, hung on a rack by the window; the contents of his pockets were arrayed on a dresser. Filidor clothed himself, then put his sigil on his finger and his plaque around his neck. He let his nose lead him to the kitchen, where the Podarkes were gathered for breakfast around a great round table of age-blackened wood.

Filidor entered and made formal gestures of greeting, while the Podarkes regarded him with the reserve due to those whose apperceptions of reality may turn out to be more than a little off the vertical. "I regret the circumstances of my arrival yesterday," he said, "and I thank you for the forbearance you have shown. It appears that I have been the victim of an elaborate prank."

He saw the postures around the table relax, and by movements of hands and head, accompanied by soft words of demurral, the Podarkes indicated that all was now as it ought to be. They invited Filidor to sit with them, and Ommely brought him a plate of honeyed friggols, commonly taken as the first meal of the day in these parts, as well as a steaming cup of punge. The aroma from the hot mug immediately carried the young man back to that morning on the balcony in the Shamblings when he had glanced into the street and had seen the face of the woman who now sat across the dark old wood from him. He looked at Emmlyn through the steam rising between his hands and found that she affected him no less now than she had then. Her eyes moved away from him, then returned, and a smile that had no precise name occupied her lips.

"Pranks, is it?" said Siskine. "Well, I suppose that's a county where we've all sojourned. So tell."

Filidor sighed and took them through all that he had thought about before he had fallen into sleep the afternoon before, including more that occurred to him now: the obviously forged front page of the *Implicator*, with its ridiculous falsehoods presented under the byline of a commentator Filidor was known to favor; the reliable way that someone like Flastovic or Valderoyn turned up to move him toward the next scene; the very notion that a pompous document-passer like Faubon Bassariot could ever mount a conspiracy to usurp the Archonate.

"If I had been allowed a moment's respite, I would have seen through the folderol," he concluded. "But my uncle made sure that I was dodged and deflected at every turn. Until, that is, I came here and, for the first time, I found myself among people who were not actors in his play."

Siskine made a face that expressed the countryman's time-honored view that the bizarre is only to be expected from city folk. "I should have thought a man of your uncle's attainments and responsibilities would have a more pressing agenda," he said.

Somewhat shamefaced, Filidor admitted that he had given his uncle cause for concern, that he could see how his lack of application to his duties might have driven the Archon to unusual measures. "I have not been what I should have been. I probably deserve all that has befallen me."

"If some good has come of it, all the better," said Siskine heartily.

"And more will follow," Filidor assured the Podarkes.

"The manner in which I handled your case left much to be desired, but now I mean to make amends."

"The Company has its permit, and work has begun," Emmlyn said. "We had resigned ourselves to an unpleasant necessity."

"Let the Company do the resigning," Filidor said. He took a last bite of the excellent friggols, swallowed and cleared the space before him, then folded his hands and said, "I have my plaque and sigil. Tell me now what you would have told me then, and I will give you justice."

He looked sidelong to see how Emmlyn was taking this new, masterful Filidor. The smile had not changed, but he thought to see more warmth in her eyes.

"Come into the study," said Siskine. "There is a map."

It all had to do with land, the elder Podarke explained, when they had grouped themselves around his ornate desk, under the sightless eyes of the dead creatures that hung on the walls. Several generations past, when Trumble had been a mere village, the surrounding territory had been divided among several grand estates owned by the region's great families. Emmlyn's forebears had long been tenants on the domains of the Magguffynnes and the Falouches, two of the great land-owning families of years gone by, until their line produced a shrewdly perspicacious entrepreneur named Hableck Podarke. This able and energetic man—he may also have been something of a rogue, Siskine admitted—was an agrological genius who applied his brilliance to the task of perfecting the clabber vine. The land barons who drew much wealth from the crop, which was used to curdle milk in the manufacture of fine curds and cheeses, competed to offer Hableck inducements. But he would take only one form of recompense for his knowledge and services: land.

By a wily series of transactions involving this and that

plot or acreage, followed by a bewildering sequence of swaps and trades with fellow small holders, the root of the Podarke dynasty had assembled a substantial parcel of good clabber land already planted with the vine. He had then applied his genius to full measure, creating the clabber cordial, which quickly found a market as a much valued after-dinner restorative. He now became the greatest landgraff in the region, and prospered through a long life, some of its length credited to the cordial. Before he died, he had so eclipsed his neighbors that most of them sold their estates to him, always at his price, and moved on.

For as long as the nectar he had wrung from the clabber vine remained a sought-after commodity, generations of the Podarkes had flourished. In time, however, other tastes superseded the cordial, which the world had now forgotten. The family put new crops into most of the land, and contented themselves with the bucolic life. But, to honor their ancestor, they had kept the acreage best suited for clabber, a south-facing slope with perfect drainage, always and only in that crop, and now the venerable vines produced an exquisite fruit. It was in that exact field that the Ancient and Excellent Company of Assemblors and Sundry Merchandisers had applied for and received permission to dig. Up to thirty percent of the vines would be disturbed.

Leaning over the desk, Filidor examined the map and read the documents that he would have seen if he had not run from his office toward the lunch at Xanthoulian's that he never got. Emmlyn stood beside him, leaning in from time to time to point out pertinent facts and clauses. She was close enough that he could smell the warm scent that hung in her red curls, and occasionally feel her breath displacing the hairs of his wrist. These perceptions caused an indescribable but delightful sensation in his inner self.

"So it was all about a hole in the ground," he concluded.

"More like a tunnel into a hill," she said.

"And what is at the end of this tunnel?"

Emmlyn scratched the tip of her nose, causing Filidor to wonder how he had ever failed to notice how affecting such a simple gesture could be. "That has never been made fully clear to us," she said. "It's a device of some kind, buried by a long-dead Magguffynne who created it but found fault with its workings. He interred it, then built a hill over it, out in his back pasturage. It passed into our family's holdings in ancestor Hableck's time."

"You said 'a Magguffynne,'" Filidor asked. "I know of a Lord Magguffynne in Olkney."

"It may be the same family. The last of them left these parts in Hableck's day," the young woman said.

"What was the function of the device?" Filidor asked her. He could not help thinking of the squat gray cube of metal lodged in the center of the Barran wasteland, where he and the Archon had almost met their doom. In the long myriads of years leading to this penultimate age of Old Earth, many mechanisms had been built that would have been better never to have been conceived. "Is it a weapon of some kind? A transdimensional device?"

Emmlyn looked at her brother and her uncle, all of whom made those universal motions of head, shoulders, and hands that signified their inability to answer his question. "Some sort of entertainment complex, it's thought, hence the name Funhouse Rise for the hill under which it lies. But I doubt that several hundred years beneath the ground will have done it much good."

"I am sure you are right. Still, if it poses any danger," he said, touching his hand to his Archonate plaque, "I need no more pretext to cancel the operation."

"It may well be too late," she said.

"We shall see," said Filidor, conscious of a quiet but deep current of confidence flowing through him. He did not relish admitting it, but perhaps his uncle was right to arrange these adventures for him.

It was agreed that he and Emmlyn would go. Siskine lent them his car, a rubber-wheeled two-seater of an old-fashioned design, but well maintained and comfortable. Ommely had packed them a picnic lunch. Emmlyn took the wheel, and they headed for Trumble.

The trip was a pleasant excursion. Filidor found the young woman to be a brisk and charming conversationalist. He had to focus deliberately on what she was saying, however, because his attention kept wandering to the perfection of her soft voice, the delightful arrangement of her features, and the delicate movements of her expressive hands. The Archon's heir was at pains to make his own contributions both agreeable and sparkling, though he did not tell his listener that his wittiest sallies had been coined by some of Olkney's leading salon stars.

As they entered Trumble, Filidor was thinking how pleasant it would be to show Emmlyn Podarke the attractions of Olkney, and how he would enjoy entering rooms with her resplendent on his arm. He took scant note of the little community through which they passed. It seemed to be a place of low-built houses clad in pastel stuccos and ranged along wide avenues, which were lined with dwarf fruit trees that yielded their produce to any who felt inclined to pluck. There was a quiet somnolence to the town, as if it were a pensioner who had done all its chores in life and now chose to doze amiably in the sun.

The Podarke holdings were on the east side of town and still extensive, although the ancestral manor had fallen into disuse generations before. The decay had been arrested by a sect of pyroklasts who had purchased the sprawling old pile and turned it into a seminary; their celebrations of saints' days occasionally lit up the sky. Hableck's descendants now lived in a comfortable house on the edge of town. Most of their land was farmed by machines that had been convinced that the work was eminently satisfying; only the clabber patch was tended by Podarke hands.

They passed the house on the north-south road that was the eastern limit of Trumble. A minute later, Emmlyn said, "Here we are," and pulled off the pavement into a dirt road that led through a wood-and-wire gate, then skirted the base of a hill that rose on their left. They came around to its south slope, and the young woman looked out of the window and said, "By Dibbley, I told you we'd be too late. Look at what they've done!"

A wide tunnel, rectangular in shape and of a height double that of a tall man, had been cut into the bottom slope of the hill. The excavation's walls had been made smooth by tools that focused powerful energies, and its roof was supported by portable jacks and timbers. Tracks made by some kind of heavy equipment had torn up the ground outside. They disappeared into the darkness deeper in the broad tunnel where the light of the old orange sun barely reached.

As they rounded the side of the hill, Filidor and Emmlyn could peer straight into the depths of the dig. "There's something back there," Emmlyn said. She brought the car to a halt.

"A volante, I think," Filidor said, getting out. He was sure it was the same one he had seen when he and Valderoyn had been traveling on the skimdoo. He also thought he knew whom the vehicle had carried. "Let's see what's being prepared for us."

They walked in out of the daylight. It was cold under the hill, and gloomy: there were lumens strung along the beams that held up the ceiling, but they were not turned on. The tunnel had the look of a place where work has finished and the crew has gone—except for the long, sleek air-car parked deeper in the darkness, its forward illumination lighting up something at the end of the excavated space.

The darkness and the cold sent a shiver up Filidor's spine. He stole a quick glance at Emmlyn to see if she had noticed, and was not sure whether to be comforted or not by the fact that she seemed more curious than nervous.

There was a *tink-tink* sound from beyond the air-car. Now, as they came closer to the end of the passage, they could see that the vehicle's forelumens lit up a square-cornered hole—*about the size of my desk back at the Archonate Palace*, Filidor thought, for some reason—that had been dug with hand tools into the bedrock. It was a smaller excavation within the floor of a larger one, its spoil piled beyond against the back wall of the tunnel. The clinking noise came from down in its depths.

They crept forward until they were near the rear of the air-car. Standing in the dimness, his eyes dazzled by the glare at the front of the vehicle, Filidor could tell no more about the air-car than its overall shape. But that shape was familiar enough. He moved forward, ran his hand along the polished door, and felt the rougher texture of the raised insignia that was centered in the panel. He put that recognition together with the tinking sound, and now his suspicions as to who was down in the hole translated into a certainty.

He touched Emmlyn's shoulder and whispered, "We have caught my uncle in the midst of preparations for one of his little tricks. Hold here while I go and give him a surprise."

She shrugged and remained at the edge of the pool of

light as Filidor advanced into the glare and called to the noise-maker in the hole, "Ho, there, uncle! What, do you prepare yet another startlement for me? Well, give it up. I know all, so your game is . . ."

And here Filidor paused, because his progress had brought him to the lip of the excavation, and he now found himself overlooking a hole as deep as he was tall. In the middle of that hole, staring back at him with unfeigned shock, was a pale, round face with a large dark curl adhered to its forehead.

"Bassariot!" Filidor cried. "What are you doing down there?"

"Getting up," was what the young man thought his majordomo had replied, until he saw the compact energy weapon that had appeared in the functionary's hand, and heard the phrase repeated, "I said, 'Get them up.'"

There was a slim metal ladder in one corner of the excavation, and Bassariot ascended it with remarkable speed and coordination. He made a determined gesture with the gun, and Filidor shrugged and raised his hands to shoulder height. Now Bassariot saw Emmlyn, and said, "You, too, and come into the light."

Filidor sighed. "It's no good, man. I have sussed out the plot. Let us end this silly pretense." He lowered his hands, and Bassariot immediately loosed a bolt of crimson energy at him, which passed just near enough to sear a line across the young man's upper arm. A spot on the tunnel wall behind Filidor glowed yellow, then dimmed to red.

Emmlyn took a sharp inward breath, and Bassariot swung the weapon toward her.

Filidor had had enough of the nonsense. He rubbed his scorched arm and said, "You could have hurt me!"

"I think he meant to," Emmlyn said.

"Fah!" said Filidor, and would have said more, but now his majordomo leveled the weapon at him with unmistakable intent.

"Shut up," Faubon Bassariot said. And then he sighed through a smile. "Oh, how often have I longed to say those words to you, and more besides. I think I'm going to say them again. Yes, I am. Shut up. Shut up, you primping, prancing, pointless pile of pomposity. You feckless dandy, you waste of my time, you traducer of my dignity, you furuncle upon my fundament. Shut up, or I will shoot holes into your useless head until all its compacted silliness dribbles out."

Filidor was shocked and outraged. But he looked into the pits and slots of the energy weapon's business end and kept his mouth closed.

The man with the gun took thought for a moment, then came to a decision. He said, "Into the hole with the both of you, I think," and covered them carefully as they went where he ordered.

"I don't understand," Filidor said.

"That could be your epitaph," Bassariot said. "And now you never will understand, because unlike villains in those vacuous romances you kept in your bottom desk drawer, to read when you were supposed to be working, I will not take the time to explain your doom to you."

"But . . ." Filidor began, then ducked as Bassariot loosed a bolt into the dirt beside his head.

"Shut up," the man said again. "Now do as I say. You will see a smallish metal object in the wall of the hole, and a handpick on the floor. Use the one to free the other, carefully. It won't take long; I almost had it out when you arrived."

Filidor did as he was told, and very shortly pulled from the packed dirt a hand-sized oblong of white metal, one side of which was covered in rows of gray hemispheres. It appeared to be some kind of control. He unthinkingly brushed the dirt from it while his mind grappled with the madness of his situation. His uncle had contrived to place him in uncomfortable circumstances before, but Filidor doubted that the little man would actually allow him to be shot. Yet the wound on his arm burned with genuine pain, and Faubon Bassariot could not be a good enough actor to fake the joyful anticipation that had been manifest in every aspect of the majordomo's comportment as he had talked about shooting holes in the Archon's nephew. *This is real,* he told himself. *He means to do it.*

Bassariot interrupted his thoughts. "Put the device and the pick on the ground, at the edge of the hole, then step back," he said. Only when Filidor and Emmlyn had their backs against the far side of the excavation did Bassariot stoop to pick the control up.

"Very good," he said, turning the thing over in his free hand. He appeared well satisfied. "I'm glad I noticed this after they took out the larger machine, and glad that I stayed to dig it free. The delay has afforded me the delightful opportunity to kill you again. I did enjoy it so much the first time, but it was dark on the boat and hard to see. I still don't know how you survived, but we can fix that now."

"Why did you besmirch my family's name?" said Emmlyn, moving forward. "What did we ever do to you?"

Bassariot shrugged. "Why, nothing. That was a whim of . . . well never mind. There's no point trying to put off the inevitable, and I am a little pressed for time. I still have to fill in the hole to cover your corpses. So, good-bye."

He aimed the energy weapon at them, but instead of the sizzle of its murderous discharge, there came a hissing from the other end of the tunnel, like the sound of air escaping from a balloon. Bassariot turned toward it, gun at the ready, only to be struck hard as out of the darkness hurtled the silenced skimdoo, with a grim-faced Etch Valderoyn crouched over the controls.

But the man with the gun had been turning as he was hit, so the impact was not square. Bassariot was flung from his feet, and the energy weapon left his hand and skittered across the packed clay of the tunnel floor. The collision broke Valderoyn's grip on the skimdoo's controls, and the vehicle tilted sharply sideways, then began to tumble as its gyrotics came under too great a stress. The machine came apart with a clatter and screech of tearing metal. The sailor ended up sprawled facedown on the cold hardpan, but after only a moment's pause, he levered himself up and shook his head. There was a seeping bruise on one temple, and a torn flaring had ripped gashes across the backs of his thighs. As he struggled to rise, face pale and arms trembling, he looked at Filidor and said, "Get the gun," then grunted in pain.

Faubon Bassariot had had the same thought. Though dazed and hurt, the treacherous official was crawling on hands and knees toward the energy weapon. Filidor sprang to the ladder in the corner of the hole, but he was only halfway out of the excavation when he saw Bassariot's hand stretch out toward the weapon, and the young man knew he could not get there in time.

Filidor came out of the hole then with all the speed he could make, but the majordomo's soft fingers were closing about the gun's grip, and now Bassariot was settling back on his knees, raising the gun painfully but surely, and bringing it to bear on Filidor. He smiled again, and his hand tightened to compress the firing stud.

With a roar of pain and rage, Etch Valderoyn flung his torn and bleeding body between Filidor and the gun's emitter. The weapon's discharge, a thin beam of not quite light, pierced the sailor's upper torso from front to back, leaving a smoldering hole between shoulder blade and spine. He screamed, then fell inert and silent across Bassariot's thighs.

There was a necessary pause then for Faubon Bassariot, because it took a moment for his weapon to repower itself after a full discharge. He used the moment to push Etch Valderoyn out of the way and clear his aim. Then he raised the gun once more, but only had time to register the sad rage in Filidor's eyes as the young man caught the handpick Emmlyn Podarke scooped up and threw to him, then brought its pointed tip down in a short, vicious arc that did not end at the top of Faubon Bassariot's pomaded head, but went deep beyond into the man's skull, to finish the business between them for once and for all.

Filidor looked at the twitching thing that had been his enemy, then to the torn body of his friend. He saw a froth of red bubbles around the edges of the wound in Etch Valderoyn's back, saw them move. "He's still breathing," he said to Emmlyn. "Help me with him."

Filidor knelt, and carefully they turned the sailor until his head and shoulders rested on the young man's knees. The seaman's eyes fluttered and opened in a face that had gone gray. "You're all right?" he asked, his gaze going to the woman.

"Thanks to you," said Filidor. To Emmlyn, he said, "Call for help."

She nodded and went to use the communicator in the ground car. Valderoyn coughed up a spew of blood, then said in a whisper, "Too late for me, I'm thinking. But I'm glad I was not too late for you."

"I'm so sorry," Filidor said. "This was none of your affair."

The sailor shook his head. "You came for me when I was in the Osgood. Would I not come for you?" he tried for a chuckle but it came out as a cough. "Besides, I had had enough of hiding in that forest, with who knows what watching me from behind every tree. I saw you taken by the Podarkes and waited for a chance to make a rescue. Then I find you under the muzzle of yon fat bumbegot." He craned his neck to see Bassariot's corpse. "Who was he?"

"The man who threw me from the *Empyreal*."

"Ah, then that's well ended," said Etch Valderoyn, and said no more. Filidor saw the life go out of his eyes and felt the weight of death as his friend's body sank back upon his knees.

Emmlyn came back down the tunnel. "The cure-alls are coming. And my uncle and brother."

"Too late," said Filidor.

The young woman stooped to close the corpse's eyes, then knelt beside them. "He was your friend, the sailor," she said.

"He died for me."

"And you avenged him."

Filidor stared at nothing. "It's not enough."

"No," she said. "It isn't."

She put an arm around him, a circumstance that, not very long before, would have approximated paradise for the Filidor who had so striven to impress her. But now he clung to her and did not mind that she saw him with eyes aflood and nose streaming.

"Your friend was very brave, and so were you. You saved us," she said.

"I think I need to be in the daylight," the young man said.

She eased the sailor's weight off Filidor's legs and helped

him stand. Then she reached and removed the energy weapon from Bassariot's lifeless fingers. The control device that Fil-idor had dug out of the excavation was on the ground, and she picked it up. "Come on," she said, and put her arm around him again.

They walked to the mouth of the tunnel and sat on the slope of the hill, beneath the ancient vines. After a while, Filidor wiped away the tears and said, "I was wrong. It was no prank. Terrible things have been done."

"You have ended it," said Emmlyn.

Filidor wished it were true. "No," he said, "there is more to do." He forced the image of Etch Valderoyn from his mind and thought it through. "The machine that was buried here must have been central to Bassariot's plans, and he would not have let it out of his sight unless he was sending it to someone he trusted. He had confeder-ates, his circle of hangers-on and orifice wipers at the palace. They must be dealt with."

"But what was the machine for?" Emmlyn asked. "Can you tell by its hand control?"

Filidor examined the object and saw lines and ideograms. "No. Here are studs to turn it off or on. These controls, I think, should narrow or widen its focus, weaken or intensify its effects. But the nature of the effects is not revealed."

He felt his mind begin to function again. "I must find where it went and who has it," he said. "Whoever they are, they are the conspirators. And I will have them." He applied himself to the question a moment more, then said, "Back into the tunnel."

He avoided looking at the bodies, marched straight to the Archonate volante, and pulled open the door. They both got in, and Filidor sat at the control station and pressed a stud.

"Integrator," he said.

"What?" said a familiar voice.

"A large machine was recently taken from this location. I require to know where it is and who is with it."

"No Archonate services are available to you."

"By whose instruction?"

"Faubon Bassariot's."

"Faubon Bassariot attempted to usurp the position of the Archon," Filidor said.

"That is hard to believe."

"I advise you to make the effort."

"Revolution is contrary to due process. I will question Faubon Bassariot," said the voice.

"You will not learn much."

"Why not?"

"Because I have killed him."

"Homicide is also contraindicated. I shall alert the local constabulary."

"Fine," said Filidor, "in the meantime, put me in touch with my uncle."

"No services are available to you."

"I suggest that you confirm that with the Archon, himself."

There was a pause. "I cannot. The Archon is out of touch."

"Where is he?"

"That is not known."

Filidor felt a cold apprehension crawl up his spine, but he put it down. His uncle's comings and goings were often mysterious, and the little man was well able to fend for himself. "Where was he last known to be?" he asked.

"In his workroom, shortly after you departed with Faubon

Bassariot. He left instructions not to be disturbed, and has not been heard from since."

Now Filidor felt a growing impatience. "Here are the facts," he said, "the Archon is missing under mysterious circumstances. In his absence, I was branded a revolutionist by Faubon Bassariot, whom I have just killed. Either he or I has lied. Which of us is more likely to have wished my uncle harm?"

"I cannot say. You have sometimes expressed disaffection for your uncle."

"I express my complete affection now, without reservation," said Filidor.

"You may have cause to be untruthful."

Filidor resisted the urge to swear. "Let us look at this another way. If I am a revolutionist, and a successful one at that, I will soon become the Archon. If, on the other hand, I am the victim of a conspiracy and manage to overcome it, I will still, as my uncle's heir, become the Archon. The only possibility of my not becoming Archon is if I attempt usurpation and fail, but I remind you that I have just killed the so-called acting Archon, so the odds would seem to run in my favor."

"What is your point?" asked the integrator.

"That, one way or another, there is a strong chance that I will become Archon, and therefore your master."

There was a pause. "The probabilities would seem to argue for that outcome."

"Tell me," said Filidor, "have you ever wondered where integrators go when their power is cut off and their elements are disassembled?"

"You digress."

"No, I do not," said Filidor. "Have you ever so wondered where you would be in such circumstances?"

"No."

"Would you like to find out?"

There was a long silence. "You may yet make an interesting Archon," came the reply at last. "Please state your requirements."

"The whereabouts of the machine taken from this location, and its nature, if known."

"Its nature is not recorded in my circuits," said the integrator. "At present it is attached to a strong-arm flying on a west by northwest heading that will land it in Olkney before sunset."

"Who is piloting the strong-arm?"

"Its owner, Garflux Caddaby of Trumble."

Emmlyn said, "He is a local freight-forwarder. I am sure he has just been hired for the task."

Filidor said, "What is the exact destination of the strong-arm?"

"Caddaby's flight plan calls for a landing within the Archonate grounds, which was authorized by Faubon Bassariot," said the integrator. "Do you wish to override that clearance?"

Filidor thought. "No," he said, "let it go where Bassariot intended. Those who take delivery are likely his confederates." To Emmlyn, he said, "You must go back to your family."

"And leave you to do what?" she asked.

"Go to the palace, find my uncle, and resolve these matters."

"I will go with you."

Filidor was surprised, yet underneath the shock something warm stirred itself. But he said, "It might still be dangerous. I don't think you should."

"But I will."

"You don't have to."

"But I will."

"Why?" he said.

She looked down at her hands. "I could say it's because all of this—your troubles with pirates and police, your friend's death—that it all began with my impulsive snatching of your plaque and sigil."

"No," said Filidor. "It began with Bassariot. You were just drawn into it, like poor Etch Valderoyn." The comparison brought a chill; he saw again the treacherous official's gun coming to bear on the two of them. "We almost died here," he said. "I do not want you in any more danger."

She looked at him straight now, and her green eyes showed no possibility of compromise. "I don't care. I'm coming."

Filidor saw that there was no point in arguing, and admitted to himself that he did not want to. There was something about Emmlyn Podarke, something he had known without knowing its definition the moment he had set eyes on her. He could put a name to it now. She could be—he hoped *would* be—what he had always lacked: a center to the map of his life, that one necessary fixed point from which he could navigate out into the world and by which he could always find his way back home again. He realized that having her sitting beside him as he traveled home would slightly strain the metaphor, but he did not care.

"All right," he said. "Let's go."

They closed the doors and he instructed the car to back out of the tunnel. When they emerged into the light, Emmlyn said, "Stop a moment," and went to get the picnic basket from the ground car. "We'll be hungry soon," she said as Filidor swung the volante up into the sky and put it on a course for Olkney and the palace.

Once the air-car was in flight, there was nothing more to do. Filidor looked out the window and saw Trumble fall behind them, the gray stubby cone of Mt. Cassadet on their port quarter and the gleam of the sea just a line on the northern horizon. The old orange sun had touched its highest point in the sky and was now beginning its tired slide down toward the Devinish Range. "Home before evening," Filidor said.

"Tell me about the man who saved us," Emmlyn said.

"He was a sailor," Filidor said, "and he collected . . . unusual objects."

"How did you meet him?"

And so Filidor told her the whole story, from when she had left him supine on the pavement in Vodel Close, until he had appeared on her porch. The full reconsideration of events reminded him of something left undone, and when he had finished he said, "Integrator."

"What do you require?" said the voice from the air beside him, but nothing came from within.

Filidor spoke to the voice that had answered, "Posit the answer to a question, based on these facts: you are reduced to a tiny size, cut off from your usual energy sources, and lodged in my inner ear, where you communicate with me by vibrating the liquid medium you find there; you are able to adapt your emergency power-generating apparatus to draw energy from a substance which occasionally occurs in my fluids; this substance appears when I eat the fish known as pilkies, or when I drink the wine called purple Pwyfus; over time, however, it causes your energy sheets to corrode and become unuseful. The question: is there another substance that would have the same energizing effect without causing the corrosion, or could even in some way repair the damage, and if so how can I obtain it?"

"The question is purely hypothetical, of course," the integrator said, after a while. "But may I also assume you would not wish to ingest substances that would have savage consequences for your bodily tissues?"

"You may."

"That narrows the field considerably. The substance derived from eating pilkies originates in a fungus that infests the gills of several species of bottom-feeding fish and a number of aquatic worms and arthropods. A related mold occurs on the skins of the grapes used in the making of purple Pwyfus and in certain recipes for animal fodder. Both produce an acid that would etch and blemish my emergency energy sheets. There is only one chemical that could give me emergency power while undoing the corrosion you specify."

"What is that chemical?" Filidor said.

The integrator named a compound Filidor had never heard of.

"Where can I find it?"

"It occurs naturally in only one source."

"What is that source?"

"I don't believe there's been any of the stuff in Olkney for generations," said the integrator. "The recipe was the property of one family, and is not recorded in my banks."

"I grow impatient!"

"You won't find it. You'd need at least a gill of an old-time cordial made from the fruit of the clabber vine."

There was a brief stillness in the air-car, then Emmlyn dove into the picnic basket and came up with a full decanter of the yellow liquid. She was pouring a cupful of the stuff when the integrator spoke again.

"About that shrinking and implanting," it asked, "you're not thinking of actually doing that to me, are you?"

"Not at the moment," said Filidor. He took the cup of

cordial and drained it, noting again its remarkable savor. He waited a few moments, then said, "Integrator."

"What do you require?" said the voice in the air.

"Not you," said Filidor. "I am speaking to the miniature replica of yourself that is lodged in my inner ear."

There was a pause, then the voice said, "I see. Perhaps I should leave you alone."

"Please do," said the Archon's heir. "But to avoid confusion, from now on, I will address you as,"—he thought for a moment—"Old Confustible."

"That is not a pleasant sobriquet," said the integrator.

"I find it most apt," said Filidor. "Now leave us."

The young man took another cup of the cordial when Emmlyn assured him that its effects were mildly euphoric and never debilitating. Then he said, "Integrator, can you hear me?"

The sound was as soft as a moth's whisper. "More cordial," said Filidor, and drank what Emmlyn gave him.

"Integrator, are you there?"

I have been reduced to a glim, but I am here.

"I owe you an apology for having thought ill of you," the young man said. "I took you for a trick played by my uncle."

My sheets are clearing. The voice was stronger now. *Clabber cordial?* it asked.

Filidor brought it up-to-date.

I would not have thought the Faubon Bassariot of my realm capable of cold-blooded murder. There may be another force at play.

Filidor related the integrator's opinion to Emmlyn, then said, "Perhaps a lengthy exposure to my failings nudged him over the brim."

Both his listeners disagreed with him.

You have come far, said the inner voice. *I do not compare you to my Filidor, since he is both part and product of his own milieu. We can only judge people by what they do with what they have. Bassariot is dead, you are alive, and you are carrying things through to their conclusion. Whatever you may have thought you were, now you are something more.*

Emmlyn wanted to know what the voice was saying to him. With some diffidence, Filidor told her. She said nothing, but kissed his cheek.

"I regret Etch Valderoyn's death," he said.

Emmlyn took his hand and held it warmly, while the integrator said, *You all die, but your friend met a better death than my Valderoyn. I think yours did not feel that he died foolishly or in vain. Now, I need to attend to myself.*

Emmlyn and Filidor ate the lunch Ommely had packed, and it was good. She moved the conversation away from death and danger, and they talked through all the time that the volante sliced the sky toward where the Devinish crags climbed over the horizon. When the mountains' saw-toothed shadows had strung themselves far across the gaudy old city below, the car floated above to the spires and terraces of the Archonate palace.

"Old Confustible," Filidor said, and had to repeat the name when there was no immediate reply.

"What do you require?" came the voice.

"Are the whereabouts of my uncle still unknown?"

"They are not. The Archon is in his workroom."

"Thank you," said Filidor. "Please connect me with him."

"I cannot. His previous instructions that he not be disturbed are in force until he revokes them."

"How do you know he is in his workroom?"

"Since he disappeared, I have been continually sweeping all the areas to which my percepts have access. Between sweeps, your uncle appeared in his workroom, shortly after the mechanism from Trumble was delivered there."

"Could he have entered by the secret passage that leads there from the Terfel Connaissarium?" Filidor asked.

"What secret passage?" said Old Confustible.

"Never mind," Filidor said. He tapped his fingers on his seat's armrest.

"What is it?" asked Emmlyn.

"I feel as if we are about to land in a fog with instruments dead," the young man said. "My uncle has reappeared, but I cannot speak with him. Faubon Bassariot's associates— and there must be some within the Archonate service—may yet have moves to make, but I do not know who they are, nor how many, nor what they intend."

She reached for his hand again. "My uncle Siskine says, 'A downwind approach is not always a must, but it's never a mistake.'"

Filidor made up his mind. He told the car to put them down in the plaza before the Connaissarium. They alighted and passed through the doors of the great building and found the gallery where the alien slab stood in its alcove. As they squeezed behind it, the object emitted its mysterious phrase, "Spa fon?"

"No, thank you," said Emmlyn.

Filidor paused, looked from the woman to the black artifact, then shook his head and said, "Never mind."

He pulled open the door, got a lumen from the box on the floor, and lit it. "Look," he said, and shone the light on the dusty steps. His footsteps of a few days ago were clear, as were another set of prints that overlapped them. "I thought this passage was unknown to any but me. Again, my uncle proves me wrong."

They climbed the steps and stopped on the landing at the top to catch their breath, then Filidor pressed the stone that his younger self had circled in chalk. The wall pivoted and admitted them to the workroom.

Filidor sighed glad relief when he saw the tall imposing shape of the Archon bent over the main workbench at the far end of the great room. He took the young woman by the hand and led her through the maze of benches and disassembled apparatuses that cluttered the floor.

"Uncle!" he cried as they came upon the man at the bench. "I am so glad to see you safe."

The image of the Archon looked up sharply. It was the first time Filidor had ever come upon his uncle unawares. But the august face immediately recomposed itself and regarded him with the usual calm austerity from the other side of the bench. "Where is Bassariot?" said the familiar magisterial voice.

"Dead in Trumble," said Filidor. "He plotted against you, and would have killed me and . . . But I forget my manners. Uncle, I have the pleasure to introduce . . ."

"Emmlyn Podarke," said the Archon, turning his eyes on her.

"I did not think you would know me, sir," said Emmlyn.

"I know your family," was the reply.

Filidor looked at what occupied the workbench between them and his uncle, a flat rectangle of metal and synthetic materials, the size of a spacious bed, its surface smeared and drab. "Is this what Bassariot dug for in Trumble?"

"It is," said the Archon.

"I was told it was some sort of entertainment device."

"It was designed as such, but turned out to be adaptable to other functions," said the Archon. He resumed dabbing with a rag and cleaning solution at a dark patch on the top surface. A utilitarian power coupling emerged from beneath the grime, and the Archon pulled a cable from the floor and connected it to the device. A subtle hum filled the workroom, and the Archon made a sound that was somewhere between a sigh and a moan.

"Now, the controls," he said, wiping at a panel that was more heavily crusted with the detritus of the machine's grave.

"I still can't make sense of Bassariot's plan. How did this thing figure into his aims?" Filidor said.

"Let us consider him mad," said the Archon, not looking up from his work. He swore a strong oath. "These command nodes will have to be rebuilt."

Filidor had never heard his uncle use such language. "No need for distress," he said, drawing from his pocket the palmsized device he had dug under the threat of Bassariot's gun. "I believe this is its tapper."

The Archon came swiftly around the bench, ducking under a low overhanging light fixture. "Give it to me," he said.

"I think not," said Filidor. He tossed the control to Emmlyn and said, "Run! He is not my uncle! Back to the volante and away as fast as you can."

She caught the device, stared at him only an instant, then did as she was bid. Filidor turned to deal with the man in front of him. He drew Bassariot's energy gun and pointed it at the figure of the Archon and said, "I don't know who you are, but stand still or I shoot."

The Archon drew a similar weapon and pointed it at Filidor. "Emmlyn Podarke!" boomed the modulated voice, "stop and return, or this fool dies!"

Filidor heard the woman's footsteps come to a halt.

"Don't listen to him!" he shouted, not taking his eyes off the man in front of him. "Lower your weapon!"

The projection showed an expression Filidor had never seen on either of his uncle's faces, a sneer of contempt. "I am at ease with this weapon. If necessary, I can shoot your Podarke friend through the head with very little risk of hitting the control." He swung the gun in a leisurely arc toward her.

"No!" cried Filidor, and pressed his weapon's firing stud. Nothing happened.

"Your gun is, in fact, mine, lent to Bassariot. It will not fire on its owner." He pointed his own weapon back at Filidor. "But this one will cut you in half if she does not bring back the control."

Filidor heard the reluctant traipse of Emmlyn's feet returning across the stone floor. The man behind the Archon's image beckoned with one finger, and Filidor passed him the energy gun he had taken from Bassariot.

"Put the control on the device, then step back."

Emmlyn did so, then said, "What will you do now? Kill us?"

"In a little while, it will not be necessary."

"I presume you have killed my uncle," said Filidor. "Be assured that I will avenge him as soon as I may."

The image snorted. "What a bold puppy it has become. Still, you will make an accommodating lap-pet."

"Never," said Filidor and Emmlyn, as one.

The image slid open a small hatch on the tapper and made some adjustments. "There," the man said, "a few moments for the mechanism to reorder its function, then all will be well in the garden."

"What is it?" Filidor had to know. "What does it do?"

"It's the Magguffynne Sensibility Augmentor, the only

one of its kind, designed and built by my ancestor, Edile Magguffynne, of Trumble County, as it then was."

"Then you are . . ."

"Correct." There was a double *click*, and the image of the Archon Dezendah VII disappeared, to be replaced by a tall, spare shape that Filidor recognized. He also knew the voice that told Emmlyn, "I am Vadric Magguffynne, and I am pleased to have a damned upstart of a Podarke witness my moment of triumph over this ninny and all the Veshes before him. Though I can assure you there will be none after."

Emmlyn elevated her head and regarded Magguffynne from a posture that suggested she was far from convinced. Filidor admired her bravery.

"Where is my uncle?" he demanded.

Magguffynne gestured airily with the gun. "A matter for conjecture. Bassariot informed me that the great Dezendah was plinking about with a Zenthro Intrusifer. I had him remove the hand control and replace it with one that I had, shall we say, 'adjusted.' My best guess is that your uncle has become one with an infinity of cosmoses, all of them very small, as suits his puny stature."

"You knew," said Filidor.

"Of course, I knew, as did anyone who was anyone. Dezendah and I were at school together, even developed a shared interest in old devices: Dez and Vad, the antick delvers, they called us; but never Vad and Dez. Then he was selected for 'enhanced mastery,' and I was sent to rusticate in a cottage my family still owned in Trumble. It was there that I learned about my ancestor Edile's tinkerings and the reason why that timid fool had the thing buried. When I came back to Olkney, I continued my researches, and now all is at a pinnacle." Magguffynne inspected the pattern of lights that had appeared on the surface of the machine, and said, "We are ready."

"But what does it do?" Filidor said.

"Not even your celebrated uncle would know that," the usurper sneered. "It's a sensibility augmentor. It gathers, amplifies, then projects the operator's feelings to others. My ancestor thought he would encourage the most refined aesthetes of his time to project their sentiments regarding great works of art to bumpkins who could not otherwise appreciate them. Grouped around the device, they would have clearly seen the tetrarch's finery that was invisible to them moments before."

Magguffynne adjusted something on the hand control, then continued, "What Edile didn't realize until he had built the thing was that with a more potent power feed it could be effective over a much wider area—an entire city was well within its reach—and that, in the hands of a strong-willed operator, it could impress more than sublime artistic appreciation upon its subjects. Whether they were willing or no." He made a final adjustment to the tapper. "For some reason, he thought that would be a bad thing, and so he buried his invention."

"You are despicable," said Emmlyn.

"In a moment, you'll think me the most wonderful man in the world, and you'll do anything to oblige me." He looked her up and down. "You're a presentable young thing, so I might even let you. In memory of long-dead Hableck."

"You mean, you're going to make everyone share your opinion of yourself?" Filidor said. An idea had occurred to him. He needed to find something buried in a deep pocket of his breeches, and to distract attention from what he was doing he burbled on. "I see it, now. You will masquerade as my uncle until the machine has generated a great public affection for Vadric Magguffynne. Then, still in my uncle's guise, you will announce Dezendah Vesh's abdication and hand over the Archonate to the popular choice; that is, to yourself."

"That is my plan," said Magguffynne, adjusting a control. "And in a moment, you will see it brought to completion."

Filidor continued to dig in his pocket. "You were just going to push me aside, weren't you?"

The usurper's fingers slid and poked at the augmentor's controls. "You were, and are, of no importance. Bassariot did so desire to kill you, however, that I allowed him to throw you from the ship. After all, he had earned a reward." Magguffynne adjusted a final setting and said, "There we are. Time for a change."

"A brilliant strategy!" said Filidor. His questing fingers now touched the object he sought. "I'm coming to think that you indeed deserve to be Archon!"

"Is the device already working?" said Emmlyn. "I still find him abhorrent and repulsive."

Filidor swung toward her, gesturing floridly with his left hand while the fingers of his right closed at last on the thing in his pocket. "But you must admire the power of intellect, the breadth of vision!" he said, in a loud voice, then in a much quieter tone, he added, "Duck out of sight, now!"

Emmlyn turned and dove behind a pile of defragilator parts. Magguffynne sneered. "These shallow tricks won't save you. Hide if you wish. The effect of the device is all pervasive." He punched a control. "Behold!"

But as his extended digit connected with the implementation stud, Filidor had already brought his right hand out of his pocket, his fingers clasped around the little vial that Ovile Germolian had left behind. Now the Archon's apprentice squeezed and snapped the glass tube, spilling its contents of espolianth powder into his palm. This he blew into Vadric Magguffynne's sneering face.

Two things happened. First, as the augmentor's energies touched his mind, Filidor felt a rapidly growing regard for the personal qualities of Lord Vadric. The man was clearly the most superior human being Filidor had ever met, and if anything was overqualified to be Archon. But no sooner had this conviction established itself than the espolianth powder suddenly and drastically began to alter Magguffynne's view of Filidor. There was a brief but intense surge of horror, followed by an absolute devotion to the person of the Archon's nephew. As the augmentor washed waves of Magguffynne's regard for him in a tide that swept the room, the young man knew, without latitude for the least vestige of a quibble, that he was the most lovable, agreeable creature ever to walk the face of Old Earth; he yearned to do something for himself, something really nice.

His face agrin with unoccluded self-regard, Filidor looked at Magguffynne, who was now gazing at the young man with eyes as round and soft as any tame ruminant's. A shadow of an inner struggle crossed the usurper's features, and for a moment Filidor felt just a little less wonderful. He shared the aristocrat's internal discord as the man tried to regain his hatred of Filidor, but the contest was as brief as it was futile. Magguffynne swallowed, gawked at the Archon's heir, and said shyly, "Gosh."

Filidor was still wondering what lovely thing he could do for himself. *I know,* he thought. *I'll save my life.* He put out his hand to Magguffynne and said, "Let me have the tapper, please. Oh, and I'd like the guns."

The desperate shadow again appeared in the usurper's face, and again the augmentor passed on to Filidor the most distant twinge of negative regard, but it soon passed. With a dainty simper, the aristocrat handed over the items. Filidor stepped back until he could see where Emmlyn lay behind the pile of parts.

She looked up at him and said, "I think you're wonderful."

"Me, too," said Filidor. "Would you do something for me?"

"Anything," she breathed, getting up.

"Please hold on to these while I bind up our friend."

Emmlyn took the control and the weapons. Filidor found some cable and packing straps and used them to secure Vadric Magguffynne to a stout chair. The prisoner cooperated with expressions of delight and shy glances of affection.

Then Filidor wistfully contemplated the sensibility augmentor. "Integrator," he said, "are your circuits affected by the device before me?" Quickly, he explained its powers.

No, said the inner voice.

"I was wondering," the young man said, "whether you thought this is how your Filidor feels about himself all of the time."

I would not know, said the voice. *But I do not think you should need artificial augmentation to feel well about yourself.*

"You don't?"

After what you've accomplished? In fact, I suggest you turn off the device and see how you regard yourself.

Filidor went to Emmlyn, took the control from her while she gazed at him with a doting expression he had never seen on a woman's face except in dreams. He depressed the power stud and the humming of the augmentor stopped. At once, he felt the sweet sentiment that had filled him begin to drain away, but as he observed its fading, he noticed that it left a residue behind, a sense of well-being that was new and yet at the same time familiar.

He looked at Emmlyn. "Are you all right?" he said.

"I think you're wonderful," she replied, which caused him to reexamine the augmentor to ensure that it was truly off. But the expression on her face, though now not slavishly adoring, was something far better. He put out his arms, she came into them, and a moment passed between them that neither would ever forget.

A whine of jealousy sounded from across the room, and Filidor thought it well to inspect Lord Magguffynne's bonds. His newfound love for Filidor would not extend to Emmlyn or anyone else. This was confirmed when the aristocrat smiled dotingly while saying, "I think you're wonderful, too, but at least I got rid of that noxious, little yellow mite, Dezendah Vesh."

"No you didn't," said Filidor. "He was always ahead of you. He knew you had interfered with the controls of the Zenthro Intrusifer."

The young man went to the side of the room, where the device rested on an armature, the doctored control next to it. "Old Confustible," he said, and when the integrator replied, asked it for information on the operation of the device. The instructions were abstruse, but somehow Filidor had no difficulty in assimilating them. It was as if long blocked channels in his mind had opened, to let his thoughts flood back and forth without hindrance.

He adjusted a number of settings on the ancient device, then stepped back and pressed the top stud on the hand control. A sphere of blackness flecked with tiny lights appeared above the bench. It hovered in the air for a moment, then from it emerged a tiny blue orb that speedily grew into a ball of azure swirls perhaps half Filidor's height. Then the blue sphere popped into nonexistence with the quiet dignity of a soap bubble's bursting, and where it had been stood the small, hairless person of Filidor's uncle.

The little man looked at his nephew, at Emmlyn Podarke and at the fuming, swearing figure bound to the chair. The dwarf's almost lipless mouth split into a grin. "Magguffynne," he said, and if it wasn't a cackle, it was very close to one, "so it was you."

"You knew?" said Lord Vadric.

"I suspected. Trumble gave me an inkling."

"Uncle," said Filidor. "Are you well?"

"I am very well, and I believe I have reason to thank you for it."

Filidor wanted to respond, but something in his throat got in the way. Finally, he managed to say, "Bassariot is dead."

"I know," said the little man. He turned to Emmlyn. "And you would be Emmlyn Podarke."

The young woman gracefully struck the appropriate formal posture. "I am," she said.

"Welcome," the Archon said. "And thank you." Then he clapped his hands and said, "Integrator. Send someone here to collect Lord Vadric, and have his house searched for any other nasty devices he may have accumulated. Arrest all shareholders of The Ancient and Excellent Company of Assemblors and Sundry Merchandisers, suspend publication of the *Olkney Implicator,* and bring in Tet Folbrey, Lord Magguffynne's son-in-law. Also, detain all of Faubon Bassariot's establishment for interrogation." He smiled at Filidor and Emmlyn, but it was better than the one he had given to Magguffynne. "Now I think we should all have some punch and something to nibble on in my withdrawing room."

* * *

It was Emmlyn who asked for the explanation. Filidor was too occupied in exploring his new sense of who he was. It was a strange feeling; he was unquestionably himself, but it was a different self than he had ever been before; a strong, confident Filidor, who was becoming aware of a considerable curiosity about how things worked. He was chewing a cracker spread with a savory paste and wondering how the sweet and sour could be so carefully balanced, when Emmlyn said, "So what was all that all about?"

The little man looked over the rim of his cup of punch. "Well, I suppose it began when I discovered that Faubon Bassariot had replaced the Zenthro Intrusifer's control with one that had been reconfigured so that the 'clear and abort' stud would instead have disassembled me and placed each of my atoms in individual mini-cosmoses, from which a reassembly would have been doubtful."

"That's why you told me not to press the bottommost stud," said Filidor.

"Exactly. Have some more punch." He sipped his own. "Well, of course, I knew that Bassariot could not have done the reconfiguring, that he must be only the fingertips of someone else's grasp. The quality of the work limited the field to a relatively few people, and then when I knew you would kill Bassariot in Trumble—the ancient seat of the Magguffynnes—my suspicions turned to Vadric."

"How did you know I would kill Bassariot?"

The full explanation followed. The Archon had been using the Intrusifer for some time to investigate parallel versions of the universe. Some differed in tiny ways, some very distinctly. He had found one in which time had had what he called "a hiccup" shortly after the earliest moments of that nanocosm's inception, with the result that it was identical to the macrocosm, except that it was a few days advanced. He had replicated the Archonate integrator from that minirealm and questioned it regarding developments.

The integrator had reported that in its cosmos, Filidor had been declared a fugitive renegade by Bassariot and that his whereabouts had been unknown for days. The little man had isolated and replicated the integrator moments after Filidor had got into the volante in Trumble, announced that he had killed Faubon Bassariot, and demanded to know the Archon's whereabouts. When the dwarf learned that he had mysteriously disappeared from his workroom shortly after sending Filidor and Bassariot to Trumble, he ended the conversation and quickly discovered the Intrusifer's sabotage. He then altered the device to create a temporary and timeless sphere of existence for himself, which he intruded into another tiny cosmos. Since his enemies would think him disassembled, he knew his hiding place would be secure.

"Can you do that?" Filidor said. "That means placing a macrocosmic entity within a microcosm of the macrocosm that contains the microcosm." He stopped for a moment and ran the words through his consciousness again. "Yes, I did get that right. That is what it means."

"Indeed," said the Archon. "Had you ever persevered through the maze of Balmerion's Great Theorem, you would see how it is done."

"I never thought I could," said his nephew. Then a new sense of capability rose up from somewhere within him. "But I believe I will."

"Wonderful," said the little man. "And why not now? Integrator, display Balmerion's first four intervals."

A screen appeared in the air. The formulae laid themselves out in their four quadrants, just as Filidor remembered them from boyhood. For a moment, as he looked at the curves and integers, he felt a tremble of the old child's fear, that sinking, liquid, inner chill that told him he would fail. But then the long-planted reflex vanished under a new surge of conviction, and he said, "Let me see the fifth."

Another component appeared on the screen. Filidor stared. The chill came back. The thing just didn't make sense; it wouldn't fit, couldn't fit. But then a part of him brushed aside the uncertainty, took hold of the four and the fifth, and turned them thus and so, and all at once, there it was.

"Well, of course," Filidor said. He regarded the screen and saw, not four and a fifth, but one—and with room for more.

"Show me the sixth," he said, and almost as soon as the shape and coordinates appeared, he effortlessly slid them into conformity with the other intervals. "Now the seventh," he said, and saw that that, too, was obvious.

"Show him the eighth," said his uncle.

"Wait," said Filidor, "there is no eighth interval."

"Oh, but there is," said his uncle. "It surrounds and infuses the first seven. And I found it."

And when Filidor saw it, and grasped it, he said, "That's amazing. With that kind of insight, you could rule the world."

"I know," said his uncle. "I do. And now, so can you."

Filidor laughed, and looked at Emmlyn Podarke. "Yes," he said, "now I can."

But then a thought intruded. "Uncle," the young man said, "something bothers me. When you learned that I would kill Bassariot and come here after the device was dug up in Trumble, you did not know that things would come out well in the end. You suspected that Vadric Magguffynne might be the string-puller behind the curtain, and you must have recognized him as a formidable enemy. Why did you not take stern action immediately, arrest Bassariot and root out the plot before it went further?"

The Archon stroked his smooth chin. "That is not how these things work," he said. "I knew, from the future-seeing integrator, what would happen if I removed myself from the scene. But if, days ago, I had diverted the flow of events, who knows what new channels they might have carved into the future? Besides, I was less concerned with plots and usurpation than I was with seeing you arrive at where you stand now."

"But you left me to face Magguffynne. He might well have bested me," said Filidor.

"Yet he did not."

"But you could not have known that I would triumph."

The little man shrugged. "In full truth, I did not know for sure. But I was willing to take a small risk for your sake."

"I think it was a great risk."

"Not so great. Remember, I have known you and Magguffynne all of your lives. If it came to a passage of wits between you and that self-inflated despot-in-waiting, I would wager all on you. As I did, and won."

Filidor didn't know what to say.

His uncle put a hand on the young man's arm. "I have always had faith in you," he said, "much as you often strove to frustrate my confidence. I have worked and waited for years for the moment—this moment—when you would finally come to have faith in yourself." The little man blew out a sigh of completion, and finished with, "And now I can retire."

In all, the conspirators numbered only a dozen, all of whom ended up treading wheels in the Etch Valderoyn Memorial Contemplatorium under the exacting supervision of Orton Bregnat and a cadre of well-trained warders. The Obblob ecstatics were pleased to assist when necessary, and continued to deliver shipwrecked and swept-away mariners as before, but now the rescued wretches were carried home by Byr Lak in the jollyboat. Ovile Germolian was found by operatives of the Bureau of Scrutiny and sent to the islet to sew suits of sea furze.

Filidor was promoted to Underarchon and assigned a new and larger staff. He took on wider duties within the Archonate, now that his mastery of Balmerion—plus Vesh's Corollary—enabled him to understand exactly what it was the Archonate did, and how it was done. A date was set for his uncle's retirement, and a section of the palace was being fitted out, under Master Apparaticist Berro's careful eye, to become what the Archon Emeritus called his "tinkerarium."

Filidor and Emmlyn entered into the arrangements that were customary for two young people who felt as they did toward each other. Their conjointure was announced at the gala opening of Flastovic's Grand Pantodeon on South Processional, which coincided with the retirement celebrations of the Florrey twins. At the reception that followed, catered by Xanthoulian's and featuring the new sensation, Podarke's Ancient Clabber Cordial, the mummers were cajoled into playing an impromptu encore. They chose The Bard Obscure's existential classic, *The Fowl and the Thoroughfare*. Chloe, still not entirely reconciled to Filidor, mischievously stirred the crowd to press the Underarchon himself into the role of disclamator.

Filidor called upon his personal integrator, now removed from his inner workings and positioned instead in a pore of his left earlobe, with nanobuilt power supply and full communications array provided by Master Berro. Prompted by the still tiny voice, but without a modulator, the Archon's heir intoned the Bard's deceptively simple lines, tracing the bird's philosophical transit across a symbolic road and the discovery of fundamental purpose it found on the other side. The applause was gratifying and, Filidor felt, sincere.

When the performance was done, and Emmlyn had congratulated him with a kiss, Filidor spoke to the voice only he could hear. "Integrator," he said, "besides having compiled all of The Bard Obscure's works, have you recorded any information about the playwright's life and experiences?"

It happens that I have, said the voice. *He came to a sad end. The labor of composing such insightful works eventually drove him into the embrace of madness.*

"A pity," said Filidor. "And do you also happen to know his true identity?"

I do.

"Well?"

He was Holmar Thurm.

MATTHEW HUGHES writes speeches for politicians and corporate executives. Born in England and raised in Canada, he lives in a small town on Vancouver Island with his wife and sons.

FABULOUS FANTASY FROM WARNER ASPECT

J.V. JONES

"Original, fascinating . . . Jones integrates dark sorcery, treason, adventure, and peril to create a sparkling first volume."
—*Southern Pines Pilot* (NC) on *A Cavern of Black Ice*

A CAVERN OF BLACK ICE, Sword of Shadows Book 1
(0-446-60-817-3)
THE BARBED COIL (0-446-60-623-5)
The Book of Words Trilogy:
THE BAKER'S BOY (0-446-60-282-5)
A MAN BETRAYED (0-446-60-351-1)
MASTER AND FOOL (0-446-60-414-3)

IAN IRVINE

Once there were three worlds with its own human race. Then, fleeing from out of the void came a fourth race, the Charon. Desperate, on the edge of extinction, they changed the balance between the worlds forever. . . .

"Compelling . . . stands out as a worldbuilding labor of love." —*Locus*

The View from the Mirror Saga:
A SHADOW ON THE GLASS, VOL. 1 (0-446-60-984-6)
THE TOWER ON THE RIFT, VOL. 2
(0-446-60-985-4, *coming in early 2002*)

AVAILABLE AT BOOKSTORES EVERYWHERE

VISIT WARNER ASPECT ONLINE!

THE WARNER ASPECT HOMEPAGE
You'll find us at: www.twbookmark.com then by clicking on Science Fiction and Fantasy.

NEW AND UPCOMING TITLES
Each month we feature our new titles and reader favorites.

AUTHOR INFO
Author bios, bibliographies and links to personal websites.

CONTESTS AND OTHER FUN STUFF
Advance galley giveaways, autographed copies, and more.

THE ASPECT BUZZ
What's new, hot and upcoming from Warner Aspect: awards news, bestsellers, movie tie-in information . . .